MURDER IN WINDSOR PARK

A BONE ISLAND MAGGIE MYSTERY
BOOK 2

The New Atlantian Library

Manhanset House
Shelter Island Hts., New York 11965-0342

bricktower@aol.com • absolutelyamazingebooks.com

Library of Congress Cataloging-in-Publication Data
Gregory, Peg.
Murder in Windsor Park. A Bone Island Maggie Mystery, Book 2.
p. cm.

1. FICTION / Mystery & Detective / Women Sleuths.
2. FICTION / Mystery & Detective / Amateur Sleuth.
3. FICTION / Humorous / General
Fiction, I. Title.
ISBN: 978-1-7330119-5-2, Trade Paper

November 2025

MURDER IN WINDSOR PARK

A BONE ISLAND MAGGIE MYSTERY
BOOK 2

Peg Gregory

The New Atlantian Library

Habent Sua Fata Libelli

COMMENTS AND REVIEWS OF PEG'S BOOKS

Starfish

"Peg Gregory paints visual images of the settings that are so real I can almost smell the Sargasso weed washed up on the beaches . . . strong visual images both of her characters and of the locale, which in this novel comes to life as strongly as her people."

—*Writer's Digest*, Cincinnati, Ohio

"I just finished Starfish and I loved it . . . wonderful and touching love story brought tears to my eyes. Peg has a wonderful talent for evoking true emotion from the reader."

—Alison McKinney, teacher, Houston, Texas

And Then There Was One, a memoir

"A fascinating account of nursing in mid-century America . . . the extraordinary story of a remarkable, dedicated lady."

—Joanna Brady, author *The Woman at the Light*

"Veritably a bible of nursing history from 1955 until recent times . . . rich narrative."

—C. S. Gilbert, Solares Hill, Key West Citizen,

and author *Mother Poems*

DEDICATION

A special posthumous dedication to Walter McLaughlin, former FBI agent who started the sex crime investigation school at Quantico, Virginia, and who, after his retirement, traveled the country teaching sex crime investigation to law enforcement and others who worked in the field. It was Walter who taught my sex crime investigation courses after I became acting coordinator and paralegal counselor to survivors of sexual assault, both adults and children, on the first team of the sexual assault assistance program in Palm Beach Country in the mid-1970s. Walter became my friend, pen pal and mentor from that first course at Palm Beach Jr. College until his death a few years after I left the program. It was through his courses that I learned of a world that, in those years, most human beings not involved in the field could never imagine existed, the world of the dangerous sexual predators and the horrifying ways they would hurt and kill their prey, and make no mistake, their victims were their prey. They'd pick them off the street at random, they'd stalk them from afar until they were ready to strike, or they'd hold them virtual prisoners in their own homes because they lived in their homes as their husbands, fathers, brothers, other relatives, friends of the family, or boyfriends of their trusting mothers. I came to know of many of them through my work with those they'd hurt by kidnapping, molesting, torturing and raping. Sometimes for periods of several years they'd do what they wanted to their victims before they'd get the courage to tell someone, despite the threats of death to them and their loved ones if they dared to tell what had been happening to them all this time, at the hands of those monsters. In my non-law enforcement position I did not work the homicide cases, but in Walter's classes, some of the slides were so unearthly horrible that more than once I'd have to hurry from the room for a few minutes because I, a seasoned registered nurse who'd seen all manner of illnesses and injury, surgeries, death and autopsies, simply could not bear to look at them anymore. Slides showing torture machines and instruments, mutilation, cannibalism (yes, in modern day America), every horrible deviation that existed Walter had first-hand knowledge of as an agent. Some of these predators were such charming sociopaths that they fooled everyone into thinking they were model citizens from every walk of life who never hesitated to lend a helping hand when needed. Ted Bundy was the perfect example. Women and children adored them – until they happened to be unlucky enough to see the face of those rapists and murderers. And no one really sees the true face of a rapist or killer except his or her victims. No one.

—Peggy Butler
writing as Peg Gregory

Other works by Peg Gregory

Starfish

And Then There Was One, A Memoir

The Bone Island Maggie Mystery Series

***Bone Island Maggie*, book one**

***Murder in Windsor Park*, book two**

***The Trial of Maggie Metronia*, book three**

ONE

Maggie sat perfectly still in the lawn swing staring out at the sunset spiking colors on the fountain water in the middle of the lake, never once looking back toward the compactor and the man she'd seen throw the bundle down into it, the bundle with a man's hairy leg, as bloody as a hunk of meat in the butcher's freezer, sticking out of it. She tried not to react as she heard the grinding of the machinery as he closed and latched the door. She willed herself not to vomit the bile rising in her throat as she realized what was happening inside that compactor. Even when the man came to stand near her at the edge of the lake, staring at the fountain as she was doing, she did not dare take a breath or turn her head.

"Nice lake," she heard him say. When she said nothing, he asked, "Don't you think it's a nice lake?"

Still not turning to look at him, she croaked, "Yes, it's – it's nice."

"Well, you have a really good day, ma'am. I need to finish my Saturday errands. It never ends, does it."

"I – no, it doesn't," she managed to get out around the still rising bile. Within moments, she heard shuffling beside her, then behind her, and then it stopped. She held her breath. She felt the swing move as the man gave it a quick push and she tightened her hold on the slats of the seat, trying not to fly out and roll into the lake to become dinner for the alligators the sign said were in it. He said nothing and neither did Maggie.

1

Just as quickly, the shuffling started again and then she heard footsteps crunch small stones on the pavement before a car door opened and closed. Time stood still before she heard the engine start. Nothing happened for a while. He just sat there with that engine idling, as Maggie's heartbeat accelerated as she wished the engine would. Finally it did and the car drove away, but still she did not move or turn her head toward the circular drive of the senior community they called Windsor Park.

TWO

When she heard the last of the car's engine as it drove out of the senior community north of Forest Hill Boulevard, she couldn't help herself; she lost her dinner and then rose from the swing as a couple of black ducks and a slew of snowy egrets went for the vomited mess. Maggie wiped her mouth on her sleeve and tried to keep from running back to the building where her friend was in case the driver turned around and came after her. She wanted to appear as normal as possible, so he would think she didn't see anything, though why come to stand beside her after throwing pieces of a body down the compactor, if he didn't suspect she saw him do it? Why give the swing a shove if he didn't want her to fly out of it and roll down into the lake? Still, she didn't hurry her steps, and walked very close to the building, so people would hear and help her if she ran into the open hallway and started screaming if he came back for her.

When she reached the elevator of her building and then the third floor, she ran as fast as she could to safety. Pounding on the door, she called, "Carolyn! Carolyn, please, let me in! Hurry."

The newly-married couple across the hall opened their door and looked out just as the other woman opened the door and said, "My goodness, Mag, what on earth?" Maggie flew past her without speaking.

"Is everything okay?" the slender brunette with the Midwestern twang asked from the open doorway across the hall, as her husband stood towering over her. He'd been widowed a few years before and seemed happy now that he'd found love again with his willowy bride, or so Vanny told them before he left on vacation. Vanny was as bad as a nosy woman when he got started, but Carolyn loved him dearly. She'd never had a gay friend before she met him in Key West. Like many before him, and more every month, he gave up on the outlandish amount he was paying to sublet the condo beneath her and moved into the beautiful roomy apartment on the mainland three years ago and pocketed the extra three hundred a month he saved by moving. He missed the ocean at the end of the street, instead of four miles away, but he made up for it by swimming under the stars in the beautiful pool across from his building every morning with his friends in the complex, leaving a couple hours after daybreak when the community came alive with those who slept later than the ten of them.

Carolyn smiled broadly at them after Maggie ran past her, and said, "Yes, everything's fine. My friend gets overly-excited sometimes. She probably saw another tall goose at the lake. Someone told her they were good luck." They seemed satisfied, returned her smile and closed the door to get back to what they were doing before they heard Maggie's shouts. Carolyn smiled to herself.

"We have to leave right now," Maggie said, throwing her things into her opened suitcase, as Carolyn entered the den with the deep red sleeper loveseat on one wall.

"Whoa – tell me why we have to leave? We have three more days here, remember? Vanny doesn't get back until Tuesday. We promised to housesit until he returns. We can't just dash back to Key West and leave his place unattended. As much as I didn't want to take it, he did pay us good money to help him out, Maggie. He doesn't know I hid it in his sock drawer." Maggie said nothing, just kept packing her things, as though her life depended upon it. "The point is, regardless of his paying us, he can't possibly come back until after his aunt's funeral and he's finished closing the house up and putting it into the hands of the realtor. His aunt had no one else and he's always been there for her. That was the last promise he made her, because it was all she had to leave him for all his years of dropping everything for her and driving up to her place when she needed him."

The woman managed to smile at her young friend. When she opened her mouth, there wasn't a tooth in it at the top and the bottom ones didn't show, but Carolyn had long ago gotten used to that and didn't blink an eye. Maggie patted her hand, and said, "You're right. But if we stay, I can't leave the apartment again 'til you have our bags in the car and the motor running."

Carolyn laughed and said, "You only walked to the lake, so what could you possibly have done to get yourself into trouble this time? My goodness, you're trembling. What on earth has scared you so?"

THREE

Two years before, Maggie Metronia was minding her business sitting in Alabama Jack's with her trusted best friend and chauffeur, Homer Wiley, eating a grilled cheese sandwich and drinking the last of her Corona as she stared out at the mangroves in Biscayne Bay, before he drove her the last lap of the shopping trip home to Key West.

All at once, Maggie spied what looked like a body hanging over a thick twisted root and asked to see Homer's miniature binoculars he always carried in his pocket. "Oh Shit," he heard her say, and knew there was trouble ahead, as she rarely swore, and when she told him about the body and directed his eyes toward it, he whipped out his cell phone.

Trouble was right. She refused to let him call 911, telling him how foolish they'd look if it was just a pile of rags instead of a body, which both could clearly see it was. Against his better judgement, he donned his wet suit in the front seat of the gold Hummer she'd had him park down the road from the restaurant and bar, hidden from the dollar toll booth with the big sign announcing, 'Welcome to Downtown Card Sound'. Jack's was all Downtown Card Sound consisted of, unless you counted the county toll booth and the occasional squatter selling his catch of the day. Maggie got into hers in the back. And then trouble really began for the two of them.

Before they reached the body via the crystal clear waters, since the sun had not set yet, she said, "Look, we can just step up onto this log and into the mangroves," which they did just as the log started moving and then dived down before coming back for its prey. She nearly lost a foot when the gator grabbed for it and got her flipper, instead, just as Homer grabbed her and pulled her up into the roots of the mangroves.

To add insult to injury, just as they almost reached the body, they were caught by a sheriff's lieutenant and his trigger-happy deputy as their boat came up to the mangroves. Of course, the two thought they'd caught the killers of the person whose mutilated body was draped over the mangrove root, a person they all knew, Key Wester Jackie Weener, the only haberdasher in the Keys.

They were jailed in the Monroe County Jail on Stock Island, as soon as the crime scene man arrived, after the deputy nearly got her eaten by the alligator because he'd whipped out his Taser and fired it at her because she wouldn't stop trying to convince them that they had the wrong people. Homer jumped into the bay after her and the disgruntled lieutenant and deputy rescued them both just as the gator grabbed at the deputy's hand, barely missing it as he jumped back, taking his hand with him as he let go of Homer, who'd landed in the roots after Maggie was pulled out by the lieutenant.

Stock Island was right outside the entrance from the Overseas Highway to Key West. They were reluctantly released when another mutilated body was found in a condo across from Cowboy Bill's on Duval Street, where a casual acquaintance, Carolyn Cramer, lived. The sheriff knew since he had them in his jail they couldn't possibly have killed the man found in the condo, whose body was still warm.

Maggie hoped she'd never see another dead body for the remainder of her life.

FOUR

"Maggie, we've got to call the sheriff's office to report this," Carolyn told the frantic woman whom she'd persuaded to unpack her bag and tell her what happened by the swing.

"Then he'll know for sure I saw what he did. We can't do that. Besides, after what we went through with those cops in Key West, do you really want to get involved with them up here?"

"I don't look forward to it, no, but we've done nothing wrong this time, and my conscience won't let me look the other way on this. This was a man's life he took and I, for one, am going to tell them so he won't get away with it. Write down everything you remember and I'll call them."

"I will, but I don't like it one bit," she said as she started jotting down the details, including the description of the car he was driving and two of the digits in the license plate, which was all she could see before he walked over to the compacter door.

"Okay, that's a pretty good description of both him and the car, so I'll call." She picked up her cell phone, after she sketched a likeness of him to Maggie's satisfaction. To her astonishment, Maggie knocked it out of her hand onto the sofabed beside her before she could plug in 911.

"Do me one favor, first. I said I wouldn't leave the apartment until you had the motor running to head back home, but you know they'll want to talk with me as the only witness. Let's just drive to the sheriff's office and we can tell them there. If they come here, he'll know for sure."

"Good thinking. Grab your purse and let's go now before you change your mind." She opened the door, with Maggie behind her and they hurried down the middle stairs rather than wait for the elevator. Maggie held back in the shadow of the building until Carolyn brought the car up to the end of the sidewalk across from the pool, and hurried into it. "I didn't see anyone outside, so I doubt he's seen us."

"This really scares me, you know," the frightened Maggie told her friend. "It's worse than it was in Key West, because he stood right next to the swing and talked to me before he left in his car. There's no question he knows where every mole and wrinkle is on my face, Carolyn."

The other woman smiled but not to belittle what Maggie said. She took her hand, which was cold as ice, in hers, and held it as she turned onto Gun Club Road not far from Windsor Park and found a parking spot in front of the tall building that housed the sheriff's office and county jail.

"May I help you?" This was spoken by a pleasant woman in the triangular lobby.

"We'd like – we need to report a murder," Carolyn told her.

"Have a seat over there and a detective will be right out," she said as she picked up the phone and spoke with someone. Carolyn sat back on the bench seat, but Maggie was on the edge of it, swinging her leg furiously, almost kicking off her flip-flop.

"Good evening, ladies, I'm Lieutenant Jackson. How may I help you," the tow-headed detective asked, as he shook both their hands. He looked like he belonged in the wrestling ring instead of in a suit catching bad guys for the sheriff's office.

"My name is Carolyn Cramer and this is my friend Maggie Metronia. We're happy to meet you, but wish it were under different circumstances. You see, Maggie witnessed a man dumping a dead body a short while ago."

"I'm sorry, Ms. Metronia. Why don't we go to my desk where we can speak in private." He smiled kindly at her as he led the way through the maze of desks in the large detectives' squad room until they reached his office. He grabbed an extra chair from the next desk and put it beside the other one across from the desk.

"May I get either of you something to drink? One of the guys just made some fresh coffee."

"Yes, please, that would be nice," Carolyn said. "Do you want one, Maggie?"

Maggie, who was looking like a deer in headlights, told her yes, as she twisted the hem of her yellow cotton top. Both Carolyn and Lieutenant Jackson felt badly for her.

"Cream and sugar?" They both told him yes, and Carolyn jumped up to help him carry it back.

"She's really scared of this guy, isn't she," he said in a quiet voice while he was filling their cups.

"Petrified," Carolyn told him. "Two years ago we went through the trauma of being witnesses to another murder – well, we didn't see the actual murder. Murders, since there were three – but the murderer saw both of us when we were staking out Duval Street and chased after him. We live in Key West."

"Oh my goodness, real live undercover angels, eh?" He gave her a small smile. "How did that turn out?"

She gave him a brief version of events and he whistled. "Maggie was just getting to where she wasn't thinking about it all the time when she saw what she did earlier today."

"I'm sorry she had to see that, but let's go sit down and I'll take some information from her so we can catch this guy."

FIVE

"Okay, Maggie, er, Ms. Metronia," he said after they started drinking their coffees.

"Just Maggie, please, detective. I don't like formality," she told him before he could finish his statement.

"Maggie it is, then. And may I call you by your first name, also, ma'am?"

"Sure, Carolyn is fine."

Just then one of his colleagues brought a large box of pastries into the squad room and over to his desk. "Here you go. These'll taste great with my fresh coffee," he said with a grin. "I'm Detective Flagg, by the way."

"It's nice to meet you, detective. These look yummy, thank you," Maggie said, as she reached for a couple of the large delicacies, as his grin spread wider. Maggie loved her sweets. She put them on the small paper plate the lieutenant handed each of them.

"Yes, thank you. We didn't take time for dinner." Carolyn took only one of them.

"How 'bout you, Jax?"

"Yeah, never turn down a bite when it's offered," he said, with a smile for the ladies. "Why don't you sit in, Lenny? Ms. Maggie here witnessed a guy disposing of a body earlier."

"Oh, I'm sorry, ma'am, I know that must have been tough for you. He didn't see you, did he?"

Maggie's lips trembled as she answered, "Yes, he even came over to stand by me as I was looking out toward the lake in front of us. Before he left he gave the porch swing a big shove from behind and I thought the chains were going to come loose from the frame and I'd be thrown down the bank into the water. They've seen gators and snakes in there, you know." She raised her head to look at him. "To tell the truth, I'm about as scared as a body – er, as a woman can be."

Carolyn put her arm around her. "Why don't you finish your Danish, Mag. I'm sure the detectives won't mind waiting a moment. I'll give them the paper you wrote up and they can ask you questions after that, if it's all right with the two of you?"

"More than all right. That's what every witness to a crime should do while it's fresh on their minds, but most don't think of it. Let's see what you have," Lieutenant Jackson said, as he reached for the paper in her hand. "I wish more witnesses would do this," he repeated. "It would make our job a lot easier."

Detective Flagg sat near him so he could see it, also. "My God, he put it into the compactor?"

"I think we'd better head over there, Len. If she heard the motor, I doubt there's much left, but those things don't grind up everything, so we might luck out and get something for CS to get some DNA and teeth from. I'll give them a call now to meet us there."

Flagg asked, "Is this everything you remember, Ms. Maggie?"

"Yes, sir, I can't think of anything else. Oh wait a minute, there is something I forgot to tell Carolyn. On the left, no, on the right side of the back window is a big Support the NRA sign, bigger than those little bumper stickers."

"Great! That should make it stick out like a sore thumb, since there are so many white Chevy Cruzes on the road around here. Good work, Ms. Maggie!" Jackson smiled at her, noticing her toothless mouth for the first time when she smiled back. Flagg grinned at her. His grandmother didn't have a tooth in her head, so this endeared her to him even more. He was thinking she must have been a beautiful lady back in the day. Except for some gray on the edges of her long hair that was the color of new mown wheat, she sure didn't look older than 50. Of course, her wheat color came from the bottle and had for many years, but he didn't know that.

"Yes, that really helps. Now, are you certain this is all you can tell us?"

"Well, now that I think about it, his voice was strange."

Flagg looked at Jackson, who asked, "Strange in what way?"

"I think his sentences all ended in something like the sound ah, sort of the audible breath you'd hear Perry Mason, I mean Raymond Burr, make before he said anything, except this one's sound was at the end not the beginning of his sentences. It wasn't really loud, but it was there. Just the slightest bit, probably not anything you'd notice if he wasn't standing right next to you by a lake with gators and snakes in it..." she shivered all of a sudden. "As he was to me. I even thought for a minute he was going to reach down, grab me and throw me in the compactor alive with the body of that man!"

"Oh my, you didn't tell me that. I'm so sorry you were by yourself. Now I wish I'd gone with you when you said you wanted to watch the sunset in the swing."

She patted Carolyn's hand. "How could you have known it wouldn't be like any other sunset here?"

"Now, let me ask you ladies, are you going to be safe where you are?"

"I have no idea," Carolyn told the lieutenant. "I mean, we don't even know if the guy lives in Windsor Park or just drove in there to do what he did."

"Has either of you ever seen that Chevy with the NRA sign before?"

"No, I haven't, have you, Carolyn?"

"No, but with several buildings in the community, it would be impossible for either of us to see what everyone drives who lives there. I've noticed some of them in our building use the left gate and others use the right and circle around, so we'd have no idea. And since we're only house-sitting, we've not been there that many times. This is Mag's first time there, in fact. Vanny, Tom Vangrift, who lives in the apartment is an old friend of mine from Key West and asked us if we'd mind staying there while he took care of family business this week in Central Florida."

13

"Okay, write your building number down for me and your friend's apartment number here, with his cell number," Flagg said, handing Carolyn a sheet of paper, "and we'll make sure there's a car patrolling for a few nights and walking the halls a time or two to make sure no one's trying to get in. Chances of his knowing which apartment you're in are pretty low, since he drove off before you went back to it, Maggie. But we won't leave you stranded while you're staying there. When do you go back to Key West, by the way?"

"Vanny's coming back on Tuesday morning, so we plan to leave shortly after he's back," Carolyn told him.

"Okay, then, we'll send a patrol car over now and we'll be leaving to check out that compactor, ourselves. How long is the office open? I'm assuming it takes a key to get into the compactor building from the back."

"They closed at 5, but they'd answer a call from you, I would think. The maintenance people on call will unlock it for you."

Flagg smiled at Carolyn, and said, "I'm sure you're right. Do you have the number with you?"

After she gave it to him, the ladies thanked them, as they did the two of them for bringing the information to their attention. They assured them they'd have a patrol car driving into and around the senior community night and day, but advised them to call the number on the card they were given, if they saw him again. They assured the detectives they would do that and left the station.

Six

"I'll tell you, I'm more scared now than I was before we reported it. What if that guy finds out we went to the cops. He'll kill us for sure."

"I think you need to talk with Homer. Why don't you dial him now while I drive us home?"

"I'd like for him to know, but why don't you tell him since it's on speaker in your car, anyway."

The younger woman smiled at her friend. "Okay, I'll tell him but he'll want to talk to you so he'll know you're okay."

"I know, but I just can't tell him after – you know." She threw her a sidelong glance, before staring out at the road again.

"I understand." She asked her phone to call Homer, and soon his voice came over the speaker.

"Hey Carolyn, how's it going up there? Is our Mag behaving herself?" They heard him laugh and then it sounded like he took a drink of something – probably his beloved Sam Adams beer.

"Uh, that's why we're calling," she answered. "Now, Maggie did nothing wrong, but she's in trouble, nonetheless."

"Aw, please, tell me it involves anything other than another murder."

"I'm afraid that's exactly what it involves, Homer. In fact, we're just leaving the sheriff's office and heading home now."

"Mag, are you okay?"

"Yeah, nothing to worry about. Why don't we call you again when we get home, so Carolyn won't be distracted while she's trying to drive."

She was stalling and he knew it, but he said, "Okay. Carolyn, call me as soon as you walk in the door, okay?" They could hear the tension in his normally cocky voice.

"We'll do it first thing. Bye now."

"Bye, Homer."

It was quiet in the car after he disconnected. Neither spoke until they pulled into Windsor Park. "Uh, Carolyn, don't go through the left gate."

Knowing she didn't want to see the compactor building, Carolyn went through the open right gate behind another resident and circled around until she came to the building Vanny lived in and parked near the sidewalk to the outside hallway and the elevator.

Maggie looked around frantically to make sure there was no man who looked like the killer sitting in wait of them. They both nodded to the young deputy parked in front of the swimming pool where she could keep an eye on all the exits of the building. She nodded back, but none of them waved. Maggie let out the deep breath she'd been holding.

After they got off the elevator, they saw another deputy. Like Jackson, he was a big burly guy who looked like he could be a star on the wrestling circuit. What do they feed these guys in West Palm, anyway? He introduced himself, nodded for them to unlock the door, but held up a hand against their coming in with him. After a quick but thorough perusal, he called for them to come inside. Carolyn locked the door behind them.

"Are – are you going to stay in here with us?"

"No, Ms. Maggie, the lieutenant just asked me to make sure you arrived okay and that your place was clear. I'll be going, but I'll be right outside with the other deputy until we're relieved tonight by two others. One of us will walk the halls periodically. We're not taking any chances if this guy might still be around."

"Thank you, sir. Please excuse me. I think I'll lie down in Carolyn's room for a while." She turned without another word and went into the back bedroom, closing the door behind her. They listened as she closed the blinds and lay down.

"Thank you," Carolyn told him. "We really appreciate that. This has scared my friend more than she's saying."

"The chief said you went through something similar in Key West a couple years ago. That right?"

"Yes, please, have a seat and I'll explain, but first I need to put some coffee on and call our friend down there so he won't worry. I can fill a couple thermoses for you and the other officer, after it brews."

"Sure, take your time. I'll be glad to make the coffee, though. I do a pretty credible job, so they tell me at the station." He smiled and noticed tears in her eyes.

"That's sweet of you. Thank you. I promised Homer I'd call, and I'll just be a minute."

True to her word, Carolyn called Homer, explaining they were both fine but that a deputy was there now and she'd call again when he left. Homer sighed. "Okay, but please don't forget. If I don't hear back from you within a half hour, I'm calling you."

"You won't have to. I'll get back to you before then, I promise." He sounded satisfied and disconnected, just as the deputy handed her a mug of piping hot coffee. She told him thanks.

"Do you want cream and sugar, Ma'am?"

"Carolyn, please. And, I'll get it. It's right here on the bar." She prepped her coffee, took a long drink and then sat across from him at the round table. It already had been a very long night and she felt drained of energy.

"You see, it was I who saw the killer first in Key West. Maggie..." She smiled, and said, "Maggie, though you can't tell it from how frightened she is today, is a detective wannabe. Of course, she'd never admit to that."

The deputy laughed heartily, "I can see that. She looks the type to want to go after the bad guy."

"Very much so, but she almost died trying to disarm one of the bad guys in that murder."

She told him the whole story, and he said, "Well, West Palm's not Key West and there're too many places up here a guy can hide and lie in wait for someone he's after. And trust me, if Maggie saw what he did and if he made a point of letting her know he knows what she looks like, he will lie in wait for her."

"Oh God, to have you echo what I've been thinking scares me to death, Deputy Ganon."

"I don't mean to scare you, but it's a bad situation. If that guy ever sees her, before we see him, you know darned well he'll get to her and then it's anyone's guess what he'd do. He could drag her into his car, drive to an isolated beach and throw her into the ocean, or he could drive west toward Belle Glade and dump her body into a deep canal or a cane field and it would be months before anyone would discover her. Or he could just keep driving north and who knows where he'd get rid of her."

Neither of them noticed that Maggie had come into the kitchen and was starting to pour a cup of coffee when she turned white and fainted dead away on the faux hardwood tile. They heard the crash at the same time and jumped up.

"Oh God, Mag!"

"I'm sorry, I didn't hear her door open."

"She came through the bathroom door that was open already, so I didn't hear her, either."

The deputy got her to come to and they sat her up on the floor after examining her and asking her if she hurt, anywhere, which she denied. "I'm sorry, Ms. Maggie. I wouldn't have said what I did had I known you were standing there. I had no business saying it, anyway."

"Not – not your fault. You were just doing your due diligence in leveling with Carolyn," she said, patting his hand that was around her waist. "Not anyone's fault. It is what it is, and I know I'm in big trouble here."

"Don't try to talk anymore, Maggie. Forget the coffee and let us walk you back into the bedroom."

"No, I was worse being in there. Every time I tried to close my eyes, I saw that horrible man leering down at me the way he did by the swing.

I'm fine. Just let me drink some of that great smelling coffee of yours and I'll sit out here with the two of you."

"It's Deputy Ganon's coffee. He made it while I called Homer."

"I'll bet he's on the way up right now." She smiled at the younger woman.

"No, he's waiting for another call. I told him the deputy was here and I'd call when he left, so he really doesn't know what's happened."

"And I won't keep you ladies much longer," the officer told them. "Here, let me help you to the couch. There now, just rest and – oh, here's your coffee now. Your friend's way ahead of me."

Maggie smiled at them and took the mug of steaming coffee, doctored by Carolyn just the way she knew her friend liked it. After a sip, she said, "That's great coffee, deputy. Thanks."

"You're welcome, Ma'am. Oh, one more thing before I go. Is there anything else about that guy you've remembered that you didn't tell us at the station?" As he talked, Carolyn fixed the two thermoses with coffee as she'd promised and put some pastries into a bag for him. He nodded his thanks.

"No, except Carolyn drew a picture of him right after I told her what he looked like. I know your lieutenant said someone would come here with a sketch artist, but she's very good and that sketch of the other man helped the police in Key West." She took another relaxing drink of coffee. The color was returning to her face, to Carolyn's relief.

"I gave that to Lieutenant Jackson. They said they wouldn't need us to work with the artist after seeing it."

After Deputy Ganon left, it wasn't long before there was a knock at the door, causing both women to start and almost drop their mugs of coffee.

SEVEN

Carolyn opened the door, after she saw him. "What on earth are you doing here?"

Homer grinned and hugged her and then walked over to the couch and hugged Maggie, who was watching a new mystery drama on HBO. "Hi Mag, " he said, his hand going to her forehead.

"I'm not sick, Homer, so stop checking for a fever. I just saw a man throw away a body, that's all."

"That's all? Mag, you make it sound like people see thugs throw away a body every day of the week." He tried to laugh, but it came out a choked sound, and he quickly looked away at the large tree covering their view of the courtyard. "That's a huge gumbo limbo out there, Carolyn."

Carolyn put her hand on his shoulder, but said nothing. He reached up and grabbed her hand with a gentle tug and said, "Come on, let's all sit down and you can tell me what happened from the beginning. I went over to the deputies to tell them my name and that I'm your friend from the rock. Deputy Ganon said he heard you call me that on the phone and to go right upstairs."

"Are you staying?" Mag choked on the words, hoping he would but afraid he was going back home in a short while.

"Are you serious? Of course I'm staying. We've always gone through everything together. I'm not ditching you now," he said with a wink at

20

Carolyn, whom he'd always been a bit in love with, but since she wasn't buying it never went anywhere. "I hopped in the Hummer as soon as Carolyn called from the car."

Maggie burst into tears, surprising both of them. They let her finish and Homer said, "If it's going to be too much for you, why don't you go in and go to bed early. Carolyn can catch me up."

"Okay, but I don't want to be alone all night. Carolyn, you've had the bed this whole time, but do you mind if I sleep in it, too. Being a king size, I'm sure there's enough room. Homer can take the sofa bed in the den."

Carolyn patted her hand, and said, "Sure, honey, whatever you want we'll do. I was going to suggest it, anyway."

"I don't know why I'm being such a wimp about it. I'll get back to normal when we're back in Key West," she said, sniffing loudly.

"Normal?" Homer laughed and she smiled at him. "Maggie, if you were normal, neither of us would want to be with you all the time. That's what we love about you. You're eccentric and as stubborn as a mule, but we wouldn't have it any other way."

"Oh be quiet. You know what I mean," she said, with a smile for this man who meant so much to her. He was twenty years her junior, but she felt protective of him, even though he was the strongest of the three of them. They were her family and she loved them like the mother she could have been at 71 years of age, although she thought she was a very young seventy-one and no one could doubt it with her trim figure and long silky hair.

The knock on the door startled them again, and Homer walked to the end of the short hallway and looked out the peephole at burly Lieutenant Jackson. Behind him was Detective Flagg. "Carolyn, take a peep. Are those the cops? If not, call 911."

She smiled and opened the door. "Hello, Detectives. Please, come in. This is our friend Homer Wiley from Key West. Homer, Lieutenant Jackson and Detective Flagg."

They shook hands and she invited them to sit. "Hello, Ms. Maggie, are you feeling any better? Young Ganon told us you'd fainted earlier," the lieutenant said with concern in his kind, but tired, gray eyes. Homer's eyebrows shot up alarm.

"Nah, I just slipped on something in the kitchen. Thought I'd mopped the floor clean last night, but guess I must not have gotten everything."

He smiled and said, "Yes, I do that myself from time to time. I'll get right to it, if you don't mind. We wanted to let you know we – we recovered some of the body from the compactor, enough that the maintenance man told us the man did live here. His name was Nelson Blake. Ring any bells for either of you?"

"No," they told him in unison, Maggie's eyes tearing up again. His putting a name to the body made him more real to her.

"Well, apparently he lived in the far north building. Turns out he's a wanted felon, so we expect the guy who offed him was wanted, also, or at least is mixed up in the stolen goods ring he ran from his apartment. We found a lot he'd been dealing in right there in his back bedroom. Quite a haul that he must have been getting ready for his fence. Most of it was from a big heist they'd done – or someone had done – in Boca last week," Jackson said.

"Yeah, we don't know what went down that caused his pal to off him, but you can take it to the bank it was over money."

"I see," Maggie told the younger detective. "And you really think he'll want to – to off me, too?" They both smiled at her language, as did Carolyn and Homer. It was nothing new to them, since she'd adopted it when she was involved with the murders in Key West.

"Well, put it this way, he's seen you and guys who commit atrocious crimes like that usually try to tie up loose ends – if you know what I mean."

She gulped and took another sip of tea from the white porcelain cup she'd been holding that was now shaking like it contained Mexican jumping beans, not tea. After she drank, Carolyn reached over and took it from her hands to put it back in the saucer. Maggie said nothing but gave her a small smile. "Well, looks like we'd better call Vanny and let him know what's going on, don't you think?"

Carolyn nodded and said, "I'll call him after the detectives leave."

"Actually we took the liberty of speaking with your friend before we came back up here. We asked whether he knew the deceased and he said if he had it would have been from being at the mail boxes or pool, and the men in the neighborhood aren't great at introducing themselves even when they saw each other every day, as though names weren't that important to them now that they were retired. We told him we'd be patrolling around the buildings for the next few days even after you've gone back to Key West."

"Well, that's good to know – in case the guy circled around and saw which apartment I went into," Maggie told them, despite not seeing any car as she made her way back to Carolyn. "I'd feel awful if poor Vanny got hurt just because I'd been staying here."

"Yes, I'm glad, also." Carolyn smiled at both the detectives who rose from their comfortable seats on the red leather sectional in front of the sunny yellow-orange colored accent wall. "Thank you both for all you're doing to try to catch that awful person."

"Yes, thank you," Maggie echoed. "If you'll all excuse me, I think I'm going to take a nap, maybe even sleep through the night if I don't wake up hungry. It's been a very long day and I'm beginning to feel it. "

"Of course, and if you think of anything else later this evening or any time before you leave West Palm, please just give us a call."

"I'll do that. Excuse me," she said and left the group standing looking after her.

"This is really hard for her, I know," Jackson told Carolyn and Homer. "It'd be hard on any of us, knowing a creep of a killer knew we saw him dispose of a body like that. He's a brazen one, too, to have done it in broad daylight and they're the worst. I have a feeling that stealing a room full of jewelry isn't what he usually does. I expect it was just to make a great deal of money quickly. Someone like that is a hard-core killer, who's probably killed several times. They don't seem to care who knows what they've done. They just take care of 'the problem' and get on with things. I don't know why he left most of it in Mr. Blake's apartment, when he could have gone back and taken it along with his money. Maybe he'd planned to go back for it, but then thought he'd better just get out of here since Maggie saw him and could report it to us."

Carolyn wrapped her arms around herself and said, "That's what worries me. I wish Vanny could come back a day early so we could get her away from here. I have this creepy feeling he's out there by the pool or somewhere just waiting for a chance to get our Maggie."

"Well, if he is, he won't get through the officers parked downstairs. And, he sure won't get through this Marine," Homer told her with a big smile. "So don't you worry, we'll all make sure he doesn't get near her – near either of you."

"He's right about that. We aren't going to remove the officers from in front of the pool. They'll have their eyes on this building the whole time you're here. Ganon's covering the sides and Aker, the middle. No one's going to get up on this floor without their knowing it and stopping him, since there are no backdoors to the apartments. We know what he looks like, thanks to you, so don't you worry about another thing. One of them will continue walking the halls every now and then, also."

She and Homer thanked them and they left the apartment. Lt. Jackson turned around and went back to knock on the door. "I forgot to tell you to call me before you leave Tuesday. I want a couple of my men to tail you down to Key West. They have months of comp time they need to use up, so I asked them if they'd mind taking it now down there." He smiled. "Of course, any of my guys will jump at the chance to spend time in Key West. They'll go to the KWPD after they see you safely home and apprise them of what's happened here, so they can be on the lookout, too."

"What? You think if he's hanging around, he'll follow us all that way to the end of the road?"

"Yeah I do, unfortunately. Like I said, these guys try to tie up any loose ends and Maggie's this creep's one loose end. It's just an extra precaution, Homer. Chances are he didn't even live here and is long gone by now, but we want to cover all our bases."

"We appreciate that, Lieutenant," Homer told him, smiling at Carolyn. "We'll just have us a three car caravan."

"Well, I need to get back so I'll leave you folks now. Try not to worry about this and spoil your whole night."

"Thank you," Carolyn told him, and locked the door behind him.

"Why don't you go in and take a nap, too, while Maggie's asleep. Who knows what's in store for either of you in the next couple of days. I'll get some dinner started in a couple hours. Would spaghetti and meat balls be okay?"

"Thanks. I think I'll do that. And that sounds good to wake up to, since we haven't had any since we came up here. You'll find everything in the pantry, and I saw a bag of meatballs in the freezer, so you won't have to make them from scratch. Do you mind if I stretch out on the sofa bed. I don't want to disturb Maggie if she's gone to sleep."

"Of course not. I have my book to read, so wasn't going to go in there, anyway. You go right ahead and I'll be here to answer the door or whatever. Unless you want company," he said, with a big grin. She just threw up a hand and kept walking into the den.

EiGHT

When Tom Vangrift returned the following Tuesday, Maggie and Carolyn were already packed and Homer had the car loaded to leave shortly after he got home. "Well, from what the cops tell me life hasn't been boring around here," he said, tentatively, after he was introduced to Homer.

"No, it hasn't, I'm afraid," Carolyn told him.

"Maggie, I'm really sorry you had to witness that awful scene down by the lake. I can just imagine how frightening it must have been for you."

"Thanks. Yes, I don't know when I've been so scared. I really didn't think he was going to leave me sitting there alive," she said, clearing her throat and tugging on her plaid shirt at the hem. He went to her and threw his arms around her, holding her for a long time.

"Uh, Vanny, Maggie and I've thrown together a little bit of a buffet luncheon, but wanted to wait for you to get here. You didn't stop for lunch along the road, did you?" Carolyn knew if they kept talking about the murder, Maggie was going to be in a funk again and not touch her lunch. They planned to drive straight to the end of the road without stopping, unless the cops wanted to stop.

Understanding she wanted him to stop talking about it, he smiled and said, "No, I stopped in Orlando and had breakfast earlier, so wasn't hungry till now. That food really looks good, hon. Thanks for waiting for me."

Homer kept glancing over at Maggie during lunch at the round dining room table, but she kept her head down throughout most of the meal, rarely commenting to any of the light banter going on around her. At least she's eating, he thought, as he chewed his roast beef on rye. He finished it and poured himself another cup of coffee, after offering to get refills for the rest of them, who didn't want one.

"How did you find things in Mt. Dora?" Carolyn asked Vanny, after things started to get quiet and tense again.

He laughed and said, "I never realized how much stuff Aunt Loni had until I got back from seeing her the first night and decided to start right in on it. I mean, besides all that antique furniture I'm sure you noticed when I took you up there a few years ago, she had three closets with clothes in them. One was entirely cold weather stuff, one was all slacks and the other was tops and dresses."

"Oh my, she was quite the organized being then, wasn't she. I loved the eclectic furniture in that house. You must have gotten a fortune from it, alone."

"No, as a matter of fact, she stipulated in her will that none of it was to be sold. All of it was to be donated to a little museum about ten miles out of town and her clothing to the local shelter. Knowing she'd planned this, the curator, who was the only person on staff, already cleared one entire room months before she died, so all her furniture could be placed in there as one great room with her ornate Japanese screens separating the bed and bedroom furnishings from the rest of the room."

"Oh my goodness," Carolyn said, as she poured another coffee. "So, you had most of the work done before she died then."

"Yes, it's what she wanted. She said she didn't want me just sitting in the room waiting for her to die. She only wanted me to come to visit her in the early evening each day and of course, they called me when things turned imminent so I was with her for the last hours." He became a bit emotional then and stopped to drink some more coffee. Maggie reached over and patted his hand and he smiled at her.

"I can understand her wanting that and I'm sure she appreciated that you were at her bedside when the end came," Carolyn told him.

"Yes, her last words to me before she became unresponsive were 'thank you for everything you've done for me'. Of course, thanks was never necessary. She was all I had left in the way of blood family, so of course, I wanted to help her all I could. It helped me, too, knowing we were together as often as I could get up there. Anyway, the museum room turned out quite lovely. She'd told him exactly how she wanted it all arranged, with an electric fireplace and mantel as the center of it all, which he provided. It was also antique so it all came together around it. He didn't open it to the public until after the funeral, of course, but since he had it all arranged before Aunt Lonny died, I took photos of it to the facility and she loved it. He leaves the fireplace turned on all the time while the museum is open. I didn't think it would all fit in there, but it did. It's like a lovely studio apartment. He has an iron plaque standing at the entrance saying it is the furniture of Mt. Dora's legendary Lona Vangrift." He laughed then, and they all smiled at him. "Aunt Loni also stipulated that she didn't want it to be on display with touching forbidden as in most museums. She wanted the visitors to enjoy the furniture as she always did, so when he has any customers, he makes tea that they take in Lona's House before they leave. That's the name she wanted the room to be called. So, they sit on the comfy furniture and chat as though they were home. Isn't that a hoot? She would be immensely pleased with the whole thing."

"Well, that certainly is different and it was sweet of you to take photos of it to her before she died," Carolyn said. "It was generous of your aunt to do that with her furnishings. So, the house is now for sale?"

"Yes, it is. Since Aunt Loni was in the assisted living facility and I purposefully stayed elsewhere, knowing all I had to do with the house, I spent the next two weeks after the furniture was out taking my time with cleaning and painting, so it should sell fairly soon, the realtor told me."

"We'll all have to go up there one day and take tea in Lona's House. Of course, we'd pick you up on the way up, Vanny," Maggie said, brightening at the prospect of going on such a pleasant excursion having nothing whatsoever to do with dead bodies – not that Lona Vangrift was alive, but at least she wasn't murdered.

"Not for a while," Homer told them, "and if we're going to get home before nightfall, we'd better get on the road now."

Looking at the clock on the console and seeing it was already three, Maggie agreed. "I'll just clear up these..."

"Oh no, you don't. You ladies prepared this delicious treat, so I'm clearing and putting everything in the dishwasher after you leave. Now, are you sure you got everything and do you need help with any of it?"

Homer said, "Thanks, pal, but it's all packed away in the Hummer, so there's nothing left to do except get these ladies home."

Carolyn came out of the bathroom and gave Vanny a big hug. "Thanks so much for letting us stay here while you took care of things up there. The pool was perfect and – well, until the incident the other day, we had a really relaxing time."

"Yes, we did and we'll let you know when we want to make that trip to the center of the state to see what you've done with the antiques." Maggie's smile came easily now.

"Most of it was planned by Aunt Loni and the curator did most of the arranging. I just put the side pieces around the room after he told me where she wanted him to put all the furniture. Anytime you want to go, just give me a call, stop here overnight and we'll go on up to Mt. Dora. I found a delightful B&B we can all stay in while we're up there. They make the best cannoli," he said, grinning at Maggie, knowing her penchant for sweets.

"Great," she told him, with another big smile.

"And it is I who needs to thank you and Carolyn. I was expecting her to die, but Carolyn can tell you I was a basket case when I realized it was really happening. I don't know what I would have done had you said you didn't have time to house-sit for me. And again, Maggie, I'm sorry for what you went through. I'll let you know when they capture that jerk who did it, though I'm sure you'll probably have been informed by the S. O. before they even broadcast it."

"You're probably right about that, which is fine, but I just want him caught, no matter who learns about it first."

29

"Thanks, hon," Carolyn told him, pressing her hand to his cheek. He took it and gave it a kiss, before releasing it. "Oh, I forgot, I need to let the lieutenant know we're ready to leave."

"Bye, Vanny, it was nice meeting you, and we'll see you the next time we're up this way," Homer told him, as he shook his hand and opened the door for the ladies. Maggie gave him a big hug before she went out the door, with Carolyn following as she dialed the number on her cell phone. Maggie also given him a gift he didn't know about until he went to bed that night. There on the top of the ebony bureau was a thank you note with $500 in it. His mouth flew open when he saw what was in the envelope. He'd paid them $200 to housesit for two weeks and ended up making $300. He smiled and said aloud, "Maggie Metronia, she always told me you were one sweet and generous lady."

He reached for his cell phone and called Carolyn on hers. "Hey Caro, can you put Maggie on the line, please." He was the only one who could get away with calling her the nickname her mother had for her. She had a contentious though loving relationship with her mother, who hated that she still lived in Key West after the murder in her condo building. She wanted her to move back to where she was born and raised in North Carolina, to the very town that housed her ex and his present wife, Delilah, whom she swore had been a stripper before he married her, since when he first saw her at Fantasy Fest one October, she wore only body paint and nothing else. Thinking Carolyn hadn't seen him, he slipped her his card. Carolyn saw it all through her mirrored sunglasses, but she'd always taken the attitude that they deserved each other and was very happy and content with her life without him on the island.

Baffled, she turned off the speaker and handed the phone to Maggie. "Hi Vanny, did something else happen? If so, that was really quick."

He laughed. "Yes, something else happened. I met a wonderful little generous lady who lives on my favorite island in the world and she left me an unexpected gift on the bureau."

"You weren't supposed to see that till we got home."

"Well, I went into the bedroom to get out of my clothes and have a soak and saw the envelope when I was taking off my rings and getting out clean socks. Thank you, Maggie, but that was certainly not necessary, since you were doing me a favor."

"You gave me a nice comfy bed to sleep in with that big thick mattress topper on it and a pool to die for, so we're even. In fact, I got so used to that pool that I'm calling my contractor as soon as we get home to start putting one in the backyard for us."

Carolyn glanced over at her, with a grin, but said nothing. After she stopped talking with Vanny, Maggie looked at her and asked, "Wouldn't you like a pool in the backyard?"

Laughing, she said, "It sounds like a done deal and sure I'd like it. What was that all about, anyway?"

Her innocent face intact, her friend asked, "What was all what about?"

"Oh stop. You know perfectly well what I'm talking about."

"It was nothing. He was just saying how nice it was to finally meet and I agree."

NINE

Carolyn chuckled to herself. She knew, unless Vanny said something to her, Maggie had no intention of telling her the real reason he called. She sighed and her attention was riveted back onto the busy turnpike. Within a few minutes she heard soft snoring, and glanced over at her friend. She had her seat reclined and was sound asleep in it. She smiled and looked back at the road and then ahead at Homer in Maggie's Humvee, as she kept pace with him feeling good that he was ahead of them. As they went around a curve she could see the unmarked sheriff's office car behind them, another comfortable sight to see. She felt quite safe and was glad to be between both cars, as they neared Florida City.

Her phone brought her out of her reverie. It was Detective Flagg, whom the lieutenant sent with them along with young Officer Ganon, thinking since they already were familiar with the case it would be easier all around, especially for Maggie, plus they really did need to use those weeks of comp hours or they'd lose them.

"Hello, Detective."

"Hi Carolyn, will you alert Homer and then stop at Alabama Jack's. Ganon and I didn't take time for lunch and I need to go over the game plan with the three of you, anyway, since we won't be stopping again before we get to the end of the road."

"Sure, I'll be glad to. We had a large buffet lunch, but we could all use some coffee and dessert before we get home." After they disconnected she alerted Homer and the three of them turned off onto Card Sound Road as soon as they got through Florida City.

"Maggie, wake up, dear." She had to call her twice. That was the deepest sleep she'd had since all the business at Windsor Park. "We're going to stop at Jack's so the guys can eat lunch and let us know what's going to happen when we get home."

"Oh, okay. I could use some coffee, I suppose," she said, rubbing her eyes with her knuckles as if that would wake her up more, causing Carolyn to smile. "Can't believe we've made such good time."

"Yes, it's been a good trip so far, not too much traffic, and we should avoid the evening rush hour if we don't stay too long at the restaurant. I'm glad you got a little sleep in on the turnpike. I know you've been exhausted and not sleeping too well since – you know."

Maggie looked at her and smiled, while patting her hand. "Well, here we are, " she told Carolyn. "I'll just run in and splash some water on my face while you find us a table."

"Okay, looks like your table in the corner by the water is empty, so I'll grab it," Carolyn said as they got out of the cars and went inside. "Over here, guys." They all followed her to the corner and sat down, leaving a chair by the water for Maggie. There were few patrons in the restaurant that time of day, so they could choose.

Ganon asked, "Is that where you saw the body, Homer?" He nodded toward the mangroves across from the restaurant.

"Yes, we could see it clearly hanging right over the thick roots in the middle where it looks like there's a pathway. Of course, there isn't, but the roots are cut in a little more there than in the rest of the mangrove." He sighed. "I sure wouldn't want to go through that again."

"Nor would I," Carolyn said, with a bit of a smile, even though she didn't get in on it until after their little stunt in the mangroves. A couple minutes later, Maggie came from around the bar to where they sat.

"You look wide awake and perky," Homer told her, as she reached the table and he got up for her to take her seat. The cops stood also, not because they were blocking her path but out of respect for this little elderly woman they were beginning to care about. Maggie had that quality in her that drew people to her almost as soon as they met her.

"Amazing what a splash of cold water will do. Have you ordered, yet," she asked, as she sat down, straightened out her top and smoothed her cotton slacks with her other hand, her eyes going to the mangroves, as much as she didn't want to be reminded.

"No, the waitress hasn't been here, yet – oh, here she comes now," Ganon told her. She greeted them with a smile and told the three regulars it was nice to see them again. They told her the same and after everyone gave her their orders, she left them alone to go for their drinks.

"Okay, let me tell you what's going to happen in Key West, " Flagg said. "First, as soon as we hit town, we're all going to the PD. We're to see a Lieutenant Butler there. You know him?"

"Yes, he handled Strummond's case," Homer told him, not adding that he wasn't his favorite person because of their teenaged history.

"Good, that's good. He's been apprised of what went down in West Palm, and he and one of his guys is going to go to your house with us, Maggie."

She looked puzzled. "For what? You don't think that guy knows where we live and came down in wait of us, do you?"

"We don't know what he's been doing since the murder, but we're not taking any chances. It's just a routine precaution we'd take with anyone and we'll be through in no time. After that, we'll check into our hotel – we're at the Southernmost, since it's almost across the street from you and we could get to you quickly."

Carolyn said, "You really are afraid he's followed us, don't you?"

"Like I said, it's just a precaution. I don't want you to be afraid, but back around the Coral Springs' exit, we noticed a tail we'd suspected when we neared Boca. Thought he'd turned off, but he popped up again right before the exit."

"Oh no," Maggie said, her face white with fear.

"Now, Maggie, please don't jump the gun, because it could just be a coincidence. Since the turnpike and the Sawgrass weren't that crowded, it probably is. But that's why we wanted to stop at Jack's – to see whether the same guy turned off onto Card Sound."

"And did he?" Homer had been quiet until now.

Ganon said, "Yes, he did, but he went on through the toll booth."

"Well, that's good, then," Carolyn told him, smiling at Maggie.

"Maybe, maybe not," Flagg told her. "If he's our guy, we think he's probably waiting at one of the little alcoves past the bridge, until he sees us go by and then he'll follow us again."

"But if you see him, why can't you just arrest him?" Homer asked. The women nodded.

"If we see him, we'll let you go ahead, and then when he pulls in behind us, we'll pull off the road, let him get ahead of us and then we'll put our light on and stop him. If it's him, of course, we'll detain him."

"Detain him?" Carolyn asked. "Why not just arrest him?"

"Because Monroe isn't our jurisdiction. We'll call for backup from the MCSO, so they can meet us and pull over into his path as soon as we put our lights on and they can arrest him."

"I see," she said. "Well, that makes sense. We certainly wouldn't want his case thrown out on a technicality."

"No, we sure wouldn't," Maggie added.

"Remember it might just be a coincidence and there might be no reason to detain him at all," Ganon, who'd been quiet until that moment, told her. "He might not be your guy, Maggie."

"Okay then, let's enjoy our coffee and eats and we'll be on our way. Oh, I do want to add one thing. If we see the guy, don't look over at him and if you see a cruiser coming toward you, I want you to pull both vehicles off to the side of the road, make sure your doors are locked and duck down until we give the all clear because if it is him and he sees we have him cornered, he'll probably start shooting at us and we don't want you caught in the crossfire. Clear?"

They all said yes, and went back to drinking their coffee and waiting for the rest of their orders to reach the table, each in his and her own thoughts.

TEN

If the suspect was the one following the detective and Officer Ganon, he played it differently than they figured he would, since they passed no car sitting in the alcoves tucked along the rest of Card Sound Road as they continued on their journey south. It was a major disappointment to the two officers, since it would have been the best case scenario to ending the manhunt and making sure Maggie was safe.

Flagg's phone rang and Homer said, "Well, since we didn't see the guy on Card Sound, what's your game plan, now?"

"We'll keep an eye out for the Cruze on our way down and will do the same thing – call the SO if we see him. I have to tell you, though, if it was him, he's playing it pretty cagey and will probably give us the slip. With traffic picking up, he'd easily be able to stay three or four vehicles behind us, undetected, and follow us clear to the island. Butler knows about the NRA sign in the rear window of the vehicle and has cars planted north and south along AIA and Roosevelt, so they might even have him by the time we get to the PD."

"Sounds like you have it covered pretty well. I won't worry about the ladies, then," Homer told him. "Thanks, Flagg."

"You're welcome, just enjoy the rest of the trip as you always do and let us do the worrying. That's what we're getting paid the big bucks for," he said with a chuckle and wink at Maggie, causing the other man to laugh, also. Actually, since it was comp time they were not getting paid for it, but Maggie made it clear to them that if they were going to be her bodyguards, she was going to pay them for it and she wouldn't take no for an answer. Of course, as she always compensated anyone, she paid them far more than they'd ever made with the sheriff's office. She'd done that when they were sitting at Alabama Jack's after questioning them about how it worked with the S.O. and when they'd protested, she told them they could just turn around and go back to West Palm if they wouldn't let her do it. After a brief phone conversation with Jackson, who laughed and approved it since they were on their own time, they took the payment.

"I'll try, but I've been worrying over Maggie for decades now and doubt the scenery I always enjoy will cause me to let up on doing it now," he said before he disconnected.

In the other car, Maggie was deep in thought, as the Keys scenery, with all its beautiful blue/green waters on either side, palm trees, bougainvillea, and colorful buildings whizzed past as they did five above the speed limit . "Do you really think he followed us? Lying in wait for me in Key West?"

Her friend patted her hand. "No, I don't think you'll see him again, dear. Actually, I personally believe he left the state when you heard him pull out of the complex Saturday. Why would he hang around, risk getting caught and find himself in jail when he could be in New Orleans or Chicago by now?"

"You make sense, but I remember what young Officer Ganon said about killers wanting to tie up loose ends, too," she said, with a bit of a shiver.

"Is this too much air for you?"

"No, it's fine. I just get the chills when I think that guy could get to me again. And this time he won't give me just a shove – he'll do me in and get rid of the body quicker than he threw that bag of human flesh and bones down the compactor."

"Try not to think that way, Maggie. It won't help you and we don't know that he's not long gone from Florida by now," she said, patting her hand, which was as cold as an old-fashioned metal tray of ice cubes.

Homer was thinking the same as Carolyn as he drove alone down the Keys. He hoped he was right and they'd not see that White Chevy Cruze on the road. He hated to think of what could happen if they did and he recognized Maggie in Carolyn's Lincoln. He could cause them to crash and have her out of the car before anyone could blink twice. Damn, trouble just seems to follow her around. She's still in her early seventies so should be able to enjoy life now, without a care, being in such good health. His frustration caused him to momentarily swerve into the other lane, but he corrected before an oncoming truck reached him.

"Hey Homer," Carolyn said into her cell phone, "are you all right? You almost drove into that semi."

"Yeah, I'm fine, just have a lot on my mind and swerved a bit before I noticed what I was doing. Don't worry, I'll stay more alert now. How's Mag holding up?"

"She's sound asleep again. Hopefully, she'll sleep the rest of the trip and won't be worrying about – things."

"My sentiments, exactly. Well, you be careful, too, and I'll see you when we reach the rock, okay?"

"Okay, see you then."

Just then her phone rang again. Flagg asked, "Hey Carolyn, have you spoken with Homer lately?"

"Yes, I just called him because I saw him almost getting hit by that 18-wheeler back there."

"That's why I was calling. Is he okay? We can stop again if he needs it."

"Yes, he's fine. Said he just had his mind on something other than his driving, and he'd make an effort to stay more alert the rest of the trip."

"Okay, just wanted to make sure. We thought for sure he was going to buy the farm there for a minute. See you in Key West."

"Yes, I did, also. We're coming up on Sugarloaf, so we'll be there in fifteen or twenty minutes. Do you still want us to go straight to the police station?"

"Yes, the game plan's the same, since it looks like our guy is too cagey to show his hand out here on the highway if it was him and with that traffic behind us, we don't see any white cars, period, much less any Cruzes."

"Okay, we'll see you there."

After they passed through Sugarloaf Key, the fourteen miles went quickly and soon they were all pulling into the police station parking lot. They got out, met at the door and Flagg pressed the buzzer on the intercom to let the lieutenant know they were out there. They were buzzed into the building quickly and the secretary for the detective bureau met them in the hallway and rode up the elevator with them.

After introductions, Butler asked Flagg, "No sign of him on the highway, eh?"

"No, we thought we had a tail before we hit Card Sound, but if so, he was playing it safe by staying far enough back to stay out of sight, once we got off the road and back on U.S.1. I'm really disappointed we couldn't have ended this on Card Sound. That would have been our best bet to nab the guy."

"Yeah, I was hoping the same. Well, are we ready to do this?"

"I'm ready," Maggie said, with a big smile. "Can't wait to get home."

He returned her smile and said, "Okay, let's do it."

He drove ahead of Maggie and Carolyn, with the other two vehicles bringing up the rear. He turned into the double wide driveway and pulled up to the house, while Carolyn and Homer pulled in on the other side of him and Flagg. As planned, the three of them stayed in their vehicles, while Butler, one of his officers, Flagg and Ganon went into the house after he took Carolyn's keys to the big historic home.

The detectives searched the first floor, which was a carport and storage room, while the other KWPD officer searched around the outside of the house, and waited off the back patio while the others searched the other two floors, coming up empty. "Well, Ganon, you can tell them to come in now," Flagg said. "Looks like he's nowhere around here."

After they got into the house, Carolyn went straight to the kitchen and started coffee brewing, and Maggie found an apple pie in the freezer that still looked okay. She'd baked it right before they left for West Palm, so stuck it in the microwave in its glass pie dish. As they were all sitting around the big round kitchen table, Homer asked what was next on their agenda.

Butler told them they just had to sit tight. "He still could have been parked on a side street and followed us on foot to your street, saw where we stopped and went on to check into a motel or somewhere to wait us out."

Maggie shivered again. "You mean he still could come after me?"

Detective Flagg felt bad for her and tried to reassure her. "We don't know that for sure, Ms. Maggie. But remember, we're going to be right across South Street from you, in a room that faces United and Duval, so we'll still keep an eye on the house and if you so much as hear a single noise that you shouldn't hear around or inside, you just call my cell, Ganon will call the lieutenant and we'll all be over there before you can blink. You, also, Carolyn. Okay?"

They nodded and Maggie said, "Okay, but I have to tell you, I don't like being a sitting duck!"

He smiled and told her she wouldn't be alone and that was the important thing. For double protection for both of them, Homer had already decided to sleep on her sofa for as long as it took and already had his bag he'd packed before he left Sugarloaf to head for West Palm after that first call from Carolyn. They would be safe. He'd make sure of that. He had a license to carry a weapon and always had it with him, so he was ready for whatever happened. He secretly hoped nothing would and that their perp was long gone from the state of Florida by now. The two women were thinking the same thing.

ELEVEN

Weeks passed with no sign of the alleged killer, and all of them had begun to relax a little. Flagg had been in touch with Lieutenant Jackson who said if the guy didn't turn up by the following week, he thought it would be safe for Ganon and Flagg to return to West Palm. "Are you sure, Loo?"

"Hell no, I'm not sure of anything, but don't know how I'll justify more than six weeks down there since you've seen no sign of him after thinking he was your tail before Card Sound. Your comp time ends tomorrow and Ganon's next week. You can stay until his ends if you want since Maggie's paid you through next week."

"That's true. I hate leaving them exposed like that, though."

"I know how you feel, Flagg, but if he were going to show, it seems like he'd have done it by now, unless he made one or both of you. Let's just see what next week turns up, if anything. And in the meanwhile, I'll have another talk with the chief to see if I can get an extension on your time down there, since she's paying for it. Take the ladies and Homer out tonight and enjoy the island, why don't you?"

"Okay, we can use some recreation. We've gone out to dinner and shadowed them a few times, but mostly we've been holed up here. Damn, I wish he'd show his face so we could get this over with and she'd be safe from him."

"I know it's frustrating, but you're an old hand at this, pal, so just try to relax for a while. Talk to you next week."

The five of them and Butler went to the Chart Room for drinks and then came back to Louie's Backyard for dinner, making it look as though they weren't together, as usual. It was nice getting away from the stakeout motel for a little while, and they all enjoyed it. "Uh, Maggie, I didn't want to say anything to spoil our night out," Flagg said, when they were all having coffee and relaxing by the ocean, a table apart, "but I spoke with the Lieutenant earlier today and he said unless the chief grants us an extension, Ganon and I'll have to wrap things up down here and get back to West Palm if nothing happens next week."

Maggie felt dismayed by this news, but she tried to not show it. "Well," she said, brightly, "you gotta do what you gotta do, I suppose. We appreciate that you've been here this long. It really made us feel safer, along with the local cops cruising around every little while. It was good of Lieutenant Jackson to let you do it."

"Well, since it was comp time we were entitled to, anyway, he couldn't very well have said no to your offer to pay us if he'd let us stay a few more weeks."

"It was the least I could do, and like I said, it was good you were able to do it as long as you could, but if you're needed back in West Palm, so be it. We'll be okay, I'm sure, either way."

Butler spoke up then from the cop table without turning to look at them. "We'll keep cruising around your place, Maggie. You won't be without police protection after the guys leave."

Carolyn and Homer looked at Maggie. They wished the Key West cops could take over the stakeout after the others left, but they said nothing, since she hadn't said anything. It was late and the tide was being pulled into shore. The moon was bright above them and left the ocean waves shimmering with satiny light. A few gulls squealed overhead as they dove for food and a couple were picking through droppings from a few tables of other patrons.

A rooster's sudden crowing startled them and they all laughed. It didn't have to be dawn for Key Westers to hear that sound. They watched as he, his hen and their brood of tiny white chicks crossed under their table and went to peck the ground around the others. As this tableau unfolded before them, they were totally unaware of the man sitting on the far side of the group of tables in Louie's, watching them closely. He was dressed in shorts, t-shirt and flip-flops, blending in with the rest of the late night crowd at Louie's.

After they all went back to Maggie's, the three cops searched carefully throughout the big house on the corner until they were satisfied he was nowhere near them. They went back to their nest at the Southernmost Motel directly across the street from where he was staying and had been ever since spotting them turning into the big white house with the red trim as soon as they left the KWPD station the day they came back into town. He'd long since ditched the Cruze and was driving a nondescript black Ford Fiesta now, and because he'd grown a longish dark beard since he first saw Maggie at the compactor station in West Palm, he'd gambled there was no way they'd spot him. His gamble paid off, since they'd even passed him on the street once or twice without so much as a flicker of recognition.

"Well, no one's here or on the grounds, so you all can sleep well tonight. One of us will still be watching the house constantly while the other one's grabbing a few winks and then we'll change places, so you can rest tonight."

"Thank you, Officer Ganon, we appreciate everything you're doing and sure hope you get that extension. It's been nice knowing you're just across the street from us."

"It's been our pleasure, Ms. Maggie," Ganon told her with a genuine smile. "This has been one of the nicest assignments we've ever had and I for one am enjoying it. Night."

They all said good night and the men left, Butler going back to the station and the other two to the motel. Carolyn went upstairs to the third floor, while Maggie went to her bedroom on the second, leaving Homer making up his bed on the sofa in the great room they rarely used. They slept the night through, never knowing how close to her the killer was. Or that he'd smiled to himself, from the top floor of his motel, watching as the detectives came out of the big white house with a satisfied look on their faces, knowing he wasn't anywhere near – "or so they think," he said aloud, and then laughed heartily, knowing he had the upper hand.

TWELVE

At eight the next morning, there was a tap on the door and Homer, who'd been awake for a few hours, put his hand on his gun and looked through the peep hole to see the two West Palm cops standing on the downstairs porch at the back of the house.

"Hi Homer," Flagg said. After exchanging pleasantries, and going to the kitchen for some of Homer's "Baby's" coffee, he said, "Well, we just got word from upstairs. The chief wouldn't grant us an extension, so we're leaving on Sunday."

"I figured as much, since there's been no sign of that jerk since we've been back. Can't blame the department. I'm sure you're needed more in West Palm than you are here babysitting the three of us."

Ganon smiled and said, "Hey, we've enjoyed having six weeks in Key West, and since we've been using our comp time, if not here, we'd have taken it somewhere else or lost it. Don't get a cushy assignment like this every day, you know."

"No, we sure don't," Flagg echoed. "Where're Mag and Carolyn?"

"In their bedrooms, but I heard footsteps above me a few minutes before you knocked on the door, so I expect Carolyn's up and ready for breakfast, and Maggie's usually awake early and just sits in her room reading her mysteries until she's sure the rest of the house is awake and hungry. You might as well have some with us."

Maggie popped her head around the corner and came into the kitchen, right after the three of them came inside. "Hi guys, what's going on?"

Carolyn also came into the kitchen at that moment and asked, "Did I miss something? Has something else happened?" Despite having a full modern kitchen in her own apartment, since the murder at Windsor Park, she'd made a habit of being wherever Maggie was most of the day. Having breakfast in Maggie's kitchen went along with that vigilance. She always helped keep her friend's fridge and pantry filled, knowing that's where the three of them took most of their meals.

"No, we were just having coffee until the two of you got here and then I was going to get breakfast started," Homer told both of them. "How about a stack of blueberry pancakes, some of your pastries, Mag, and eggs and bacon?"

"Sounds great," they all told him and Carolyn said she'd do the eggs and bacon. The detectives had been awake for several hours and both were ready for a meal.

"What's on your agenda for this morning, ladies?" the detective asked.

"I was just thinking maybe Carolyn and I could go grocery shopping. We haven't been since we got back home and we're starting to get low on some things."

"Sounds like a plan. We'll let Ganon tag along with you, staying in the background, of course, while you do your shopping and I'll go back to the motel and keep watch on the house. Are you going out, too, Homer?"

"No, I thought I'd get the mower out and start working on the yard while everyone's gone. Don't want the weeds to get much more of a head start or I'll end up pulling them before I can mow the grass."

"Okay, sounds like a plan. Ladies, give me a call when you're ready to pull out of the drive and I'll have Ganon follow behind you."

"Okay, thanks," Maggie told him. "There's something none of you aren't saying, though, isn't there?"

"Well," Flagg said, after swallowing a mouthful of eggs, "we wanted to wait until after you'd eaten, but since you ask, I'll tell you. The chief wouldn't okay more time down here. He thinks that if the guy hasn't been seen in six weeks, he's probably nowhere near the Keys. And, Maggie, I'm inclined to agree with him. If he were down here, you'd have seen him by now."

After she cleared up in the kitchen and she and Carolyn went back to their respective bathrooms to freshen up, they met downstairs and went out to the car, their pursuer's eyes on them the entire time. He started to go out to his own car, but changed his mind when he saw Ganon pull out behind them. He doubted the West Palm cops could stay much longer, since he'd stayed well out of sight while they were doing guard duty on the ladies and their friend. He had plenty of time and could easily wait them out.

He decided to go to the appraiser's office while they were out. Once there, he asked to see the records for the United St home. He learned Maggie Metronia had bought the house just a little over a year ago and that Carolyn Cramer lived in an apartment on the third floor. He had no idea whom the man was, but that wasn't important. He was probably a local cop, but when both the detectives left to go back where they belonged, their in-house cop would probably leave the house, too. And then when they were all gone, he'd pay a visit to Ms. Maggie and Ms. Carolyn, and then he could get the hell out of Dodge and not have to look over his shoulder, anymore. He had a big spread out in the wilds of Wyoming and couldn't wait to get back there with the dough he found in Blake's toilet tank after he realized the guy stiffed him for the heist and got rid of him. One woulda thought the guy woulda come up with somewhere more original than the tank. He laughed at the thought. It was only the second time he'd deviated from his murderous crimes and done a heist with someone. Too bad he wasn't very bright or he might have still been alive instead of stuffed in a garbage compactor. That thought sent him into a fit of laughter, to the point he was wiping his eyes from the tears. His only regret was that he couldn't go through with the second part of his plan and go back to the apartment to get as much of the jewelry as he could stuff in Blake's luggage. Had that toothless old bag not seen him, he would have, but he knew she'd call the cops as soon as she got back to wherever it was there that she lived. At the time he didn't know she was just visiting. He'd gone back periodically to Windsor Park to see if he could spot her and as luck would have it, a few days later he saw the two women and the man coming out of building six and getting into their cars. Good thing he'd gassed up that morning, since he didn't know he'd be following them all the way to Key West.

THIRTEEN

While they drove to Fausto's on Fleming, since they also wanted to walk over to Island Books before they shopped, Maggie said, "You know, I'm tired of waiting for something to happen, aren't you?"

Carolyn laughed and said, "Oh no, you don't! I'm not playing undercover cop with you again, Mag, so just put that thought out of your head. I don't even want to hear what you've come up with this time. "

"But ... "

"No, no buts about it. We've been safe so far, and we're going to keep it that way. Besides, we haven't gotten out much these past few weeks since we got home. Don't you want to enjoy the island like we always did, catch up on the city commission meetings and get back to living a normal life again?"

"Sure, I've missed getting out and about. You're right, it'da be foolish to start staking out the island, especially when the guys haven't even seen hide nor hair of that awful man. Sorry I brought it up."

"Don't be silly. You don't owe me an apology. I just don't want to see you get hurt. All the cops in town and all over the Keys have a sketch of him and put out the BOLOs before we even got home, so if by chance he's holed up somewhere else up the road, don't worry, they'll get him. And for all we know he still might be hanging around West Palm and they'll find him there."

"You're right. Well, here we are. Are we still going to go over and browse through the bookstore before we get groceries?"

"Sure," Carolyn said, as she finished parking the car.

Maggie smiled at her friend and told her she felt almost normal again doing the things they always had, before they got out of the car at Fausto's and walked across Fleming to the bookstore, dodging a local on his bike in one of the few bike lanes in town. Island Books was one of two independent bookstores on the island and the oldest one. Marshall, the longtime owner of the store, was no longer living, but people kept his legacy alive by continuing to frequent the little place overflowing, as always. With best sellers, local's fiction and nonfiction, and a large section of older books and first editions. Island Books was the go-to place for locals who wanted quality books and to attend their friends' book signings, of which there were many.

As they walked through the doors, Maggie visibly relaxed. They exchanged pleasantries with the owners and clerks and went each in her own direction to find a few new and used books to take home with them. Both were voracious readers. Carolyn always accused Maggie of being a speed reader, since she usually finished a couple books a day and during the night if she couldn't sleep, but she always denied it, saying she just read at the speed she talked. Which isn't all that slow, Carolyn had told her once with a big laugh. When they were through with their books, they always donated them to the library on Eaton for their monthly book sales by Friends of the Library.

After the two finished their book and grocery shopping, they headed for home with Ganon right behind them. While in the bookstore they both forgot he was tailing them and seemed genuinely surprised when they saw him get into his car when they came out of Fausto's. They did not acknowledge him, but finished loading the Lincoln with groceries and drove home.

As they got to the house, Ganon turned onto South Street and parked in front of the Southernmost Motel, waiting until they got inside to go to the suite he shared with Flagg. "Any sign of him?"

"No, and to tell you the truth, pal, I think he's holed up in Chicago or somewhere in the northeast right now, and we're just out here spinning our wheels. Surely he isn't that good at the game that he wouldn't have fouled up sometime within the past six weeks. I think the chief's right in calling us back to West Palm. The ladies'll be fine without us."

"Yeah, I tend to agree with you. This has been a nice diversion, but we do need to get back to work and see some action soon of some kind."

"You got that right. Did they get all their shopping done?"

"Yes, they went to Island Books across the street first and were in there quite a while before they settled on the books they wanted. I got us a few, also, so we'd have some light reading to keep us alert for the rest of the week while the other one's watching the house."

"Hey, thanks for that. I can only watch so much TV. Meant to pack some books before we started out, but there just wasn't time for all that."

"Here's the stack. Take what you want. I'm going to read Haskins' latest Mick Murphy, though, so don't take that one. Why don't you go in and get some shut eye and I'll take this shift."

Flagg tapped him on the shoulder. "Thanks, I'll do that." He picked up another thriller by James Patterson, an old friend from his days on the force across the water in Palm Beach, and went into his room. Ganon settled into the chair nearest the window looking across United at Maggie's house, leaving "Right As Wrong Can Be" on the coffee table to start reading after his shift. The first glance at the house showed nothing amiss, not that he expected to see anything.

FOURTEEN

Actually, there was plenty amiss. The man who killed Blake in West Palm had spotted Ganon leaving the bookstore after the old woman he was after. He'd just driven from the appraiser's office when he passed the bookstore. He had been at the game so long he could smell a cop from a mile away, even if she didn't acknowledge he was with her and the other dame, who wasn't bad to look at. Maybe if he could nab them both, he'd have himself a good time with her. Of course he'd known where the cops were staying and felt perfectly at ease so close to them, knowing they wouldn't think to check all the motels, hotels and B&Bs too thoroughly on this two-bit island. Neither would the local yokels. The locals had checked all of them once right after everyone got back to the island, but that was it. They wouldn't figure he'd be smart enough to hole up in one so close to the West Palm cops and the women that he could spit on them, so didn't check them every day. One local cop came by to check the rooms in the motel he was in a couple times after that, and he'd even said hello to him but didn't bat an eye of recognition. He played it up, even asking what he was looking for and the guy shrugged and said he wasn't looking for anyone in particular, but said they checked for drug dealers every now and again. This gave him a secret laugh after the guy left his room. Drug dealers, my ass. You're looking for me and haven't a clue you found me twice.

In no hurry to get out of there, though, he was biding his time, learning the old broad's routines and where she liked to hang out when not at home in her big classy white house on the corner. Bet that cost her a bundle. He forgot to check that when he was in the appraiser's office. She probably carries a wad with her everywhere she goes, so when he nabs her, he'd make out with some dough, too.

As he was thinking about how and when he'd grab her and maybe the younger pretty one, before heading out of town and out of this god-forsaken torrid as the depths of hades state, he was getting ready to go to lower Duval and have a good time, maybe pick up one of those young half-naked tourists for the night. He'd never seen so much skin since he left Tahiti. Now there was the place to find the babes, and he did. A different island girl every night. That was before his first kill. Seems after that his taste for gorgeous women just wasn't as strong as before. What was it about taking another person's life that changed a man? Damned if he could figure out the connection, but he knew it had, not that it would ever stop him, though.

Hamilton Jacques, though certainly a killer, was a gentleman. His French mom had taught him right. Poor Mom, if she'd lived, she'd not be happy with how his life had turned after he killed his girlfriend in Missouri and then several more women after that. She knew about the first one and told him it didn't sound like an accident to her. She was a shrewd one, his mom, but he never admitted it; just shrugged his shoulders and walked away. She was never the same after that. She never told anyone or mentioned it again, but he knew she was depressed about it until the day she died. Blake was the first man he'd ever offed. He couldn't explain it; that's just how his life had turned. He thought again that if Blake hadn't been so greedy and just given him his rightful share of the money for the haul in the first place, he'd still be alive instead of in pieces in that compactor. Why'd he have to try to hold back some of Ham's stash, anyway? He was gonna get more than enough when he fenced it all. Such a fool.

He grabbed his keys and glanced in the hall mirror. Last night he'd dyed his red hair coal black and shaved what little bit of beard he had, just leaving a bit of goatee, which he also dyed, after dyeing his small mustache. Then he bought a pair of horn-rimmed clear glasses. He looked pretty darned scholarly, if he did say so, himself. A respectable English professor if anyone asked, teaching in a small college in the Midwest no one had ever heard of, Karling U in the heart of Kansas. Yeah, that's sounds like a snobbish little school to which the rich would send their brats. Karling University. He laughed to himself and checked his black and red plaid shirt opened over a black tee shirt and untucked for a more casual air. A pair of black Bermuda shorts completed his look. He stepped into black flip-flops before he went out the door, deciding to walk to Sloppy Joe's. If he were a local, he wouldn't wear anything that coordinated with anything else, but tourists always did, so he made sure he was wearing a coordinated outfit. Might as well go there to blend in with the other drunks out for a good time before heading back to their own dull little lives. Hamilton didn't like being drunk. He liked to be in total control, but he could act the part with the best of them.

The bar was noisy and raucous when he walked in. Not a place he'd enjoy himself, but plenty of young scantily clothed babes sitting with guys and other girls. He saw one sitting alone, sipping on a drink with one of those stupid umbrellas in it. He watched her for a while, had no idea why someone who looked like her would be alone, but for the half hour he observed her, she talked to no one and shooed the guys away who approached her. He made a bet to himself she wouldn't shoo him away, as he approached her table.

"Hi there," he said, with his shyest smile and a finger to his glasses. "It's so crowded in here. Do you mind if I sit at your table. I promise not to bother you."

She pretended to think about it for a moment and then shrugged and said, "No of course not, please have a seat. I just didn't want to sit with any of those college types. They only have one thing on their minds and then they end up passing out as soon as they get it, anyway."

Good, she wasn't a virgin. He laughed easily with her. "Well, that might rule me out, too."

"Oh? You're in college?" Her pretty mouth turned down just the slightest bit when she said that. He almost laughed at that, but checked himself.

"Not in college, but I teach at one, a little school in the middle of Kansas, Karling University. Ever hear of it?" He laughed, then and said, "Probably not. No one has."

She laughed then, too, showing nice teeth, a little bucked, which he thought would do him nicely. "Sorry, I haven't, either. What do you teach?"

"English lit. Freshmen English lit, which makes it doubly boring," he said with a smile.

"Your accent doesn't sound Midwestern. Where are you from originally, if you don't mind my asking?" She noticed he had a little bit of an 'ah' sound at the end of his sentences, that sounded as though he were more sophisticated than he let on.

He laughed again. "No, I'm actually from Tahiti."

Her eyes widened. "What? Tahiti?"

"Yes, my dad was in the Navy and he met my mom in Hawaii one summer. She and a girlfriend, French Polynesians, were visiting from Tahiti. They got to talking, went back to his hotel where he was taking some R & R and one thing led to another."

"Did she marry him?"

"No. Since he had a longer leave than they had vacation, he followed them back to Tahiti. He went to Mom's little house she'd inherited from her parents and stayed another week with her. She actually never saw him again or even wanted to. She was pregnant before he left, had me and we had a pretty good life, living among her big family over there, some from northern France, but mostly the native French Polynesians. Pretty nice place to grow up. Of course, I was in the ocean most of the time I wasn't studying. I knew I wanted to go to the United States and become a teacher. Never thought I'd end up teaching in a university, but that's what happened." He sure could spin a yarn, if he did say so, himself. Almost had himself convinced it was all true, too.

"You must miss your mom and Tahiti a lot. I can't imagine leaving there if I ever had a chance to go there."

"Maybe I'll take you when I go back for my next visit."

She laughed and said, "Oh, you're expecting us to keep in touch?"

"Sure, why not. I'm single, no girlfriend, no strings to anyone or anything, except my job. I see no ring on your finger, either. In fact, I was thinking maybe I'd extend my vacation and go over to the South Pacific before I leave here next week. How 'bout it?"

She really laughed then. "You sound so serious. Here you're taking me to the South Pacific and we don't even know each other's names. You're really the clown, mister."

He didn't like that, but kept the smile on his face. "Well, we can fix that right now." He held out his hand. "Jordan Mace."

She said nothing, at first, and he said, "Your turn now. That's how this works, no matter where folks live." He was finding it easy to get into this folksy Midwestern way of speaking.

With a smile, she extended her hand. "Lana Carter, coed and aspiring model from New York. Nice to meet you, Jordan."

He took her hand and kissed it. "I'm sure you'll have a great modeling career. You're a natural. How long are you staying in Key West, Lana?"

"I'd planned to stay two weeks, but if you're going to take me to Tahiti," she laughed at the joke, "I guess I'll leave when you do."

"You think I'm kidding, don't you."

"Well, I've never had a man come up with that original a line, but yeah, I think you're kidding."

"Well, I'm not and I'll prove it to you. Where are you staying here?'

"The Pier House." That was a surprise. He figured her to be an impoverished coed who could barely afford the Days Inn at the triangle as one came into town. Interesting.

"Let's go to your place and talk about this. Game?" He threw some bills on the table and drank the last of his bourbon.

"I – I don't know, I'm not really comfortable doing that. Maybe we'd better say goodnight now."

"No, I really like you and I do want to take you to Tahiti. If I can get us a flight out, we can leave tomorrow, if you'd like. Do you have a laptop?"

"Yes," she said, looking puzzled.

"Well, when we get back to your room, I'll get online and make a reservation. Seriously, Lana, I'd really like to take you. My mom's been gone for a while and I have no one there, now, but I still love the place and love to show it off to friends. And I feel like we could be friends, don't you?"

She tugged on her lower lip with her teeth for a few moments, making him suppress a groan, before she said, "I think we could be. Sure, okay, let's walk over to the Pier House."

As they walked, he held her hand. She was one of the most gorgeous women he'd ever seen. Her dark wavy hair kept getting in her eyes and she'd reach up and pull it away from her face as the breeze blew around them, exposing how creamy her skin was everywhere since she had on one of those skimpy little halter tops. She could almost pass as French Polynesian and he couldn't wait to get her alone. He was serious about Tahiti and he had his Jordan Mace passport with him. It would be a perfect break from the monotony. Fly over there for a few days before coming back and getting that old bag out of the way.

"Well, here we are," she said, as she inserted the key card and opened the door to the room, with him behind her.

He couldn't help himself. He reached for her as soon as the door closed, pulled her close and they kissed. "You're so beautiful, Lana," he said, and meant it.

"You're not so bad, yourself," she said as he backed them toward the bed. He pushed her down on the bed and sat down beside her, pinning her arms over her head. She gasped and he started touching her bare skin down to her barely there halter top. "Oh God."

He leaned down and his fingers touched her and kissed her rougher than before, as he undid the hook at the back of her neck and pulled her dress down and onto the floor. She wore no bra and her breasts were exquisite. "Oh yes," he said, as he pulled off her panties. She was already so wet he could enter her easily, but he took his time with her, never once letting her put her arms down. He liked dominating his women and letting them know he'd take what he wanted when he wanted. So far, she seemed fine with that.

After he'd had his fill of her, he asked, "Where's the laptop?"

Barely able to speak because he'd been at her for so long, she motioned to the small desk across the room. Pinning her down again, he started touching her breasts until she was moaning hard, and then entered her once more before he went into the bathroom. When he came back, he sat down at the laptop.

She took a shower while he made the reservations. They'd fly to LA in the morning and then to Tahiti the next day. He was going to enjoy this trip. She was so young and gorgeous and he could go at her all day without stopping to eat. He hadn't had anyone this young for a long time. She'd told him she was nineteen as they walked to the Pier House. And her body told him she was telling the truth. He couldn't believe his luck.

When she came out of the shower with just a long towel around her, she went to him and draped a soft arm over his shoulder. "You weren't kidding, were you? Oh my gosh, I'm actually going to Tahiti," she said, like a high school girl instead of college coed. At first that irritated him, but then he thought, if she's that excited, it will make for a good trip.

He finished the reservation, put the card back in his wallet, turned around and pulled her to his lap. "Yes, Lana, you're really going to Tahiti. You'll fit right in with those gorgeous Tahitian girls."

She laughed, "Oh I doubt that, I've seen pictures of the island girls."

He pulled her hair from her neck and kissed it. "You're as gorgeous as any of them with all this dark wavy hair down your back and that body that never quits. Speaking of which."

"Not again, surely. Haven't you had enough?"

He backed her toward the bed again, "Not nearly, girl. Not nearly enough of you." He threw her down roughly on the bed and started touching her slowly. She moaned and arched every time he touched her, which excited him more. He hadn't gotten dressed and entered her immediately this time, making her scream and tears popped from her eyes, because she wasn't that ready for him. He liked that. You always have to let them know who's boss so they don't get any ideas about holding out on you. Yes sir, she was really something.

She fell asleep before he left, leaving a note that he'd pick her up at 6 in the morning to drive to Miami to catch the next flight out. He looked down at her before he left, and wished he didn't have to leave, but he had to pack a bag before he came back. This time he walked back up Simonton, so he didn't have to pass the Southernmost and maybe be spotted. He slipped easily into his motel room. They'd passed three cops on the way to the Pier House and not one looked at him with suspicion since he really did look like a nerdy college professor. This was going to be a cinch. He'd take Lana to Tahiti, but from there he wasn't sure. He'd have her check out of her hotel so if he decided to get rid of her after they got there, she'd leave nothing in the room to raise suspicions. Yeah, as much as he liked being with her, as gorgeous as she was, it probably wouldn't do to bring her back to the states with him. He knew plenty of places on the island to stash a body if he decided she was going to be a liability and then he'd come back for the old broad. Get that over with so he could stop looking over his shoulder. She went downstairs to check out as he'd asked, but something told her to leave her reservation as it was, since she wasn't sure how this trip with him would work out. She might have to fly back early if it turned out he wasn't as nice as he seemed. She had plenty of money, not from teaching, but from her wealthy parents. She didn't mention to him that she'd made no changes. She just told the clerk to hold her room. She said she had to attend to something for a few days. She'd pack up all her things so Jordan wouldn't be suspicious but that was as far as she'd go.

FIFTEEN

Ganon and Flagg met the ladies and Homer at Mangrove Mamas on their way out of town. "Well, Maggie," Flagg told her, "I think we can be safe in saying the perp wasn't interested in hurting you, after all. I guess he just wanted to give you a good scare. It's been a whole six weeks, Ganon and I've searched every inch of this island and haven't seen hide nor hair of the guy. Neither has the PD or SO, so he's nowhere around."

"I think you're right, Detective," she told him. "I guess he's hightailed it back to Chicago, New York or wherever he came from." She twirled her stirrer around in her drink.

He smiled. "You don't look too happy with that. Surely you weren't hoping you'd spot him here, were you?"

She looked almost sheepish, as she had planned to do some sleuthing after they left, with or without Carolyn. "Oh no, I'm glad he's not around. I guess I was just hoping the cops – you, Lenny Doan, the rest of them – would have put him away by now. No matter where he is, he's still out there."

"True, but the good thing is he's not after you and that's all we care about. He'll be caught and prosecuted for Blake's murder sooner or later. These things don't happen overnight, you know."

"I know. It's just that since he didn't follow us down here, we'll probably never know if he gets caught and put away. That's what would make me feel better."

Homer patted her hand, and said, "I expect we'll hear when he's arrested, Maggie. Like Flagg said, these things take time, but you can be sure he'll make a mistake and get caught one of these days."

Carolyn shivered. "Yeah, but how many other poor souls are going to be chopped up in the meantime."

SIXTEEN

Thousands of miles away, in a little hut far away from everything else, a beautiful young woman was lying on her back sound asleep, as the man looking down at her tried to make a decision. They were due to leave Tahiti day after tomorrow at three and he had to get rid of her before his plane left. She wasn't aware he'd made the return reservation for just one passenger.

She was so gorgeous, lying there with nothing on. He wished he could just take her away somewhere and live the kind of life they'd lived for the past week and forget all his obligations. Why not, he wondered. Who's to know if we don't go back to the states? No one would find us out here. We could live like royalty here among these friendly people who minded their own business. Who's to know what he left behind? He had enough money he'd stashed in the bank downtown and he'd learned she was rich. No one would ever dream of looking for him on this island. She moaned then and he couldn't help himself. He lay down beside her and touched her until she awakened and smiled at him.

"Hi," she said with a huskiness to her voice. "How long have you been awake?"

"Not long. I was going to get dressed and go get us something to eat, but then I looked at you again and well, you know," he said, smiling as he took a breast into his mouth, his hand spreading her legs as he did so. "Hmm, so good," he murmured as she moaned loudly again.

Afterward he got his shower and left to get their food. When he returned, she'd showered and dressed and was putting silverware on the small table. "That didn't take long."

"No, I went to that little fish hut we said we were going to try. They had some pretty good looking mahi mahi, so I got some of it and some lobster tail so we'll eat well tonight. You know we only have another day here before we have to get back home."

She looked sad all of a sudden. "I know. I don't want to go, Jordan. I want to stay here with you for the rest of my life." She sighed deeply. "I guess that isn't reality, is it. And I have to get back to New York and finish school if I'm ever going to have that modeling career."

He smiled at her. "I've been thinking about that."

"My modeling career?" She pulled off a big piece of lobster tail, dipped it in the hot butter and put it into her mouth, eliciting another moan from the man and she laughed.

"No, about staying here. Just chucking it all and staying here. We could have a happy life, you and me. I've never been married, but I sure felt like it this week. How about it? Would you like to stay here, continue this happy life with me?" He was almost praying she said yes, because in his heart he knew he cared deeply for her and didn't want to kill her.

"How I wish that were possible. But we both know it isn't."

"I think it is, Lana. My god, you're so beautiful like that." She smiled and fed him a piece of mahi mahi."

"I'll get old and then you won't think so," she said, with a small laugh bubbling up from her throat. "I can't imagine it now, but we both know I will and then you won't want me."

"Are you kidding? I'll want you till the day I die." He got up from the table, realized again that he meant what he said and pulled her up with him. He started undressing her again, though she had on so little, it was accomplished within seconds. He pulled off his shorts and stepped out of his flip flops, as he carried her over to the bed.

"I'm sorry, I really care for you," she told him, "but I have to do what's best for me right now. Maybe after I finish school, if you still feel the same, we can come back here to live and I'll model for a store or two here."

"If you think that's the way to do it, then I'll just have to wait to marry you and bring you back here as my bride." She smiled and leaned over and kissed him, not having any idea how disappointed he was at her decision that meant she wouldn't ever leave the island.

After they were sated, both from making love and eating, he suggested they take a drive. He wanted to show her something. They dressed quickly and left the little hut. He opened the rental door for her and went around to his side. He'd made his decision, as much as he didn't want to. He knew he had to go back, but he couldn't take Lana with him. She would be a liability and sooner or later, she'd discover what he really was and try to get away from him. He'd rather she'd do that here on a remote part of this beautiful South Pacific island instead of back in the states where she could get help easier. He drove them to the most remote part of the island he knew of and close to a cliff. He couldn't bear to kill her and chop that beautiful body up as he had all the others. No, he'd not be able to bear that. They walked out to the edge of the cliff.

"It's so beautiful out here, isn't it," Lana told him, looking out to sea as his arms tightened around her from the back. "Let's make love right here."

He laughed. "You like that as much as I do, don't you."

"You've made me insatiable," she answered, turning around and tugging at his belt. Why not, he thought, one more for the road. "And don't think our going back home will be the end of us. I won't let it be."

"Of course it won't be the end, baby. Our love will never end."

"You love me?" Her eyes widened and her smile softened as she looked deeply into his eyes.

"Yes, I love you very much. I realized that during dinner last night. I've never felt this way about any other woman, Lana. You're it for me."

"Oh Jordan, you are for me, too."

He found a soft pad of grass and lay her down, after finishing undressing her. He took his time, touching her everywhere he knew would ignite her for him and she didn't disappoint. They made love longer than they ever had, several times, for what he knew was the last time, before standing again. "Let's walk over there. I want to hear the water below," he told her. "We can get dressed later."

"Okay," she said, never suspecting it was the last walk she'd ever take. "I love being here with you like this. I hope we can come back one day."

"Or never leave," he said, smiling at her.

"Oh if only that were possible. I'd love nothing better, but I have to make my way in life, Jordan."

"Oh, you will. You will, don't worry about that. I think you were made for this island, Lana Carter," he said, as she turned to face him. At that moment, he pushed her, and with widened eyes, she showed fright for the first time.

"Why?" was the last word she uttered, as she fell screaming to the rocks below. She broke her neck as soon as she hit the first jagged rock which split her back open by the edge of the sea. Lana Carter died instantly. He could see her beautiful crippled body lying there and had a moment's regret that he'd had to do it. But there's no question he had to. He couldn't have taken her with him and built a life together in the states, where he had so much to lose. He wondered what it would have looked like to have lived a normal life with such a beautiful woman as Lana had been. Had been. He almost cried when he thought she was no longer alive and moaning to his touch. She was probably the only woman who could have loved him completely, but there was no way she wouldn't have eventually learned what he was. Not whom he was, but what he was. Not a scholar; an animal who killed every woman in his path. But he had to, didn't he? Of course he did. That's the only way he survived.

He glanced down once more at the twisted limp body of the dead girl he'd loved touching and making moan with pleasure. He shook his head, dressed and got into his car where he sat still for a moment. There'll be another Lana somewhere. Plenty of them, he was sure, but regretfully, none like the real one ever again. None as sweet and trusting, but there will be others he can use for a while and then get rid of just as he had her. That's how it would always be. Had to be. He sighed and turned the key.

He drove down the mountain after he'd packed his things and burned all of hers. No one really saw them come up here to this isolated cottage, so no one would come looking for her. When he got down to road level, he knew he had to see her again, touch her again. It was risky, but he had to do it. He drove into the thick seclusion of the bushes, parked the car and walked around to the spot where he saw her fall. She was still there, but closer to the water, her legs both broken and twisted in awkward positions, and her arms spread out grotesquely over her head, as though she were waiting for him to touch her again. The rock had broken and was no longer sticking in her back. And he did touch her. Every inch of her beautiful twisted and torn body, ignoring the blood beneath her as it was being diluted by the salt water and washed out to sea. He made love to her once more, even though he couldn't hear those soft moans from her again. Finally, with a big sigh, he got up, pulled on his shorts and drove away, leaving her to the birds and fish as the tide took her out into the deep waters. He'd never think of her again. He'd done what had to be done and now it was over. Looking back wasn't something he ever did. Once he was through with anything and discarded it, he never had regrets.

SEVENTEEN

Maggie and Carolyn were sitting alone on Carolyn's porch, watching the sunset. "Hey, Carolyn, do you believe in God?"

"Whoa, what brought that on?"

"I was just wondering."

Carolyn had been worried about her before this, but now, she was beginning to be a bit on the frightened side as she looked at her friend who was watching the sunset. "Well, since you were just wondering, I'll say, yes, I believe in God, but I can't tell you what I believe about him, except that I think he's a benevolent spirit."

"Hmm, I think that, too. But what do you think he thinks of us? I mean there are so many things to consider."

"Like what?"

"Well, take your friend, Vanny, for instance. He's very nice and doesn't seem like he could ever hurt a soul."

"That's because you're right. He's one of the kindest men I've ever known and he'd rather die than hurt anyone. What has you on this kick tonight? I've never heard you so serious and – what? Philosophical?'

"I've just been thinking about it, that's all. I mean, on Facebook the other night, someone posted something about gays and showed a slurry painted sign about them that wasn't nice at all."

"That's been known to happen."

"Well, it wasn't very nice of them to do it. And then, to top it off, down about halfway through all the comments, which had been empathetic to the gays, this man types, 'Well, gays are an abomination to God! They all need to be strung up by their heels in a forest somewhere and left to the animals!' I'll tell you, I was shocked at his tone."

"Some people do believe that, dear, not that they all want to see them die a horrible death like that. Not everyone has the opportunity to meet gays or any other group of people who are different from them to get to know what they're like. To know they're just like them, trying to get through their days as best they can. All those other people think of is the sexual side to gays and lesbians, which those of us who do know them never ever give a thought to, any more than they think it when they see, talk with or think of us. It just never crosses the mind."

As though she didn't hear that, she said, "Then, when a couple of other people gently asked that he not do that because the gays, all of the LGBT community, were worried enough about some of the people the new administration was hiring and what that meant for them, the guy came back with, 'Well, don't you ever read your Bible? It says it's wrong.' I just had to say goodnight and log out of Facebook. Why do some people think they're the religious policemen of the world? That everyone has to believe and live the way they say they do because someone is supposed to have said it thousands of years ago? We all know that Bible was changed multiple times, not just by the Catholic Church under Constantinople, but when it was translated into other languages."

"I'm sorry if he upset you. Just try to ignore people who are on a crusade like that and realize that the world is changing for the better and for the most part, people are becoming more accepting of how other people are and are kinder. After all, no one asks to be born gay – or straight, for that matter. It just happens. Or Arabic, Jewish, African, etc. If he believes, and I'm sure he does, that God created us, it's like he's saying God made a big mistake when he created all these gay people. Of course, if he's that dogmatic, he probably believes being gay is a choice, as though our friends wanted to be persecuted and hated by many in the straight world who don't understand them."

"It's kind of hard to ignore it when you're the target as most of my friends on there were. I felt so badly for them. And I wondered what God thought about it." She laughed a little and said before she logged out, she just typed 'WWJD?'

"WWJD? What's that?"

"What would Jesus do?"

"Oh, of course, I've seen that. Well, I think we know what Jesus would do, whether you think he's the son of God or just a wonderful spiritual person who lived back in the day."

"Yes. I've seen that same man put down the homeless and refugees on FB, saying there wasn't enough room for the people who have a right to be here and they're criminals, probably, all of them."

"That's awful. So many of them are tiny children, orphans. Or veterans who've fought to keep them free. I've not spent much time on there, so I guess I've been pretty sheltered from all this," Carolyn told her. "I'd much rather read or go out with friends than sit at a computer talking with them, some of which I've never even met in person, but I suppose there are some who become friends through getting to know each other on social media."

"Yes, I've met a few I think will be good friends from being on there a lot. Well, getting back to what I was saying. I don't know if Jesus was the son of God or if, as some have said, it was made up by the Catholic Church in the 4th century to bring people under its thumb more."

"I didn't know that."

"Oh sure, that's what people suspected they'd done. There's a lot of researched papers I've read online about it. And some books in the library that discuss it. Archeologists have even discovered old parchment gospels that were never allowed in the Bible, because they didn't go along with what the Catholic Church was teaching about God and Jesus. They even found the story or gospel of Mary Magdelaine stuck in crevices of rocks they were chipping away at. And the gospel of Thomas. But it doesn't make any difference to me. I'm a Christian and I try to follow what Jesus taught those who followed him in the day. I try to treat everyone as though they are worthy human beings – I say try to, because I find it hard to think of that horrible killer in those terms or to find a saving grace in bigots like that guy on Facebook. "

Carolyn shivered suddenly, and said, "I hate to think of him at all. The killer, I mean. " She tried to smile, but it fell short of her eyes.

"Same here. Getting back to Jesus. He told those men and women who were his followers and admirers that he had only one thing he commanded them to do and that was to love each other as he loved them. I sort of feel like he meant every man and woman who came after them, too, which includes me. I've always tried to love everyone as much as that is possible. Jesus was homeless after he gave up all his worldly goods and didn't seem to have much if any money, but when he fished, he'd share what he had with the rest of them and told them to do the same with everything. It was like a commune, where everyone was to share everything with everyone else. I guess I couldn't say that to just anyone, as I'd probably be accused of saying he was the first communist."

Carolyn smiled. "Yes, I guess you could say that, Maggie, but he did seem to be like that, the sharing part I mean, not the mean part of it, and I would say he probably was the first socialist, though, not communist."

"Well, the point is he didn't say love everyone except that gay man bartending at 801, those Syrians over there on that crowded boat or that black family down on Julia Street. He said, 'Love one another' – period. No conditions. So, I think if that man said something like that to Jesus, he'd tell him he was supposed to love gay men, lesbian women and transgender people, not persecute them or single them out as being horrible people."

Carolyn laughed softly and said, "You really are the cream of the crop, my friend. And I adore you."

Maggie looked embarrassed. She could never take compliments very well and never had been able to, mostly because she'd always been put down so much as a young person that she never really thought she was worth much. Homer always sensed that, especially after meeting some of those fellow former cheerleader friends of hers, and he tried to help her build up her self-esteem. She never quite got there.

"That brings me to my earlier question. What do you think God thinks of us? I mean, what do you think happens to us when we die? Is God there to take us by the hand and say, 'you did good, Billy'?"

This got another chuckle from her friend, although Maggie never said it to be comical. She meant it as a valid question, and soon Carolyn realized that. "I have no idea what happens when we die. Some people think we just go into a sort of deep coma that we never come out of and we never know another thing. That's it. Caput! It's over."

"I'd hate to think that, wouldn't you?"

"Sure, I like what other people think, some of them, at least. They think that when we take our last breath, although our old sick body stays right there, we get up from that bed or that ground – wherever we've died – take the hand of someone who's come for us, someone we knew and loved, and walk off to this beautiful other plane no one else can see but those who are gone, because everyone is a spirit, instead of a human with a body you can see. And that even though we don't have bodies, anymore, we'll know each other as we'd know them down here if we couldn't see them."

Maggie smiled. "I like that. It wouldn't be so bad then, if that's what happens."

"Well, no one will know for sure until he or she dies, but some who've died and been brought back to life by resuscitation have said it's like that. That one minute they were in their old sick bodies and then the next minute they're walking off with their mom, dad, spouse, sibling or a lost loved one they never got to marry before he died, toward this place that's so beautiful no one could ever describe it."

"Wow, I'd love it!"

"Yes, so would I."

"I wonder if it hurts horribly, though." She shuddered as though picturing it.

"Well," Carolyn told her, "those who've been brought back also say that the moment of actual death is not painful at all, and then like taking another breath, there they are with that happy – and dead – person who looks perfectly fine, except in a wispy, ethereal-like form instead of a body like he had when he was alive."

"Hmm, I wonder how they know it's him or her, whomever the person is. I mean do you think their hearts, their souls know each other?"

"I've never thought about that, but let me ask you this. When you think of someone you've loved in your lifetime who's already gone, do you picture that person exactly as he or she was during life?"

Maggie tipped her head and glanced out into space, thinking about it for a moment. "No, come to think of it. I just think of the person but not of a body or face at all. It's just an awareness of the person and I know that's whom I'm thinking of or dreaming of. That's cool, Carolyn, "she said with a big smile. "I never thought about it before, but that's true. The person doesn't have a body or a face, but I know it's him or her."

Carolyn smiled but said nothing more about it, as they both looked at the last trace of colors on the horizon. It was a beautiful bright splash of orange now, with a lot of gold and some red further west. Truly a glorious sunset tonight. She sighed deeply with contentment. She loved living up here in her secluded apartment, able to enjoy all this without the noise of lower Duval. And because Maggie was so wealthy, she would never even discuss Carolyn's paying rent. Carolyn made up for it in other ways, buying groceries since Maggie hated to shop and treating Maggie and Homer to dinner somewhere or a trip somewhere else. And she was always buying things for the house, backyard pool and patio area and more beautiful plants for the front lawn.

"Well, you've made me feel a lot better about dying. Now I won't be so afraid if it does happen. Thanks, Carolyn." She smiled broadly with her toothless gap of a mouth.

EIGHTEEN

"Hey, wait a minute. You had your checkup last week. Did the doctor tell you something you didn't share with Homer and me?"

"Oh no, nothing like that. He said I'm fit as a fiddle, as always. No, I was just thinking if something happened to me that wasn't a natural death..."

"Oh Maggie. Honey, nothing's going to happen to you. That man is long gone back to the hole he crawled out of and he's nowhere near here. Why, I'll bet he's even forgotten you were on the swing that day."

"What day?" Neither of them heard Homer come up the stairs, being so engrossed in their serious conversation, and they didn't even hear the door open and close when he came into the house from the front porch on the second floor.

"Oh, hi," Maggie said, brightly. "Carolyn and I are just discussing life – and death."

"What? Whose death?" What the hell?

She laughed heartily, because he was frowning so. "No one's in particular. We were just having a philosophical discussion, that's all. Nothing to worry about," she said hitting him lightly on the shoulder, as he leaned down to give her a hug.

Carolyn said nothing and motioned for him not to ask any more questions. "Well," Maggie added, rising and moving her back and shoul-

72

ders around to loosen up, since they'd been out there for hours, "I think I'll go down and heat up some of that apple pie I made last night. Anyone care to join me? I'll throw some vanilla bean on top?"

They both did, but Homer looked quizzically at Carolyn behind Maggie's back. She just smiled and shrugged her shoulders. In her heart of hearts, though, she was scared for her friend and wondered whether they were right that the killer was nowhere near Key West.

After they finished the pie a la mode, Maggie was ready for a nap, so excused herself while Homer and Carolyn were having another cup of coffee. "So, what was that death talk all about?"

"I think she believes that horrible man is going to find her and kill her." She raised both eyebrows and blinked hard in an attempt not to tear up again.

"My God, I didn't think she even believed he's down here. I thought the guys had convinced her that he was up north somewhere or down in Mexico having a grand old time and forgetting she ever saw him with that body." He took a big gulp of the coffee and looked at her. "That's the way they were talking at Mangrove Mama's the day they left and I thought she believed them. Damn."

"No, I'm afraid they fell short on doing that. Although she didn't say it, she's as scared today as she was the day it happened and I don't know that she's ever going to feel safe again until she learns he's been caught and in prison. I'm sure she believes he's here on the island somewhere just waiting for a chance to 'off' her." She got up from her chair and went to stand at the slider facing the back of the house.

He walked over and stood beside her, squeezing her shoulder gently as he said, "Seems like she isn't the only one who thinks that."

She turned and stared at him for a few moments, before looking back at the painted canvas before them that was now fading to purple and pale yellow. "Truthfully, I'm not sure what I believe at this point. Every time someone walks up onto her front porch, I get chills down my spine, wondering if it's him coming to do something horrible to her."

He put both hands on her shoulders and turned her to face him. "You know what. I think maybe it's time for the two of you to come back to Sugarloaf with me. You'd be safer there as you were the last time."

She mocked him with a small laugh and said, "Oh, you mean the time one of the killers was guarding us when we all thought he was just another nice young cop?"

"Touché."

She smiled and went back to the coffee pot, started to pour more for herself, but then took the cup to the sink to rinse it and put it into the dishwasher. Then she went to the table to gather their ice cream bowls before going up to take a nap, herself, and try to put the killer and his whereabouts out of her mind for a while.

NINETEEN

Even though the PBSO detective and deputy had been gone from Key West for a couple months now, the KWPD officers and detectives paroled with eagle eyes around Duval and United more often than they used to and occasionally, Lieutenant Blake Butler stopped in to say he was in the neighborhood and ask for a cup of Maggie's coffee. Of course, she always filled a plate with donuts and other good pastries and set it in front of him at the table as she joined him in enjoying the coffee.

"Lieutenant, I know you aren't just in the neighborhood as you always say you are. Why don't you level with me and tell me you believe, as I do, that man is still on the island."

"Never kid a kidder, eh, Maggie?" He laughed to try to get her to relax.

"That's right. So tell me the truth about these frequent visits and don't pretend anymore that they're just to sample my coffee and pastries." When she looked him straight in the eye like that, he couldn't lie to her any more than he could have his mother, God rest her soul.

"You're right, Maggie. Just as the other officers are patrolling more often, I'm here so much because I'm not convinced he's not here." There, he'd said it. When she started to say something, he held up a hand. "Now, with that said, I have to say I don't know that he was ever here. None of us know that for certain. And with his not showing himself in all these months, I have a feeling he never followed all of you that day. With Carolyn's good sketch of him, we were able to ID him. We saw no need to reveal this to any of you since it would serve no purpose and, too, if you were right that he did follow you, you saw him again and blurted out his name, who knows what he'd do then. So, we're keeping that to ourselves for that reason."

He laughed quietly after saying that, remembering all the trouble Maggie got Carolyn and herself into by playing undercover angels more than a year ago after the Key West murders. "You're a good little detective when you want to be, but you're also spontaneous and we wouldn't want to take that chance with you."

Maggie smiled at him over her coffee cup but didn't say anything for a while. Neither did he. His eyes were glued to the marching of a mother hen and her chicks out by the patio and pool. When she came to the large gumbo limbo to one side of the pool, she, with her brood following, went inside a tunnel like opening between the low branches. They didn't come out for a while, so he suspected Maggie kept them well supplied with chicken feed back there out of sight in case the chicken cops happened to come around. He grinned to himself. She smiled again, knowing what he must be thinking.

"Lieutenant?"

"Yes?"

"Do you maybe this man – and I won't ask his name since you're withholding it for now – might have pulled what that other awful murderer did when Carolyn and I chased him to the back of Fausto's? Gone to a boat and sailed for Cuba?"

"No, we haven't entertained that thought this time, because he didn't commit the crime down here so. It'd be unlikely he'd have a boat stashed anywhere. We've circulated his photo to all the commercial fishermen, the Coast Guard, the Navy, the port chief at Houseboat Row, and everyone else who works or lives on the water. That was at least three months ago and we've not had a single nibble from anyone."

"Oh," she said, not hiding her disappointment. "I thought maybe he'd make it easy for you all to find him by doing what the other guy did. And then you could send Homer, Shirley and young Davidson back over to be undercover until they found him."

He smiled at that. "If only it were that simple this time, but it's not. He's nowhere near Cuba. That we know for sure, even if he knew someone with a private plane, since we've got the deputies and everyone else at the airport here and in Marathon also keeping an eye out for him."

She shrugged and said, "Well, it was just a thought. I remember how dead-on right Homer was to tell you that's where the man in black was the last time."

Butler laughed as she was reverting to her tough gal talk as she always seemed to do when it came to talking about a murderer. Then he got up from his chair, gave her a quick hug and said, "It's sure been nice visiting with you, Ms. Maggie, and I thank you, as always, for the delicious coffee and donuts. Those eclairs were mighty good, too." He never said it, but he was thinking they how lucky they would have been to have her on the force had she ever thought of going into law enforcement back in the day.

She grabbed a baggie and threw all the rest of the pastries into it and handed it to him over his protesting. "Are you trying to make me fatter? I'll never pass the next mandatory physical if I keep eating all these," he said laughing again.

"Well, then, just take them back to the station house and share them with everyone else, why don't you," she told him with a big toothless smile. "I'm sure the other guys and Miss Ellie probably would enjoy having them on their breaks, if you ever let them take a break, that is."

"Come on, now, I'm not that bad a boss. Even Lenny lets us all relax sometimes," he said with another smile for her before heading for the front door. "You be sure to call us if you suspect anything's wrong, now, no matter if it's only a feeling you have. Okay?"

"Okay, you know I will." She followed him out onto the big wraparound porch with its gleaming white railings and bright red shutters on the windows.

He walked down the steps but then turned around, looking at her sternly. "And no undercover work, you hear?"

She crossed her heart and said, "I promise. No more of that." He didn't see her other hand behind her back with its fingers crossed.

TWENTY

*L*ieutenant Butler smiled, waved to her and got back into his unmarked car, just as a man across the way returned from another
brief vacation, this time to Bermuda. A man with coal black hair, a tiny
goatee and horn-rimmed glasses, who called himself Professor Mace.
Jordan Mace. He easily cleared customs everywhere he went. Nothing
on his passport made him suspicious. Just your average Joe, enjoying
Key West and other islands in other parts of the world. He almost went
back to Tahiti, but thought better of it, since he'd just been there recently and that might raise a red flag, so he stuck to islands off the east-
ern seaboard and the tip of South America, like St. Thomas.

He noticed the unmarked car and figured it was one of Key West's
finest consoling Ms. Maggie Metronia with the fact that the big bad
killer was nowhere near the island. He laughed to himself as he took
his bags up the back stairs to his room at the new B&B.

As he watched out his window facing United and Duval, Maggie and
now Carolyn Cramer were sitting on the porch swing, and then the
same man he'd seen there so often drove up in that ghastly gold Hummer and joined them. They were all relaxed, he thought, which was a
good sign for him. The guy must have said something funny because
they all laughed hilariously, not acting like they were scared something
bad was going to happen to them.

Maybe he'd just get his trusty rifle with the accurate scope, load it with plenty of ammo and just start shooting them, one by one. He could pick them off easily out there on the front porch. He'd get the guy first right in the middle of his forehead. The two women would be so shocked they would be unable to move and he'd pick them both off real fast, before they had a chance to run and hide. With the music from the beach restaurant across the way, it probably wouldn't register to anyone that they heard three shots.

By the time someone walking by found them all dead up there on the porch, he'd be in his rental heading for Miami, only he wouldn't drive all the way to Miami. He'd stop in Islamorada, a good eighty miles away but still in the Keys. They would never think he'd not drive straight to the mainland, those dumb excuses for cops. When he was on the island, he walked around in plain sight, frequented the bookstore and grocery store and spent a lot of time in Sloppy Joe's where no one ever suspected he was any more than that shy college professor he pretended to be when he wanted another young woman for a time.

TWENTY-ONE

Carolyn came downstairs from her third floor apartment and saw that both Homer and Maggie were home, she with her nose in a James Patterson thriller, as usual, and he reading the sports page of the Citizen. They all needed to get out of this house for a while. "Hey Homer, what do you say I treat you and Maggie to dinner up the Keys somewhere?"

"Sounds great to me. How about it, Mag?"

She was thoughtful for a moment, but then brightened and said, "Where did you have in mind?"

Carolyn smiled and told them, "I was thinking somewhere on the bay side in Largo. We haven't left the island for a while. It's a gorgeous afternoon and by the time we reach Key Largo, it'll be dusk and we'll all be ready for a good lobster dinner or any other good dinner you'd like tonight."

"Well, okay then, but do you mind if I get a shower and change? I haven't cleaned up since Lieutenant Butler caught me digging in the flower beds earlier. I was going to wait until I finished the book, but if we're going out, I'll have to at least smell better."

Laughing, she said, "No, of course not, take your time. What did the lieutenant want? Did he have some news for you?" This was the first Carolyn had known of the detective's visit.

"Oh come on, you know if there was anything new I would have shared it with both of you before now. No, he just stopped by for his usual coffee and donuts. I sent all the pastries back to the station with him. I doubt they get to eat a regular meal very often, so figured they'd enjoy the donuts, eclairs and cannoli."

Homer laughed. "Yes, I'm sure they're enjoying the heck out of them. Go on in and get your shower and change. We'll be right here when you're ready."

Carolyn stood, also, and said, "You know, I think I'll get into some long pants before we go. It's supposed to be a little cooler tonight and since we'll probably be eating somewhere on the water, I guess long pants, a top and a sweater wouldn't hurt anything. I notice you changed out of your shorts, too."

"Yeah, I'd been working in the yard all day, so just put on the slacks when I got my shower and heard the weather forecast. You both take your time. I'm going in and listen to the news while you're getting pretty." He smiled at both of them, as he followed them into the house and turned on the TV in the large living room, after he called to them to pack an overnight bag as he was going to treat everyone to a hotel room on the gulf side for the night. He'd let the lieutenant know they'd not be back until tomorrow.

When he called Blake Butler to tell him, he said he'd have the undercover officers they knew, Savage and Davidson, follow them, and they were sitting in the KWPD drive waiting when they saw the Hummer passing and then got in back of them.

It had been a while since they'd seen the two detectives, so they were looking forward to dinner with them. Since they weren't eating in Key West, there was no reason they had to pretend not to know one another. The detectives were prepared to get rooms in the same hotel or motel as they, so they wouldn't have to worry about Hamilton Jacques.

"Glad you two could tag along with us, Shirl. It's been awhile since our little escapade in Cuba last year."

"Seems like yesterday, Homer," Joey Davidson said with a big grin on his handsome face. "We've missed your company when we're on stakeout."

"Sure you do," he said, laughing.

"Well, at least this time, we have the ladies for company, too, so we have something better to look at across the table than just you."

They all laughed and Homer pretended to be wounded in the heart. "Well, I'm not kidding that it's good that you're both here tonight."

"Hey, if you're worried about Hamilton Jacques..." Joey's eyes widened as he realized what he'd done.

Homer looked at him, puzzled for a moment. "Who's Hamilton Jacques – oh, is that the jerk we're trying to protect Mag from?"

Shirley looked at Joey and said, "Guess you'll have to let Loo know what you did, pal."

He hung his head for a moment with his eyes closed. When he looked up, he said to Homer, "Look, I'm sorry. That just came out. The lieutenant didn't want Maggie to know the guy's name for fear she might blurt it out if she saw him."

Maggie waved his apology away. "Don't worry about it. I'm not going to say his name even if I do see him. You think I'd want to scare him off so he could continue eluding you guys?"

"No, we don't think you would, Mag, but Joey does have to let him know that you know the perp's name." She paused for a moment and looked out to sea and the beautiful canvas that was being painted in the sky. "And for that matter, it's a moot point, anyway, since none of us think the guy is anywhere near the Keys, much less on the island."

Maggie looked at Joey again. "You do what you think you need to do, but I assure you his name won't cross my lips."

The young detective smiled and squeezed her arm as he took a bite of his lobster and quickly wiped the butter off his chin.

TWENTY-TWO

As all this was going on, Hamilton Jacques left his window where he'd been watching to see whether the gold hummer had returned, and prepared to go to Sloppy Joes to pick up a dinner companion among the cute young half-clothed women. Since the untimely but necessary death of his young and beautiful Lana, he never chose one for any kind of lengthy dalliance, but just took them to dinner and maybe dancing out in the moonlight if he felt up to being with them all night.

Since there was a bit of a nip in the air as the weather people had predicted early in the day, he chose a pair of lightweight dark blue corduroy slacks and a dark blue long sleeved pullover sweater, the perfect professor outfit. When he added his horn-rimmed plain glass spectacles, he had to admit he looked the part. He combed the little bit of goatee on his face after combing his coal black hair and was quite pleased with himself. He never feared he'd not have a dinner companion if he wanted one. He'd lost quite a few pounds since he murdered that loser Blake in Windsor Park. He was sure even if he had a clean shaven face and his naturally red hair, he'd not be recognizable by the old woman across the street.

It was obvious he didn't know Maggie Metronia or he'd know how doggedly she hunted down her prey and how she never forgot a face.

He put a small revolver in the bag he always carried with him along with a book he pretended to read until he made his move on another woman. One never knew when he'd need a gun to protect himself if an unusually astute police officer thought he recognized him, though he had no idea how that could happen because of his great transformation.

Grabbing his room key and taking one last glance in the mirror by the door to his room, he climbed down the two flights of stairs and started walking through the alley to Simonton Street, as he'd been doing of late to avoid all the cops walking the beat on Duval. He'd stay on that parallel street until he reached Greene Street and then he'd just slip in the side door to Sloppy Joe's.

As usual by the time he got to the bar it was packed with drunken tourists, nearly all of them young the way he liked them. Right away he noticed a red-headed Susan Hayworth of about twenty-one or twenty-two. Her hair looked thick and luscious, as it draped over her shoulders and a big wave fell over one eye. He stood along the side wall with dozens of other patrons watching her for at least fifteen minutes and when it seemed she was alone, he made his move. He went to stand, not sit, at the bar right beside her, but never spoke to her. "I'll have a draft", he told the bartender. "No, make that a stout ale – any kind will do. Thanks."

Noticing him and seeing he was standing in back of but not sitting on the stool beside him, the young woman looked up and said, "Hey, mister, no one's sitting on this stool if you'd like to sit down." Her smile was mega-watts of white sweetness.

"Well, thank you, young lady, I appreciate your pointing that out and I'll certainly take you up on it. Of course, I saw it, but didn't know if you were saving it for your boyfriend or someone else."

"No, no boyfriend. I'm here alone," she assured him.

"It's hard to manage not to spill half your mug with a crowd like this pushing in on you when you're standing," he said with an equally bright smile, not alluding to its being odd she was alone. Why do women so readily announce that to a stranger? Don't they know it's a dangerous thing to do? Don't they realize the world is filled with perverts and killers? He sighed as though that description had nothing to do with him.

"True." She smiled broadly again.

"Jordan Mace," he told her, as he held out his hand to shake hers.

She hesitated for a moment and he gave her his usual line, seeing her sudden shyness. "This is how this works. I tell you my name and you tell me yours." He half-laughed when he said it and his laughter was contagious.

"Okay," she said when she stopped laughing with him. "My name's Holly James."

"What a pretty name for an equally pretty young woman, who is the spitting image of a movie star of my day" he said, and she actually blushed. "Do you know who Susan Hayworth was? You remind me of her." He was going to enjoy this one, all night if he could work it out.

After the bartender handed him his ale, he smiled at her and then was quiet as he drank a little of it. "Ah, that's good and cold."

"My Corona was ice cold, too," Holly told him. "And yes, my mom loved her and my dad always said she resembled her. She took out a photo from her wallet and handed it to him, and then said, "So, are you what they call a local, Jordan?"

"Guess the apple doesn't fall so far from the tree, then, since you're the image of your mom. She's gorgeous." She blushed and he gave her another big smile, as he handed her wallet back to her. "And no, I'm not a local. I'm from out west, just here on a little vacation to get away from my students."

"You're a teacher then?"

"A college professor, actually. I teach English Lit to freshmen, so it might as well be high school," he said with a laugh. "They're a pretty rowdy bunch of kids."

"I'll bet you're a great professor, though, and they're probably very lucky to have you."

He laughed again, easily. "I don't know about that, but I do enjoy teaching them. My life is boring, though. What about you? Are you a student or a career girl in the big city?"

"How – how did you know?"

"Oh, so you *are* from New York City, eh?" He could always spot them.

"Yes, I live in Manhattan and work at Macy's," she offered.

"Let me guess, you're a floor manager in perfume and cosmetics."

She looked at him as though he'd hung the moon. "Wow, you sure you're not a mind-reader or magician?"

Bingo! That earned her another big laugh. "No, I really am a college professor, but as gorgeous as you are – and don't look so embarrassed – you're a beautiful young woman and you just look the part of a floor manager in that department."

"Actually, it's just in perfume. Cosmetics is across the aisle from perfume and fragrance. I really enjoy my work. I especially like to help these little old ladies who come in every now and then, trying the different sample fragrances, but looking as though they couldn't buy one because they're living from one Social Security check to the next."

"How do you help them then, if they can't afford to do more than try the samples?" He loved to watch her talk. She had the loveliest lips, almost as beautiful as Lana's were. He sighed deeply.

"Is something wrong, Mr. Mace?"

"Please, call me Jordan. Mr. Mace teaches my students," he said, with a smile. "And no, there's nothing wrong at all. My mind just wandered for a moment, thinking of my own dear mom, rest her soul. She couldn't afford nice perfume, either, so I gave her a new bottle every Christmas."

"Oh, I'm sorry you lost your mom. I knew it had to be something like that. You just looked sort of sad there for a minute or two, and I thought I said something wrong."

"Absolutely not, but you never said how you help those little old ladies." He put the hand that was resting on the bar under his chin to appear even more attentive to her boring talk of old ladies and perfume samples.

"Well, we always get a lot of small samples of everything we sell and when I see one of those ladies – I can always tell by the way they're dressed if they're really poor – I say to her, would you like a sample to take with you. Her face just lights up and she always says yes, sure if you think you have any. I tell her to wait right there and I go searching for just the right one. If we're out of that particular one, I offer her a sample of Chanel #5 or something like that I'm sure she's heard of but never been able to buy. I feel like Santa Claus as I load her up with four or five different samples. She's always so grateful. One woman even hugged me and had tears in her eyes. That really makes working worthwhile to me, as hard and hectic as it can be sometimes."

Damn, she has tears in her own eyes. I'd better do something to bring this conversation back up or I won't get anywhere. "I'm sure it makes you feel on top of the world to do that. Hey, I was just going to grab a quick drink and then head up the street to get dinner. Would you be so kind as to accompany me? I always travel alone, but I really don't enjoy eating alone."

"Uh, I – I don't know about that. I don't make it a habit of going somewhere with someone I just met. Maybe I'd better just finish my beer and go back to the hotel."

"Look, I don't want to force you, but I've loved talking with you and really all I'm asking is for you to sit at a table and eat a nice dinner with me; my treat, totally."

"Uh, well if you're sure that's all you're expecting, because if it isn't, I'm just not that kind of girl, you know?"

"That doesn't surprise me in the least. That's why I started talking with you, because I like young women who, like some of my students, are not fast and easy with men. I hate that in a woman."

"Well, okay, then since you put it that way, I'll be happy to join you for dinner, but I'll pay for my own meal, thanks."

"Absolutely not. I was the one who issued the invitation and I'll feel badly if you paid for your dinner, so please, allow me?"

She laughed a tinkly little laugh that so reminded him of Lana that he knew he gave a bit of a start, but hoped she didn't notice. "Okay, I'll be happy to join you for dinner."

He threw a large bill on the bar, got off the stool and offered her his hand to lead her out through the still thick crowd in the bar. It was not that sparse on the street, but he managed to find a small but elegant looking restaurant on a side street between Duval and Whitehead and opened the door for her.

"This is lovely. I had no idea a restaurant like this existed in this town," she said, with another laugh.

"There are a few of them but you have to either search for hours or know where they are and I happen to have discovered this little gem my first week here." Just then the maître d' came up to them and showed them to their table, laid with a white tablecloth and elegant silverware. As he seated Holly, she leaned over and took in the aroma of the single red rose in the vase and smiled her appreciation. After he asked for their drink order and they both ordered a nice Bordeaux, he sent their waiter over to take their dinner orders.

TWENTY-THREE

"Thank you for walking me to my door, Jordan. I appreciate it. There seem to be a lot of drunks in that crowd on the street," she said with a little nervous smile.

"It was my pleasure, Holly. I'm so glad I met you and I loved having dinner with you tonight. It's early yet, though. Do you think I could come in and we could enjoy a nightcap out on the terrace before we say goodnight?"

"No, I think I'd just like to say good night here and go to bed, early."

"That's nice, too," he said, pushing her into the room and slamming the door behind them.

"My God, what's going on?" She looked positively terrified, which delighted him.

"I'm sorry, I didn't mean to be rough. I just feel compelled to stay with you a while longer. Won't you let me fix us a drink and then I'll be on my way?"

"No," she said, adamantly, "I meant what I said, I'm tired, it's been a lovely but long night, I thank you for dinner, but now I just want you to go, so I can go to bed."

"Actually, that's what I had in mind, too," he said, as he kissed her roughly and pulled her very close to him. She tried to avoid his mouth but he forced her to take his tongue. And then she did something unexpected and which made him very angry. She bit his tongue quite hard.

"Well, you little bitch!" He slapped her hard across one cheek and then the other, as he forced her back onto the bed, tearing off her nice little black dress in the process. She tried to scream, but he hit her again and put his hand over her mouth so tightly she couldn't bite him as she tried to do again. When he had her naked, he took out his large handkerchief and tied it around her face as a gag in her mouth. Then he pulled out scarfs he'd hidden deep in his bag and tied her arms and legs to the bed, while her eyes widened even further than they had been and large tears started popping out of her beautiful violet eyes.

"Aw baby, I'm sorry, please don't cry. I just want to show you how much I love being with you and how beautiful I find you. I don't want to have to force myself on you. I just wanted to make love to you," he said as he started touching her lightly. "Now, if I take off the gag, will you not scream and just let me love you the way you deserve to be loved?"

She nodded her head yes, too quickly to satisfy him. "On second thought, maybe not. I'd love to keep kissing you, but I can't take a chance you'll not scream. I'm not a rapist but the police might think otherwise, so I think I'll just stick with plan A."

More tears came streaming down her face and he slapped her again. "Now, just stop that stupid crying, Holly. It's not like I'm going to hurt you. I like to take my time with my women." She couldn't stop crying, because actually she was a virgin as he'd first suspected and she tried to scream that at him but he couldn't tell what she was saying through the gag in her mouth. It wouldn't have made any difference, anyway. He loved to take virgins. If he couldn't make them suffer, what was the fun in that? There weren't many women he really wanted to be gentle with as he was with Lana, whom he fancied himself truly in love with, despite sending her naked body careening off one of the highest cliffs in Tahiti, before he came back on his way to the airport and made love again to her naked and very dead body. He loved that memory. As lovely as she was, though, Holly was no Lana. Suddenly that thought made him quite angry and he slapped her again, telling her to calm down. "You should be Lana, not this poor imitation."

This made her more hysterical and she knew he must be crazy. She didn't care who Lana was, but she was so scared she'd never come out of this alive. She was flailing around so much as he started touching her again, so he reached into his bag and pulled out his magic drug that would make her not only compliant but give her total amnesia of the entire night and she wouldn't even remember meeting him, even if she were so sore she would have a hard time walking in the morning. He smiled and put the powder in just a little water, moved the gag just enough to force it down her throat and it immediately went to work, despite her choking and losing some of it. After a few minutes, he was even able to take off the gag and start kissing her again as he had his complete way with her.

She started screaming again when he penetrated her without preparing her, so he moved the gag back over her mouth and kept at it until he broke that tough but prized little cherry of a membrane she was so proud of still having at 24 years of age. When it broke, she passed out and that suited him just fine. He could do more damage with her unconscious. And he did until she was pouring blood all over the bed because of his destruction of her body. When he finally had enough and pulled out for the last time, she momentarily came to, but he slapped her hard and her head banged against the bedside table, rendering her unconscious again. He made sure she was still breathing, but there was so much blood, he had to take a shower before he left her room. He wrapped the bloody condom in the small plastic bag he had in his carry-all and let the hot water wash all the blood off him and down the drain for several minutes. Before he dressed, he mixed alcohol with a little bleach and cleaned the entire room of his fingerprints and put the glass with the drink he'd fixed before his shower into another plastic bag he put into the carry-all. After that he went back into the bathroom before dressing, after taking another look at the bloody naked woman on the bed. How disgusting she looked now. Nothing like Susan Hayworth.

He knew he'd have to stay away from Duval Street for a few weeks, since he had no idea how long she was staying on the island. He decided to drive up to Coral Gables and hide out for a while. But before he could do that, and before he left the hotel, he had to change his appearance again, all because of stupid virginal Holly. This time, he'd have to become platinum blonde the hard way with pure bleach instead of hair dye and then he'd get a crew cut and maybe even go to a thrift shop and buy some camouflage fatigues and play the part of a veteran for a while. He whistled softly as he rummaged through his bag for the bleach again, wrapped a towel around his neck and began to strip his dark hair of color. He winced as it started burning, but he figured if it burned that much, it would probably work quicker.

So Jordan Mace, the former Jacques Hamilton, disappeared that night and in his place, Army veteran Jerry Stamril drove an old jeep back into Key West three months later, not knowing or caring whether he'd left a dead girl back in that hotel room. He'd burned the Jordan Mace ID and passport after making sure he had Stamril's in his luggage. He'd darned near burned his scalp to pieces the night he transformed into the veteran but the results were astounding. With the addition of the crew cut and a bleached mustache with no goatee, he looked every bit the part of a veteran of the second Iraq War, which is what he told folks who saw him and thanked him for his service. Yes, he was going to enjoy the rest of his time on this godforsaken island the stupid tourists liked to call paradise and the equally dumb locals called the rock. So stupid, both of them.

But, no more hitting the tourist spots. He'd go to little local bars like the one called Don's Place on Truman and clubs like Bare Assets a little further up the street but on the opposite side of Don's. He enjoyed quiet dark strip clubs. After all, they were gentlemen's clubs and he was a gentlemen, so he knew he'd fit right in. He pushed the things that were not very gentlemanly out of his mind and decided he'd not take any more women home. He just couldn't control his urge to violently rape them so he'd just do the touchy-feely stuff in the darkened bars and a lot of passionate kissing but that would be it. If he got them alone, he knew it would happen again because he just loved to hurt women. Man, how he loved to hurt them, but he had to stick to the plan this time and toe the line. And no more Duval Street clubbing or even dinner. He'd stick to Truman and the little side streets like Elizabeth and Margaret. He didn't lie and say he was a conch, because birth records were too easy to check down here, but he'd say he just was visiting here and was thinking of putting down roots if he liked it as much a month from now as he did already.

Of course, he hated the place and couldn't wait to get that last loose end tied up so he could head to Wyoming and his quiet and isolated little spread out there. He took a lot of gorgeous chicks there and did whatever he wanted to them, and it didn't matter how long and loud they screamed. There was no one remotely close to hear them. And there was plenty of wild range to bury them on if things got too out of hand and they caused him to kill them, damned broads. Just thinking of it made him hard as a brick, though. He kept an ear open for any talk of a vicious rape in the little hotel in Old Town, but there was never a word mentioned by anyone anywhere he went on the island. Had he bothered to read the back issues of the Citizen, he'd see that was the main topic of conversation and print on the minds of Key Westers for weeks. Maybe Holly bled to death that night, but then he never heard anything about that, either. Nothing. It didn't matter to him whether she lived or died. All that mattered was that he'd drugged her so heavily that if she did manage to live, there was no way she'd ever remember that college professor named Jordan Mace who was so sweet to her at dinner. She'd certainly never see him again. Nobody would.

Holly did live that night, but after the hotel maid found her the next morning, the doctor at the emergency room had to take her to the OR to remove her uterus and one ovary. He told his colleagues and Lt. Butler he'd never seen such damage in his 28 year career as a gynecologist. He nearly cried just thinking about how horribly mutilated that beautiful little woman was. And her parents did break down and cry when he told them about it. He didn't know what besides a very large penis the monster put up her vaginal tract that ripped her apart like that and he didn't think he could handle finding out. He wished he knew where that sonofabitch was, because he'd certainly like to do unto him as he did to that innocent young woman. He had no use for rapists, especially the kind that inserted all manner of crude things up a woman's body. It made everyone involved with the young woman's case even sadder when something went very wrong two nights after her emergency surgery and despite all their heroic efforts, she died, never having regained consciousness since she was found by the maid that morning in her hotel room.

TWENTY-FOUR

Three weeks before Jerry Stamril showed up in Key West, Maggie was having a lovely day triking around the island. She gradually was getting back to doing the things that made her happy and relaxed, and no longer worried that the murderer from Windsor Park might be nearby. He would have shown himself by now, she knew, from the brazen way he acted the day he threw the body parts down the compactor when she was sitting right there on the swing. Although there had been that brutal rape and murder several days ago at the Pier House, the cops must not think he had anything to do with it or they'd have put bodyguards back in the Southernmost Motel to guard the house and her.

She pushed any thought of Hamilton Jacques from her mind and sat on the trike at the edge of the seawall, watching the gulls and people. The beach certainly was crowded today and it wasn't even winter or a holiday. Most of the sunbathers, swimmers and kite surfers must be locals. She smiled as she watched the sight before her and felt so blessed to be able to live in such a place where on any given day, rain or shine, she could get on her red trike and within moments be right there beside the sea.

As it was getting dusky, she decided to turn back toward home and get dinner started. She'd invited Homer, Carolyn, Lt Butler, Police Chaplain Sgt. Terrance Stevens and Chief Doan to dinner and she wanted it to be relaxing and unhurried for all of them, including herself. She had already bought plenty of lobster tails, yellowtail fillets and shrimp she was going to make cocktail sauce for and she had two dozen good sized ears of corn and sweet potatoes wrapped in foil to put on the large triple grill Homer had bought her for Christmas last year. She would do the broccoli in cream sauce in the kitchen while everything else was grilling. She and Carolyn had made plenty of apple and key lime pies all week, so she knew they'd have plenty to eat. The thought of having an intimate dinner party outside under her huge sapodilla tree in the back yard made her happy. She hadn't done anything like that in a very long time.

As she rode the trike up the ramp to her second floor wraparound porch, Homer was just pulling the Hummer into the drive. Carolyn was waiting for them in the porch swing. "Hey, you two, I thought I was going to have to pull off this soiree all by my lonesome," she said, with a hearty laugh.

"Nah, I knew when to be back," Maggie told her. "I wouldn't miss having this dinner for anything."

Homer said hello to both of them with a big hug and kiss on the cheeks. "I haven't seen you this happy and excited in a long time, Mag," he told her and Carolyn added an "amen" to that.

"Well, I don't know when I last felt this happy and excited. It's time we got back to normal living, don't you think?" They both nodded. "I just got tired of being scared and looking over my shoulder all the time. Really tired of it!" No one had told her that officers Joey Davidson and Shirley Savage were always following her ever since the rape and death of the lovely young woman a few weeks ago. Discreetly, of course.

"I'm glad to hear you say that, dear," Carolyn told her. "And it's about time you had a break from doing it. I think everyone's going to enjoy this dinner tonight. I know for certain I will. Homer, if you'll fire-up the grill, I'll help Mag carry the food outside and get it started."

"Sure thing, but I can help carry some, too, after I get it going. Doesn't take long to fire up an automatic gas grill," he said, laughing. "Best gift I ever gave you, Mag, if I do say so, myself."

"I couldn't agree more. I love it and who wouldn't love eating out there with this breeze that's blowing tonight! Oh, Carolyn, will you please get the citronella torches lit, also, before we take any of the food outside. I know the breeze helps keep those skeeters away, but I want to be sure. None of us needs to deal with their nasty bites tonight."

"Skeeters?" Homer walked outside, laughing. She ignored him with a smile and checked to make sure everything was ready for the grill. After a few minutes Homer called that it was ready, so the two women carried out the food for him to start grilling.

TWENTY-FIVE

It wasn't long until Lenny Doan and Blake Butler walked out to the back yard and patio. "Well, hello Chief, Lieutenant," Maggie said. "Glad you made it. We just put the food on, so what can I get you to drink while we wait?"

"Sam Adams for me, thanks," Chief Doan told her. The lieutenant asked for the same.

After she handed them their beers, she asked, "Chief, while dinner's grilling, do you mind talking shop with me?"

"I'd prefer not to, but sure, I'll talk with you. What's on your mind?"

She fidgeted with the tie strings at the neck of her summery blouse for a moment and then said, "I just want to talk about that young girl's murder, you know, the one at the hotel."

"Oh, right. What do you want to know that you haven't read about?" He was sure he knew what she was leading up to.

"Well, for one thing, when have you had such a gruesome murder on this island?"

"We haven't had any like it since I've been chief, thankfully, and that's been since 2006, as you know. Why do you ask?"

"Do you have any idea who did it; I mean did you get an ID from the DNA? From what I heard, it was either a brutal stranger rape or a date gone horribly wrong." She hesitated a moment. "Don't you always get DNA from a rape or even if someone had normal consenting sex?"

"Actually, we don't always get DNA. This killer went to a lot of trouble to clean up behind himself and he used a condom so there was no DNA at all, except the poor victim's."

"Not even really deep in the bathtub and sink drains?"

The lieutenant's eyebrows shot up. "Maggie, I swear, we ought to hire you for the crime lab or crime scene team." He had a guilty look on his face, despite teasing her.

Lenny Doan laughed but then he turned serious again. "He's right, Mag. Sometimes I think we should hire you. Of all the specimens the crime scene guys turned in, there should have been some from the bathroom drains – I just now realized I saw none. Excuse me, I need to make a call." He turned and went further away from the rest of the small group.

"Yeah, Smitty, it's the chief. Did any of you guys take a specimen from the bathtub drain in the Pier House murder scene? That's what I thought," he said. "Of course I want you to tonight. For heaven's sake, man, you all know better. Our resident detective wannabe, Maggie Metronia, just asked me if we got DNA from the bathtub or sink drains! Yes, right now and you'd better hope they haven't cleaned that thoroughly, yet. I know it's been a week, but do it, anyway. Let me know right away. Thanks!"

When he returned to the group, he scowled at his lieutenant, who should have picked up that omission, as well. Butler shrugged and said out of range of the others, "Sorry, Chief, I took for granted they'd done it. I should have double-checked. I realized at the same time you did that I saw no report on them."

"That dinner is smelling mighty good!" Doan told Homer, to try to get back into a lighter mood for Maggie's sake. He didn't say any more to his second-in-command. They'd discuss it later.

"It sure does," his chaplain said, as he walked out to the patio, where everyone said hello to him, and Maggie welcomed him to her home. Like everyone else on the island, who knew him, she adored Terry Stevens, who didn't have a hateful bone in his body. And he was always smiling and joking with everyone when he wasn't on the job. He even pastored a little church by the cemetery and his congregation couldn't be happier he'd agreed to take the job a few years ago.

The chief was thinking it seemed she'd pretty much put what happened out in the straits last year out of her mind. It was good to see her back to her old self again, enjoying the island and its people. Of course, knowing Maggie it could be just a façade to get everyone else to think she was okay, so he didn't buy it completely. And he was going to do his part tonight to keep her mind off the West Palm murder, too, if that was even possible, judging from the first question she'd asked a few minutes ago.

"Yes, it does, doesn't it," Carolyn said, with a big smile for the cook, also trying to steer the conversation away from the murder, but Maggie was having none of it.

"It just seems to me that you have an extra vicious killer on your hands. Can't get much more vicious than to cut up a body and throw it into a compactor," she said to the group, before she took another long sip from her icy Corona.

"Aw, Mag, come on." Homer knew this was why she'd opened the subject and hated for her to spoil her own dinner party. "You wanted to have a nice party tonight. We don't need to hear all this right now."

She put her hands on her hips and glared at him. "I'll have you know, Homer Wiley, my mind is never off that murder back in West Palm and if I want to draw comparisons for the chief at my own dinner party, I think I have a dad-burned right to do it!" She stomped off into the house, leaving everyone looking aghast and a bit contrite as they sat or stood around the grill area.

"Maybe I should..." Carolyn got up from where she'd been sitting.

"No, you shouldn't. When she gets like this, whether she's right or wrong, you just have to let her cool her heels for a while and she'll come around. Trust me, I've been joined at the hip to that little woman for decades and I know how she is." He turned back to his cooking on the grill and Carolyn sat back in her chair. Everything would be ready to eat soon and he hoped Maggie would come back out before it was.

After about fifteen minutes, all of them turned toward the slider, as she came out lugging a large dispenser of lemonade, which the chaplain quickly took off her hands and carried to the large buffet counter. "Lots of fresh lemonade here if anyone wants some," she said as though nothing had transpired earlier to make her angry. That's what Homer had always loved about her. She could turn on a dime and get back into a good mood even when she was mad enough to chew nails – or make a pin cushion of his body with them, one or the other! He smiled to himself.

"Don't you say a word, Wiley. I'm still mad at you," she said, hiding a grin from him. She knew him as well as he did her and knew that's what he was thinking. He smiled and held up his hand in defense.

"Great idea, Mag. I think I'll have some now. I've had enough Corona for the night. Does anyone else want me to pour a glass for your dinner? Mag makes the best lemonade in the state, as you all know," Carolyn said with a big smile, glad for the tension to have dissipated.

"Sure, I'll have some, thanks," Butler told her. "It sounds just right with all that good food. It is almost ready. Right?"

Homer smiled as he looked up. "If you vultures can give it another ten minutes, it'll be on the table."

Lenny Doan remained quiet throughout the meal, only speaking when drawn out. Butler knew his boss was pissed with him and the CS guys, and rightfully so. He didn't know how they'd missed checking those bathroom drains, especially when they saw the trail of blood from the bed to the bathroom. That's CSI 101, for heaven's sake. And every cop on the beat knows you check the drains. Smitty must have had something on his mind other than the crime scene to have messed up that drastically. Maybe Beth wanted that divorce, after all. The last time they spoke about it, she'd asked for a reconciliation and said she wanted them to go to counseling together. He thought it was all settled, but maybe she changed her mind. Oh well, if something was wrong and he wanted to share it, he'd find out then. He was there for his guys but he never meddled unless invited.

A few minutes later, Doan's cell rang. He excused himself to take it in private. "Really? Well, that's just great. We'd never have known it had Maggie not brought it up. Good work. How about blood, though? Yes! Thanks, Smitty, I'll look forward to hearing back from you after you've run it."

"Well?" Butler said as he walked over to his boss. He looked nervous to Maggie. But she kept quiet.

"Thanks to Maggie, we now know that our perp – if he is the hotel murderer – is now a blonde. And besides bleach with some dark hair in it, there is blood further down in the sink drain. Not much, but enough and only part of it's the victim's."

"That's great news, even if my head's going to roll right along with the rest of the team's. Glad they found both of those specimens. I have a gut feeling about this guy and that Maggie's right and the perp she witnessed throwing the body away in West Palm and him are one and the same, Chief."

"I expect you're right about that. And no one's head is gonna roll. I don't know how the mistake was made and neither do you. I'm just thankful our little wannabe over there thought of it or we'd still be looking for him as he was before he decided to change the hair color. If he's on the island, that is. But we'll know soon enough. They walked back and sat down. "Pass me the yellowtail, please." Maggie said no more, but she couldn't keep from smiling when she passed him the large platter of fish. She didn't ask, but knew they'd found blood or hair. He winked at her and smiled broadly.

TWENTY-SIX

The day after Maggie's successful dinner party, Lieutenant Butler came into the chief's office. "Len, you won't believe this. I just got a call from law enforcement in Tahiti."

The chief's head snapped up from the budget he was working on. "Tahiti? What would they be calling us about?"

"Apparently they found a young woman dead on one of their beaches, below the highest cliff on the island. Apparently, she was pushed. They said they would have thought it was just an accident had they not found evidence of both pre-death and after-death coitus. There was a blanket someone left not far from the edge of the cliff that had the same semen on it as was in her body and they're sure the same guy had sex with her after she fell and was killed. They figured if he hadn't killed her he would have called for help when she went over the cliff instead of going back and having sex on her dead body."

"Makes sense, but what's that have to do with Key West?" He stood up, stretched and then sat down on the couch. He pointed to the chair beside Butler and he sat in it.

"Apparently, when they traced this young woman's parents back in Iowa, they told them they'd been trying to find her ever since she went on vacation down here. Remember that call we got a few weeks ago about a college woman from New York named Lana Carter?"

"Aw, dammit!"

"Yeah, it was the same woman. They didn't know she hadn't returned to work until they received a call from her roommate, asking whether they'd seen her. She said she hadn't come back to school or to her part-time modeling job after her vacation was over, and that's when they called us. The Pier House said she'd left the week before but hadn't checked out, so they'd assumed she'd gone back to New York when she didn't show up again after a week. She didn't mention extending her vacation to Tahiti or anywhere else, for that matter. She just left a few days early to attend to something urgent that had just come up, she told them at the desk, but made sure they understood she wasn't checking out. Figuring the urgent matter must have been so serious she'd forgotten about the hotel, they didn't charge her for the unused days when she didn't return. They said something odd, though. After they figured she wasn't coming back, they checked her room but saw she'd taken everything with her. Strange when she made a point of telling them she wasn't checking out. Maybe the guy she was with told her to check out, that she could fly back from L.A., and she became suspicious and thought she'd better not lose her room in case it didn't work out with him. When we checked the airport, they said she'd taken a plane to LA, so we called the parents and told them that, so they said she'd probably call them from there just any time now, but of course, it was the Tahitian authorities who called them."

"Did they ID the suspect?"

"Yes, the semen belonged to Hamilton Jacques."

"My God, who hasn't that sonofabitch killed!"

"God only knows, Chief. LA also checked the airlines for a reservation for Lana Carter and there was only a one way ticket bought by a guy who said his name was Jordan Mace, who bought a round-trip for himself. They checked the airport CCTV and it caught them on film. Jordan Mace is Hamilton Jacques. He probably picked her up in Sloppy Joe's, too, the same as he did poor Holly James. We're checking the CCTV there for Lana Carter's image, like we did for Holly. I'm sure we'll see her. Here's the faxed photo of her with Jacques at the airport."

"She looks like a beautiful Polynesian in this. I expect she fit right in with everyone else in Tahiti. You wonder how this monster can convince these young woman to go anywhere with him. He must have really fed her a line of it to get her to go all the way to the South Pacific like that."

"Her mom told the Tahitian police they'd never heard of Jordan Mace and were sure had their daughter planned to meet him here she would have told them," Butler said. "Apparently she and her daughter were more like sisters than mom and daughter, and she confided in her mom a lot."

"Like she confided that she was flying halfway around the world with him?"

"My thoughts, exactly. Apparently she wasn't as open about her life as they believed." He stood and said, "Let's go down to see if Smitty has anything for us, yet."

Just as they walked into the crime lab, they heard the ding telling them the search was finished. "Hey guys," Jerry Smith said, with a broad smile, "you're just in time. We have a match."

When they looked at the image, Doan pumped the air with his fist. "Yes, I knew it. Maggie was right. Jacques did kill poor Holly James. Well, it doesn't matter what he calls himself or how he cuts his hair or anything else. We know he's a platinum blonde now and I wouldn't be at all surprised if he's still hanging around the island. Let's get a new photo out with blonde hair this time and let's catch this monster! Make the hair different lengths, starting with a crew cut and ending with waves. And we won't put this new information out to the general public just yet."

"Understood. I'll get Tomlinson on it right away," Smith told him. "Uh, Chief, got a minute?"

"Yeah, what's on your mind?"

"I – I'm really sorry about messing up. I let my personal problems get in the way of my job and I promise you it won't happen again." He ran a hand through his thick black hair and his eyebrows raised, as he bit his lower lip.

Doan put his hand on his shoulder and said, "Look, you're human and we're all fallible. But if you want to talk about it, you know my door's open."

"Thanks, I appreciate that, but we'll work it out, one way or another." He gave the chief a relieved smile and turned around to go see Detective Tomlinson about changing the composite to reflect the hair change. He was relieved his boss took his failing the way he did. He could just as easily have disciplined him for overlooking such a basic part of the crime scene investigation or gotten rid of him, altogether, and he didn't think he could have handled that with all that was going on with Beth right now. For the life of him he couldn't figure out why she backed out of the counseling all of a sudden, after telling him that's what she wanted. Could there be another man? No, he couldn't picture his by-the-book wife suddenly deciding to have an affair while they were trying to work out their differences. They'd been together since middle school and he knew her too well to believe that. Maybe it was just too many long hours and not enough time at home, like she told him. He'd try extra hard to change that as soon as this case was closed. Oh well, he needed to get their personal life off his mind if he expected to stay alert to everything now and not mess up on the job again. He'd never done something like that before and to him, no matter what the chief said about not being infallible, it was a stupid move on his part after eighteen years in crime scene.

TWENTY-SEVEN

The next morning, Chief Doan made a call. "Hi Maggie, I wanted to thank you for the great dinner the other night. I really enjoyed it."

"You're welcome, Chief, but I know and you know that's not why you called me. You have news, don't you."

"You're always one step ahead of me, woman. Maybe I really should put you on the job," he said, with a chuckle. "Okay, here's what we found in the drain, thanks to you. There was some blood, yes, and also some bleach and hair."

"Huh? Bleach? You mean the killer used it to clean up behind himself?"

"Well, he did that, too, but with the hair being found in the drain with the bleach, we're pretty sure he bleached his dark hair before he left the hotel, so he wouldn't be recognized on camera, since the hotel has cameras in the elevators and stairwells."

"Oh, I see. But what about the blood. Was it all that poor girl's?" She was twisting the end of her shirt as she always did when she got nervous. "You didn't say."

"I have to tell you the truth, Maggie. No, it wasn't all the victim's and..."

"And it belongs to that same man, Hamilton Jacques," she finished for him. He was taken aback at her naming him and wondered how she found out that's who committed that murder in West Palm, but didn't ask. He'd have Butler take that and run with it at the next roll call. When he did, of course, Joey Davidson spoke up and told him he'd meant to let him know the week before that he'd slipped up and called him by name to Maggie. He wasn't disciplined for it, since both Butler and the chief figured it was an honest mistake any of them could have made.

"Yes, it does. But don't you worry, we're going to double our efforts on the island and get new drawings out to all law enforcement statewide and give it to the FBI in case he's left Florida. Uh, we're not putting the new information out to the public just yet, though, so please don't speak of it while you're outside and away from the house."

"Why on earth not? You don't want another poor unsuspecting soul to get with him and then get herself killed by the fiend!"

"No, Maggie, we don't, but if we tip our hand right now, and he is still on the island, he'll just dye his hair another color and change his appearance again." Then he figured he'd better level with her about the FBI. "Also, I've spoken with the FBI since he took that young woman out of the country from here."

"Are they taking over the case, then?"

"No, they said they were going to sit on it for a while to see whether he turns up again. It was on their advice I don't release any more information about him."

"Even to let the public know he's a serial killer?"

"Not even that, just yet. Again, none of us wants to let him know that we know about his changing identities and looks. As I say, it just might cause him to change it again, before we can nail him. He apparently was in Key West for a while, since he's killed two young women he met here, and he must be pretty good at changing his looks to cause all our guys to miss him."

"Oh, I didn't think about that."

He smiled with relief and told her, "I need to go now, but I wanted you to know we're putting some undercover guys on all three of you again. I won't have them introduce themselves, because I don't want him, if he is nearby, seeing cops go into your house. He probably knows Butler and I have been around, but if he does, he'll also figure out it was just socializing. On second thought, I might put a couple of folks on you whom you already know, but I won't share that till it's a done deal, since they might not be free, yet."

"Okay, I understand," she said, a little curious as to whom he was thinking of, but let it go for now. "I'll let Carolyn and Homer know. Will they just be watching the house and if so, do you want Homer to stay here for a while longer, so you don't have to have them on Sugarloaf, too? He's thinking of moving back home."

He thought about it for a couple seconds and then said, "You know, that might not be a bad idea. Yes, please ask him to wait until this thing's resolved. I'd say for you and Carolyn to go to his place, but then we'd have to relinquish your protection to the SO, but I think you'd be safer here in town, if that's okay with you. Homer's place is pretty isolated out there."

"Yes, I'd prefer that. I think I'd be able to relax easier if I stayed at home where I have plenty to do and I have plenty of space here so Homer wouldn't have to be stationed on the couch at night, as he's been doing. Thanks, Chief. We'll be talking to you."

"Bye, Mag." Well, at least we won't have to be so worried about the women now with Homer staying and with our guys looking after them, too, hopefully we can catch this guy without any of them getting hurt.

He went into Blake Butler's office next. "Hey Chief, what can I do for you?"

"Are Savage and Davidson still on the Spivey case?" Butler had assigned both Detectives Shirley Savage and Joey Davidson to go undercover with Homer Wiley in Cuba last year, which culminated in the takedown of the lowlife who'd helped one of their own murder the guy who'd lived in Carolyn's condo building.

"You okay, Lenny?"

"Sure, I'm fine. My mind just wandered for a minute. Getting back to Savage and Davidson."

"Oh, yeah, they're still on it, but just the paperwork now since he's pled out. Why? You need them for a new case?"

"Not a new one. I want them to check into the Southernmost Motel and keep an eye on the ladies for us. I'm having Homer stay there with them until this is over, but I want them shadowed by Savage and Davidson, nonetheless. I have a feeling Hamilton's not too far away. Since he's been here all along, he's proved he's not the kind of guy to walk away and leave a loose end dangling."

"I agree with you there. That's one vicious killer and I'd sure hate like hell for him to hurt Maggie or anyone else, for that matter. He's done enough damage between West Palm and Key West. And unfortunately in Tahiti. I'll get them settled into the motel right away." He picked up the phone.

"Thanks, Blake, I'll feel a lot better when I know they're over there keeping an eye on the three of them." He walked back to his office and got back to working on the budget. He hated that part of his job, but it was a necessary evil and sometimes the mundane paperwork relaxed him and he could do with some relaxation. Hamilton Jacques had him tied in knots and he didn't like giving him that much power. Before he started working on it, though, he picked up the phone and called Butler again. "I think it'd be a good idea to tell them to ask for the same room the West Palm deputies had if you remember the room number. They had a great view of the whole house from up there. He doesn't have to know why. If he asks, they can just say they were in the room years ago and wanted it for sentimental reasons or something. Tell them to register under, oh, I think Connie and Luke Farmer will be easy to remember. They can pay in cash as soon as they sign in so he won't need ID. And they don't have a rental so he doesn't need a tag number."

"You got it, Chief." After he disconnected, he dialed another number.

Joey Davidson answered on the first ring. "Davidson here."

"Hey Joey, I have a new assignment for Shirley and you. Could you both come to my office as soon as you're finished with that paperwork?"

"We just finished ten minutes ago and were heading out for some dinner, but we'll come by there first, if it's urgent."

"Yeah, it's pretty urgent," their lieutenant told them before disconnecting.

When the two walked into his office a few minutes later, they looked excited to be getting a new case, despite having been undercover as a homeless couple and being grungy for over seven months on the last case. He smiled and told them to have a seat. "I'm glad you aren't upset over not getting some badly needed R&R before going to the next case."

"You said it was urgent and we're available, so no problem, Loo," Shirley Savage, a leggy redhead told him. Besides being gorgeous to look at, she was a damned fine undercover detective, who could have been the head of their special victims unit had she not enjoyed undercover work so much. She'd been offered the position twice but turned it down both times.

"Yes, Shirley's right, Loo, we're fine with another case now." Joey Davidson, another fine undercover detective who'd never had another job with the KWPD since he graduated from the academy just a few years before, told him. Joey was one of the best snipers the department had.

"Okay, I want the two of you, Connie and Luke Farmer, young married couple from St. Augustine, to get room 632 at the Southernmost this evening after you've had dinner. Ask for that specific room when you make the reservation and if you're questioned as to why, just tell them you stayed in it many years ago and for sentimental reasons, you'd like it again. Tell them you want to leave your departure time open-ended if they don't mind, and they won't. It's the room the two deputies from Palm Beach SO used that had the best view of Maggie's entire house."

"Oh no," Joey groaned, in mock disappointment. "Should have known it would have something to do with that pain in the butt Wiley." Then he grinned at Shirley and the chief knew he'd be fine with it.

The lieutenant smiled, and said, "Hey, that worked out just fine with Homer, but yes, the chief asked that he keep staying with the ladies for a while longer, because we think Jacques is still on the island."

"Oh, I thought everyone was sure he was long gone by now, if he was ever here to begin with?"

"No, Shirl, we've just ID'd him for the brutal rape and murder of Holly James last month. And he's been ID'd as the perp who killed another young woman we'd all been looking for before that. Lana Carter was her name."

"Damn! That's great that you've ID'd him, but sorry to hear he was on the island, after all. And God, those poor women." She glanced at Davidson for a moment and then looked back at the chief.

"What is it?"

"Oh nothing. I'm just wondering whether we'll spot him. Maybe he's given up on getting rid of Maggie."

"I don't think so. He's pretty dogged about things like that. Doesn't quit too easily, from all we've heard about him."

"Well, if we're going to check into a motel, I guess I'll get home and get a bag packed. Are we supposed to be honeymooners or can we be married for several years."

"Since your cover story will be that you want the same room because you were there several years ago, I guess you'd better have been married a couple dozen years."

"Hell, Loo, I wasn't even born then," Davidson said and then laughed riotously. Savage laughed at him, punched him on the shoulder and they walked out the door, waving goodbye to their lieutenant, who was smiling at their backs.

Chief Doan walked back into the office right after this and asked his number one in command what was so amusing, and he told him. "I sure wish it were possible to clone those two. Some of road patrol could use an attitude adjustment and it would be nice to have another set of them out there working with them."

"I couldn't agree more," his boss told him. "And they've gotten so they work easily together, so pretending to be a married couple will probably be a piece of cake. Did you give them plenty of cash?"

"Yes, since there wasn't time to get credit cards and drivers' licenses for them, they'll just pay everything in cash. I gave them a thousand spending money besides that for a week at the hotel when they check in and they'll ask to keep their departure date open-ended."

"Good job. Sounds like you've got it all covered. Now we just have to sit back and see what his next move is going to be. I think we'd better put some men on the docks, too, and get them the composite printouts with the blonde and dark hair, just in case he does have a boat."

"Already have that in place, Chief. So far, negative, but I told them to hang around for a few days and make it look like any other time they patrol on foot. I can almost smell that monster. We're gonna nab him soon, I just know it."

Doan patted his number one on the back as he was leaving the office. "I hope so, Blake. I sure hope so!"

TWENTY-EIGHT

Maggie was sitting out on the porch swing, reading her James Patterson when Homer came out, holding a large cup of coffee. "Hey Mag, what's that you're reading?" He sat heavily in the swing opposite her.

"It's his latest, 'Black Book', she answered, without looking up.

"You sure are a cop wannabe," he teased. "All you think about is solving murders."

"Well, I suppose more than 350 million other people are cop wannabes, too, then, smarty. He has a bigger following than any other writer in the world."

"Wow, you really are uptight about Jacques, if you can't take my teasing, anymore. Wanna talk about it?"

"No, I just want to be left alone to enjoy my book," she answered, clearly miffed at her closest friend.

"Okay, but the offer stands if you decide you want to," he told her as he groaned and grasped his knee while he was getting off the swing. She still did not look up from her book, which also was not like her. She was usually a mother hen when it came to his aches and pains, and going so far as to get him a heating pad and telling him to get off his feet and let the heat work on his knees.

"Maggie, are you..."

"I said go away and leave me alone, Homer. I mean it. I just want to read in peace."

"Okay, I'm going," he said, as he went inside through the open French doors. Maggie enjoyed airing out the house every day by leaving all the doors and windows open. A strong breeze was causing the clear panels in the living room to blow out onto the porch until they were standing horizontally in the air and then flowing back in again, repeatedly, and this always calmed her. Well, that and the latest James Patterson. With Homer in the house and the detectives, whomever they are, across the street watching the house, she felt safe with everything opened again. She'd battened down all the hatches right after she came back from West Palm, even with the Palm Beach County Sheriff's Office detective and deputy there in the motel.

"Good morning. How's she doing?" Carolyn was eating a croissant with jam when he came back into the kitchen for a refill a few minutes later, holding an analgesic pad in his hand.

"Morning, Carolyn. She's out on the porch reading Patterson and under no uncertain terms does not want to be disturbed." He leaned over after taking the backing off the pad and stuck it against the side of his knee. He winced as the icy cold pad came into contact with his skin, but it wasn't long until he started to feel the effects of the medication in it, so soon forgot about it.

"Wonder what happened to put her into such a funk, besides the obvious."

"I think, despite her bravado, she's petrified again now that she knows he's still around – or probably is, since the cops don't know for sure. At least, she knows for sure he *was* here, as she suspected months ago." He put the cup on the table and sat to her left, working on the stack of pancakes he'd made earlier and Carolyn heated up right before he came inside.

"Doesn't she even want to eat?"

Peg Gregory

"She had scrambled eggs and toast earlier. I saw her plate in the drainer when I came down and there were remnants of the eggs in the fry pan before I cleaned everything and started mixing the pancakes."

"Which were delicious, thank you," she said with a smile. He loved her thousand watt smile as much as he loved her, but she wanted no relationship like that, so he had to be content with just her friendship, which he'd never jeopardize by insisting upon more than she could give.

"Carolyn, may I ask you something?"

"Sure, why not?"

"Do you think she's working up to going out on her own to find this guy?" He finished the pancakes and settled back with his second cup of coffee, watching her.

"Oh lord no, not after the last time. I'm sure she's not entertaining such an idea. Why do you ask?"

"Well, I just know how she gets when she's thinking of doing something she shouldn't and it worries me like crazy. I remember the trouble the two of you almost got into last year by chasing after that other guy. Had I not seen you and driven into the lot at Fausto's, as I called the cops, who knows what he might have done."

She patted his hand for a moment before speaking. She thought about the prospects of that, also, from time to time. "Well, we both learned a valuable lesson from that, my friend, and you can rest assured it won't happen again."

"But what if, knowing you want no part of staking out this guy, she goes it alone to try to flush him out thinking if he shows, the guys across the street who'll be tailing her will take care of him? And don't say she's beyond doing that, because I know it's exactly what she'd do if she were tired of sitting around waiting for the cops to catch him. After all, the only reason he's down here, if he still is, is to get her."

"That never crossed my mind. Do you really think she'd go it alone and make herself bait for this monster? Oh God, Homer, I hope you're wrong. Maybe we should confront her."

"No, let me sound out the chief on it, first, and we'll follow his lead on it. I don't want to spook her and get her to take immediate action instead of just thinking about it. If she is, that is."

116

"Mercy, what's our girl going to do next!"

He said nothing more. Just smiled at her. He really didn't want to know what Maggie was going to do next. It was just too frightening to allow that thought to surface.

TWENTY-NINE

"Hey Lenny, how are things?" He reached out to shake his friend's hand.

"Progressing, Homer. Progressing," was all the chief would admit. "What brings you down here?"

"I want to run something by you."

"Okay, come on into my office and talk. I've probably ten minutes before I go into a meeting with the mayor. Have a seat," he said, indicating the small sofa to the right of his desk. He sat, also, in the chair opposite Homer.

"Maggie's very quiet and tense, despite trying to act otherwise."

"That doesn't sound good, knowing how she gets. Do you think she's thinking of repeating last year's shenanigans? Is Carolyn saying anything to indicate they've discussed it?"

"No, I spoke to her after talking or trying to talk, rather, to Maggie about what had her in such a depressed mood that she couldn't even take my teasing. Of course, she's worried sick about his still being around, but she's always been able to talk it out with us before."

"So, Carolyn denies Maggie's brought up the subject of staking out the island again with her?"

"Absolutely and I believe her, because she's just as concerned as I am that it might be in her head again." He accepted the coffee his friend handed him as he sat back down with his own and took a big swallow of the hot liquid.

"Well, maybe I'll drop around, just pay a casual visit to see how she's holding up. Maybe I can get her to admit she's thinking of it, again."

Homer looked relieved. "I'd really appreciate that, pal. She's made it clear she doesn't want to discuss anything with Carolyn or me, but maybe she'll open up to you." Homer thought the chief, who'd always had almost a baby face with his part Hawaiian ancestry, had aged ten years since this monster Jacques first appeared on his radar. His hair that was coal black just a year ago was now tinged with a lot of gray and he just did not look good to him, as though the stress of it was really doing a number on him. He hated to see that happen, since he was one of the best chiefs the department had ever had. Another reason for them to catch and stop that guy.

The chief smiled, took a final gulp of coffee, and then stood as did Homer. "There's never a guarantee with our Maggie, but I'll come by after my meeting with Bert and have a little chat with her. Try not to worry. It's a great day with the ocean being so smooth. You ought to take the ladies and go fishing."

"Ha! Fat chance of getting Maggie or Carolyn either one on the boat when I'm fishing. They've made it clear they want nothing to do with killing innocent sea life," he said, with a hearty laugh, as he went out the door ahead of his friend. "Mag said once, if you came upon a bunch of tiny kittens, would you kill them? Of course, I said, no, I wouldn't dream of doing such a thing. She just put her hands on her hips and said, I rest my case. She still loves her yellow tail and mahi mahi, though." They both laughed as they parted ways at the front door.

Lenny Doan, still laughing, called to Homer, "Maybe you should tell her to read Jesus' parable about fishing and how important it was to him." Homer just laughed and threw up his hand to wave goodbye. Doan was still chuckling about Maggie when he showed up at City Hall a few minutes later. He enjoyed coming to this new building they'd renovated from Glynn Archer School on White Street just a few years ago. The inside of the building had changed drastically but the outside was still reminiscent of the old school building that had stood in Key West for many decades until they found the building that had served as the school for more years than he could remember was not safe and built the new one not far from it, which had more than one story and lacked the character of the former one that was now City Hall.

THIRTY

Maggie was the only one in the kitchen as Lenny Doan knocked on the kitchen door. Of course, she'd heard him coming up the stairs to the back porch and peeked out the window to make sure it was a friend. She smiled and opened it for him.

"Hi Maggie, I could smell that apple pie from the street."

"Maybe so, but it has another 30 minutes to go, so I'm afraid you'll have to settle for a Danish and coffee." She went to the coffee pot, but he stopped her.

"Thanks just the same, but I'm Joe'd out for the day, I'm afraid."

"Okay, then, how about a tall lemonade. I just made it fresh a few minutes ago," she said, as she went to the fridge.

"That sounds perfect and I think I'll take one of your bear claws, since you offered," he said, with a big smile. Stopping in at Maggie Metronia's was always a pleasant break from his work and the infernal heat of the summer. He'd been born and raised in Key West, though, and wouldn't trade it for anywhere else on earth. At least they nearly always had the good ocean and gulf breezes.

"There you go, then." She handed him the glass and a small bread and butter plate for the Danish. Then she sat opposite him. She, too, thought he'd aged in the past months.

Not one to mince words or beat around the bush, Doan said, "I need to ask you a question, if you don't mind."

121

She knew what it was and didn't want to answer, but she'd never say no to Lenny Doan. "Sure, I don't mind a bit. Ask away."

"We've all noticed how quiet you've been lately, and I need to know if you're thinking of making yourself bait for Hamilton Jacques."

Well there it was. Now how was she going to answer? Not knowing, she did the only thing open to her; she stalled. "I'm not exactly sure what you're asking." She sipped from her own glass of lemonade.

Of course, the chief knew what she was doing, but went right to it, anyway. "Are you planning to go alone, out in the open without Homer or Carolyn, in hopes of luring him out so the guys can grab him?"

"Would that be such a bad thing?" She looked directly at him over the rim of her coffee cup.

"Maggie, if that's what's on your mind, please, you can't do this again, especially alone. And I'm not suggesting Carolyn or Homer do it with you, just pointing out how terribly dangerous it would be for you. This guy is like no other killer I've ever encountered. He scares me to death, to tell you the truth. I have no idea what he'll do next, because he's so damned brazen." She started to say something else, but he interrupted her. "We haven't told anyone else, but he picked up another beautiful young woman here on vacation, convinced her to go to Tahiti with him and ended up pushing her off the highest cliff on the island."

She gasped and said, "Oh, that poor little thing." She was quiet for a while, as was the chief, but a few moments later, smiled her most innocent smile and leaned over to take his hand in both of hers. "Lenny Doan, I've watched you grow from that shy little boy I used to baby sit to become the police chief of this beautiful city at the end of the road and I'm very proud of you."

"Well, thank you, Ms. Maggie. That's a nice thing to say." Damned woman had a habit of trying to distract anyone who was trying to keep her from hurting herself.

"Well, I just want you to know that I promise not to cause you to worry about me. Besides you have two big burly men sitting up there in a window of the Southernmost Motel with a bird's eye view to my house and probably everything inside it if they have a telephoto lens or stronger on those binoculars or rifles, whichever they're looking through, so there's no reason for me to do that."

He didn't seem convinced – and he wasn't. He said, "And I don't have two guys sitting in that motel window."

"Oh, I see." That was disconcerting to hear. "I didn't think you'd take them off so soon."

"I didn't take them off, but like I said there aren't too men up there. Joey Davidson and Shirley Savage are up there looking out for you. You remember them from last year."

She breathed a big sigh, and said, "I sure do. That makes me feel better. Thanks for letting me know that. They're good people and I know they wouldn't let anything happen to me."

He stood and took her hands. "Yes, they are, so let them do their job and let the rest of us do ours. We're going to get him, Maggie. I promise you." Kissing her cheek, he left the kitchen and went back outside to his patrol car sitting in the back driveway. "Lord have mercy, woman, I think you really were thinking of going out on your own to try to lure him out."

THIRTY-ONE

"**B**as that Lenny I just saw driving away?"

"You know dang well it was," she told her friend, "since you probably called him yesterday."

"No, I didn't. I haven't talked with the chief since we were both there last week to get an update from him." At least she could tell the truth about that.

"Well, if you didn't, I know Homer did and he probably told you he was going to, didn't he." She looked her friend straight in the eye and Carolyn couldn't fib.

"Yes, he told me he was going to go see him, but Maggie, please don't be angry with him. We've all been worried about you. You've been so quiet and wouldn't tell us what was on your mind," she said, reaching across the table to take her hand.

"I know," the other woman said, with a big sigh. "I'm just so tired of waiting for him to make his move against me – and don't say he isn't still planning to off me, because even Lenny thinks he is."

Carolyn's eyes filled with tears, just as Homer walked in from mowing the lawn. "Hey, what's going on," he said when he saw her. She just shook her head and grabbed a tissue. "Mag?"

"Sit down, Homer."

"Let me run in and get a quick shower, first. I'm sticky and grimy right now and really need to get changed."

Carolyn poured another cup of coffee and sat silently with Maggie until he returned.

"Now, will you tell me what's happening," he said, fresh from his shower in a clean white tee shirt and dark brown shorts. He walked over and poured a cup of coffee before he sat down.

"Lenny was just here to see me," Maggie told him.

"Oh, anything new? Have they caught Jacques?"

"No, but they've proven he killed that poor girl in the hotel, so that means he's been here lately. And because they found that bleach and hair, along with the blood in the bathroom drain, they think he's a blonde now, as you know. But there's something else neither of you know, because he just told me."

"What's that?" Carolyn looked frightened.

"He picked up another poor young woman here, took her to Tahiti and pushed her off a high cliff to her death."

"Oh dear God, that poor girl," she said.

"Bastard. He sounds like he's getting worse by the day," Homer told her. "Well, I know they've alerted everyone who works the docks and lives in the houseboats. They'll get him, Mag. Just try not to worry and let them do their jobs."

"That's what Lenny said. But do you know how hard it is to just wait and do nothing? I feel like a sitting duck and he's holding the pellet gun."

"Well, with the two guys over in the Southernmost, you aren't a sitting duck. They'd take him down before he got to you."

"There aren't two guys in the motel," she said.

"What! When did he take them off? He never mentioned a word about that to me!" He started to call Lenny on his cell when she reached over and put her hand over the phone and his.

"There never were two guys over there." Then she smiled and said, "Your two Cuba cohorts are over there."

He smiled then and said, "Joey and Shirley are the lookouts?"

"Yep, that's what he said. And you know they wouldn't let anything happen to me, Homer."

"You have that right. Well, that's a huge relief to know those two are there."

"It sure is," Carolyn echoed. "They're both first rate cops and Joey, especially, is a real sharpshooter."

"That he is. Well, this makes me feel so good about it that I'm taking you two out for an early dinner."

"Where're we going?" Maggie asked.

"How about La Te Da? The garden's probably nice and breezy today, so what do you say?"

"Sounds great to me," Carolyn told him. "And Joey and Shirley can walk behind us and keep an eye out in the restaurant."

"I'll give them a call now. We can go as we are, okay?"

"Sure," they both said.

"Hey Joey, how's it going over there?"

"Haven't seen hide nor hair of the guy. Lenny thinks he's a blonde dude now, so we're paying extra close attention to any guys with blonde hair now."

"Yes, he told us the same. Hey, listen, we're going to walk up to La Te Da to have dinner in the garden. Wanna follow us?"

"You know it. We'll leave as soon as we see you all come out your front door. Don't look at us, though, and be sure to tell Mag and Carolyn not to, either, while we're on the street or in the restaurant. We'll grab dinner, too, while we're there, since we've about had it with takeout."

"You could come over here to eat now and then, you know. Oh right, I forgot for a minute there. We'll see you down there." He disconnected and said, "You ladies ready to walk down the street?"

"We are," Carolyn told him, as she picked up her purse.

"Uh, Joey reminded us not to look at them on the street or in La Te Da. It would blow their cover if he really is around."

"Don't worry about that. We're old hands at this, now. Come on, let's go," Maggie told him. He and Carolyn exchanged smiles and the three went out the door, without glancing toward the motel or looking behind them as they were walking down the street toward the bar and restaurant.

After a good meal and relaxing with their drinks, and starting the walk back, Maggie asked Carolyn if she could think of any groceries they needed. "I want to run to Publix tomorrow afternoon and pick up a few things for the weekend, in case anyone comes over."

"No, I can't think of anything off hand, can you, Homer?"

"Looks like you're running a little low on coffee. I can take a drive up to Baby's and get that and more pastries and cookies while you two are at Publix, if you want, and then just swing back there and wait for you to come out."

"I'm not going to get much, so neither of you have to go to Publix. I can take my little shopping cart and walk up there."

"Mag, I know it isn't far, but I don't think it's a good idea for you to walk there by yourself, do you?"

She looked at him disconcertedly. "Nothing's going to happen to me in Publix, for heaven's sake. He's not that stupid, Homer. And remember I won't exactly be alone. We can call right before I start walking and they can shadow me all the way there and back. Please, I need this. I feel like I'm in prison having to have one or both of you with me all the time. Let me at least do my grocery shopping alone?"

Carolyn looked at Homer and he at her, but neither said anything. Homer opened the front door after unlocking it.

Maggie's hands were on her hips, a sure sign she was exasperated, as she stood on the porch. "Well?"

"Okay, I suppose if you have your heart set on some alone time out, we can't do anything about it. What time are you thinking of leaving, so I can alert Joey?"

"I want to leave at 10 in the morning. It won't be too hot then. And on second thought, I'll just trike over there and use my baskets instead of my cart." She walked inside so he could close the door.

"Okay, I'll tell them to watch out for you at 10 so they can bike along after you, but don't worry, they'll give you plenty of space. Now, do either or both of you feel like some gin rummy before we call it a night? There's nothing worth looking at on TV tonight."

"Why don't the two of you play? I want to finish my grocery list and then I think I'll turn in early so I'll be fresh tomorrow morning."

"Okay, Mag, g'night. Carolyn, you up for a game?"

She smiled and said, "Sure, why not. I don't have a hot date or anything."

With a grin, he told her, "I could easily remedy that if you'd say the word."

"Start dealing the cards, Homer," she said, feigning disgust.

He laughed as he picked up the deck and started shuffling the cards before dealing them out to the two of them.

THIRTY-TWO

The next morning Maggie announced that she had a headache and was going back to bed after breakfast.

"Give me your list, then, and I can pick up the groceries after I get the coffee," Homer told her.

She said nothing, just handed him the grocery list. He and Carolyn exchanged glances as she left the table and went back to her room.

"What was all that about?"

"I don't know," she told him. "Maybe it's just what she said and she has a headache."

"Since when have you seen Maggie with a headache, much less going back to bed right after breakfast?"

"Well, I never have, but there's always a first time for everything. She's under a lot of stress and it can bring on physical symptoms. I'm going upstairs and work on my bills while she's lying down and you're at Baby's and Publix. See you later."

Maggie listened as Carolyn's steps faded up to the next floor and her own apartment. Even though she lived up there and had a kitchen, Maggie had always wanted the three of them to take their meals together like a family, so they'd done it for as long as Carolyn lived in the big house on United, especially since the incident with the murderer in West Palm. After a while she heard Homer go out the front door, down the steps and then heard the Hummer start up.

Quietly she slipped her shoes back on, closed her bedroom door and left the house by the back door. She tip-toed down the back steps, crossed the yard beyond the pool, went through the fichus roots to Whitehead. She walked up to Caroline where she went into the Bull and sat by the window sipping her club soda with a twist. If no one else wanted to find Hamilton Jacques, that was fine, but she was sick of staying home.

It felt good to be out and about, relaxing with a Perrier with no one shadowing her. There was no way Joey and Shirley could have seen her go since she slipped out the back door and through the roots of the big tree that hid everything with its massive roots and branches.

Like a prisoner the first day out of prison, even the air smelled better to her through the open window of the bar. She knew there was no difference but it seemed like it. Why didn't she do this months ago instead of obediently sitting in the house or having someone follow behind her every time she ventured out of it? She was seventy-one years old and didn't need anyone looking out for her. She wasn't scared of Jacques anymore. He wouldn't dare try to get to her in a crowded public place like this, even if he were back in Key West, which she doubted. She'd sat here long enough to eyeball every man who walked by the bar and every man who came into it and no one remotely resembled Hamilton Jacques with blond hair.

After she finished her drink, she tipped the waitress way more than she'd make in a month as she always did, and walked out the door. She continued on Caroline until she reached the Historic Seaport and then she went into the Rawbar. She had only had coffee earlier in her ruse about having a headache so painful she just wanted to go back to bed.

She ordered a huge breakfast and was really enjoying it. She hadn't felt this alive in months and she was going to milk it for all it was worth. Why not? This was her home and she'd always enjoyed it until that murder in West Palm, if you didn't count the three murders in Key West last year. Well, the days of being cooped up and shadowed were over. It was her life and she'd decide how to spend her days.

After leaving the Rawbar, she went out and sat on a bench watching the fishermen working on their boats and the entertainment boats taking people out. She thought that glass-bottomed boat ride looked like fun and decided to go out on it one day soon. Maggie couldn't dive because of a breathing problem so she never got to see what was under the surface of the ocean. She never saw the reefs that were supposed to be so beautiful and she heard the boat took people out that far so they could see them. Yes, she was going to buy herself a ticket and do that one day very soon.

"Beautiful day, isn't it, Maggie."

She sighed, looked up and saw Chief Lenny Doan standing there looking out to sea. "Well, hello, Chief. Yes, it is beautiful today and I'm really enjoying it, so why don't you leave me to it."

"I could do that." He continued looking at the activity in the Gulf.

"Then, go, please."

"I said I could do it, but that doesn't mean I'm going to."

She sighed and stood to go. "Well, if you're not leaving, I guess I will."

"That's fine, Mag. Enjoy the rest of your day."

"Just like that? You're letting me walk away?"

He laughed and said, "Well, why not? It's not like you're a prisoner."

"I've sure felt like one the past few months."

"Mag, sit back down and let's talk."

She looked at him long and hard before speaking again. "I don't want to talk. I just want to live the life I've always lived on this island."

He sat down and patted the seat. "Please, just hear me out."

Reluctantly she sat down on the bench, again, looking out to sea, where the catamaran was just leaving the dock with its load of laughing and happy tourists. Right now she envied them, something she'd never done before. With a sigh, she said, "Okay, I'll listen."

"Thanks. You and I go way back, as you said not long ago, to the days when I was a little boy and you were babysitting me."

"That's true. What's your point?"

"My point is that you're very dear to me, always have been since that time when I depended upon you to take care of me and I don't want to see anything happen to you. Neither does anyone else in this town."

"I've been away from the house now for over four hours and nothing's happened to me. No one paid me the least bit of attention, except to smile as I passed if they knew me. Or if they didn't. No one's out to get me. I don't believe for one minute that Hamilton Jacques is anywhere near this island."

"I wish I believed it," he said, "but the evidence points to his having been here very recently and I really doubt he dyed his hair just so he'd look different when he went back up north."

"You really think he did it so he could get around the island without being recognized?"

"I'm afraid I do. It's the only explanation. If he intended to stay away from here, he'd have just left as he was and gone far from here. There would have been no need to change his looks so drastically."

"Oh drat, I suppose you're right. But do you mind if I just walk back home by myself rather than getting into your car?"

"I'm on foot, Mag. I don't mind if you walk home. I was going to call Homer to come pick you up but if you'd rather walk, that's fine with me. On one condition."

"What's that, as if I didn't know?"

He smiled and said, "I'll stay back a block if that will make you feel better, but I am going to follow you home."

"Okay, as long as you stay back. You have no idea how nice it's been being able to walk around town, knowing no one was following me."

He took her hand a moment and said, "Yes, I think I know how it felt, but until he's caught, we can't let you do it. Please, try to understand that we don't want to do this, but we have to for your sake."

She patted him on his cheek and said, "I do understand. I'll see you later, Lenny. Enjoy the rest of your day."

She started walking from the seaport and true to his word, the chief stayed back almost a whole block, after calling Homer to let Carolyn and him know she was okay. He'd been quite upset with his two detectives over in the Southernmost Motel because they didn't see her leave, but they swore one of them had been at the window constantly all day and the only person who went out that door all morning was Homer, when he left to get the groceries after calling to tell them Maggie was lying down with a headache so he was doing the grocery shopping.

They all figured she'd slipped out the back and through the fichus roots, since they'd have seen her if she'd gone out her side gate to United. The chief agreed that must be what happened and they'd have to figure out how to prevent it in the future.

Everyone was out looking for her and they were all relieved when the chief called to say she'd been found. They hadn't put it out on the radio in case Jacques had a way to monitor police calls, but each of them used their cell phones to contact each other. Homer had called all of them to say the staff at the Bull had seen her several hours earlier. Carolyn called to say a friend waved hello to Maggie on William St not long after that. Joey and Shirley were told to stay put in case she came back before any of them got back. They knew the chief was upset with them at first and didn't argue with him.

Now that they saw her walking back up United to the house, they were all relieved and glad to know nothing had happened to her on her little private outing. Homer and Carolyn did not berate her for her early morning ruse, but just welcomed her home and asked if she'd had lunch. She said no, she'd eaten a late breakfast, but worked up an appetite on the long walk back, so she'd love some lunch. Carolyn already was in the process of fixing a big grilled chicken and strawberry salad and Homer got the iced tea everyone wanted. Life was back to normal, thankfully and nothing had happened to their Maggie!

THIRTY-THREE

Someone else had seen Maggie walking home, and with his binoculars he saw Chief Doan walking a block behind her. "One day I'll catch you unaware, Ms. Metronia, when there's no chief, bodyguards or friends anywhere near to see it. I'll grab you so fast, no one will even notice you've disappeared. And then I promise you I will see to it that you're fed to the biggest fish in the Gulf and then I can get back to my nice life in Wyoming!" He smiled to himself after he said those words aloud.

Granted, Hamilton Jacques was getting antsy and bored sitting around waiting for the opportunity to get rid of his only remaining problem. This was his illusion, since despite his name and face altered with a blonde crewcut, out there in law enforcement land, he had multiple remaining problems. Like any other criminal, he rang high on the stupidity gauge. All the men and women in law enforcement from the Keys to Maine were counting on this collective criminal stupidity, just waiting for him to show his hand when he least expected them to be on the alert.

He took a quick shower, dressed as casually as possible in shorts, tee shirt and sandals, and went out through the back of the motel and over to Truman, where he went inside Bare Assets. He noticed after he'd paid his fee and ventured back into the cool, comfortable and dark room that there was a new dancer on stage whom he didn't recall seeing the last time he was here, so he took his drink and walked up to sit in an empty seat in the front of the club nearest the stage. As she twirled around and caught his eye, he smiled in his best seductive manner.

After her act, she came down and walked to the bar, where she was given her usual drink and then she went over to him. "Hello there, handsome." She smiled a million dollar one to him and her fingers playfully reached to touch his bare lower arm.

"Hello yourself, gorgeous. I haven't seen you in here before. Are you new in town?" His eyes never left her face.

"Not exactly, but came in over the weekend and was lucky enough to be hired on the spot."

He leered at her, knowing she was probably among the other European women the traffickers brought into the country. "I'll just bet you were. What time is your shift over?" he asked, still keeping direct eye contact with her.

Smiling again, she told him, "I'm off in ten minutes. Meet me at the back door – not the side door. I have a little Smart car parked out back. It isn't very big of course, but I don't think that would matter, do you?"

"Not in the least," he said, as he downed the drink and watched her walk back toward her dressing room. He waited twelve minutes and then after leaving several bills on the table, he left the room and the club. He walked around to the back of the building and, sure enough, there she was in the smallest road vehicle he'd ever seen. Without being told to, he opened the passenger door and without a word to him, she drove off.

He thought she'd go home to a place in Old Town, where she lived in a dorm with lots of other girls, but no, she went on toward the triangle and drove over Cow Key Channel and up the Lower Keys, until she came to a small dirt road north of Cudjoe Key. This is interesting, he was thinking, since he'd been almost certain she was one of the Russian girls who were flown onto the Island, expecting a new wonderful life in this beautiful place in the United States, only to find themselves sex slaves and working just to give all their pay to the master who sponsored them. He always allowed them to keep their tips. Otherwise, he ruled them day and night, showing up unexpectedly on their job to make sure they were towing the line for him and then he'd pick them up after their shift and it was his party from then on. Jacques had watched these young women very closely for about a week and figured this out, so he wondered why the cops hadn't. Or maybe they had and were just waiting to catch someone at the top. Who knew about cops, anyway? As always, he felt a step ahead of them at all times and so far he had been.

Jacques was glad this wasn't the case with this girl, since no way would she be allowed to have a car and she certainly would not be living off the island if she were someone's property. So far neither of them had uttered a word. She was continuing back the old dirt road, bouncing him around in his seat, but he didn't mind as long as the end result was that he got his hands on her. The hell with staying hands off. He was getting way too bored not to have someone to dally with.

"Well, here we are, home sweet home," she said with a sideways glance and smile for him. "Come on in and make yourself comfortable. I'll pour us a drink. Be careful, though, as there are rattlers out here." This surprised him, but he watched where he walked until they got inside the small house. I came home one night to find one sprawled out on my living room floor!"

"Good heavens, what did you do?"

"Shot it, of course," she said, laughing. His eyebrows shot up at that. He smiled but didn't comment.

He watched as she made a pitcher of martinis with the expertness of the best bartender there is, so he figured she probably danced on the side but bartending was her regular job. She looked over and smiled, saying, "Bartending is what I do for a living. I just needed a little extra money to take a trip down to Rio for a few days, so asked if they could use me at the club."

"Well, lucky for me you wanted to take that trip. When do you plan to leave, if you don't mind my asking?" He accepted the glass she proffered. "Thanks," he said, as their fingers touched.

"This is my last night to dance. I have enough to make that reservation now. I already told my boss at the little bar up the road I was taking a couple months leave. I plan to go on Wednesday."

His eyebrows shot up. "That soon, eh? Are you traveling with a boyfriend or is this a solo gig?"

She smiled again, "Yep, a solo gig. I don't have a boyfriend – not even a husband following me." She laughed lustily. "Why? You wanna join me?"

Did he ever! Not wanting to appear too eager, he asked, "How long did you plan to be gone?"

"At least thirty days. I'm going to leave the return date open. Who knows, I might see a club I'd rather work down there instead of up here and just stay there. I have no ties up here or anywhere in the states, with both parents and my only sibling gone. I own this little place outright, so it and my car would be waiting for my use whenever I decided to come back."

"Wow, a girl after my own heart. I'm a free spirit, too, and love leaving things open-ended like that. Were you serious about my going with you or was that just a tease?"

"Mister, you'll learn that I might be a lot of things, but a tease isn't one of them, even if that's how you met me. Sure, I meant it when I asked if you'd like to come along."

He put down his drink and patted his bare knee. "I sure would. But let me make that reservation for us. It'll be fun treating you to the trip."

Her eyes widened. This was even better than she'd hoped for. She wanted his company but never dreamed he'd pay for it. "Oh, I couldn't let you do that. After all, it was I who offered."

"Nonsense, of course you can. I haven't had a trip out of the country since I got back from Afghanistan." He fished his credit card out of the wallet, flashing bundles of cash in the process, as her mouth watered at the thought of how rich he must be. He smiled, knowing exactly what was in her head. "Now, write down your full name so I can make that call."

She wrote Sophia Mackowski on a slip of paper and gave it to him. He smiled and got out his cell to call the airline. "Yes, Stamril, S-t-a-m-r-i-l, Jerry. No, not Gerald. I was born Jerry, with a J. It's not a nickname." He looked over and smiled again at her. She'd been grinning constantly since he offered to pay for the trip. "Hold on a second."

He covered the mouthpiece and said, "Are you sure you can't go tomorrow? It's cheaper then than it's going to be on Wednesday. I have the money, just like bargains."

She smiled, shrugged and said, "Sure, why not, I'm already packed."

"Okay, we'll change that to tomorrow then. No, we'll probably be there a month but let's leave it open-ended for now until we decide. Neither of us has visited Rio and we might enjoy it more than we think we will and want to stay longer. Sure, that'll do. Yes, Sophia Mackowski." With an Mac, not Mc."

After he finished paying for the plane, he asked if she had any preferences as to hotels. She said no, so he called the number for one he enjoyed staying in and they were able to get accommodations readily for a month, possibly more, he told the reservation agent. He smiled to himself. They all used to be plain old clerks, then ticket agents or representative, and now nearly all of them had the title reservation agent. As long as they were efficient and competent, he didn't care what their title was. Finally, he was finished and stood.

"You aren't leaving?"

"If we're going to make the airport on time, I need to get packed and ready to head for Miami by eight, at the latest, so yes, I'm leaving." He held out his hand. She looked shocked that was all he wanted and shook his hand. Just as quickly, he reached out and snaked an arm around her neck and pulled her to him, kissing her roughly.

"Hey, take it easy, Jerry. I'm a woman, not al Qaeda."

He grinned. "Sorry, didn't mean to be rough. I've wanted to kiss you since I first laid eyes on you on that dance floor. Here's a milder sample," he said, and put his arms around her, planting a gentle kiss on her lips. "See you at 8, Sophia."

"Wait, you didn't drive here. You're not walking 30 miles in the dark, are you? Remember the rattlers."

He laughed and said, "No, I'm calling a cab as I walk. I'll be fine. See you in the morning. Night." He opened her door without a backward glance and started walking up the road, shining his keychain flashlight on the ground in case there was a slithering critter or two out there in the boondocks. If there were, they stayed hidden from his sight.

THIRTY-FOUR

"Good morning, Sophia. Are you all set?" He looked around the living room of the small bungalow and didn't see a bag of any kind.

"I – my bag is in on the bed, but I've decided I want to go another day – alone."

"What? Is this about the rough hug I gave you last night?" Right now he felt like breaking her neck, but kept his temper from surfacing.

"No, nothing you did. It's just that we just met and I don't know a thing about you and you know nothing about me, either, for that matter."

This definitely was not how he wanted to start his day. Not at all. "I'll give you my complete family history on the way up the Keys. Come on, it'll be fun being together. I haven't really had any fun to speak of since I left Afghanistan." He purposefully dropped his voice and looked down at the floor.

She bit her lower lip and felt conflicted. On the one hand she didn't think she trusted him, but on the other, he was a veteran just back from the war and he deserved a good time with someone. It might as well be her as someone else. She smiled and said, "Oh, all right, I suppose I'll be safe with you. I'll get my bag and purse."

He smiled as she walked into her small bedroom that he wished he had time to get acquainted with, but they were on a deadline and one never knew what would happen on that two lane highway out of the Keys, so he wanted to give them plenty of time.

"All set," she said with a smile, as she brought a single medium sized travel bag out of the bedroom.

"A girl after my own heart," he told her, motioning toward her bag. "Never knew one who could get a month's worth of clothing into a single bag like that."

She laughed that lusty laugh again and said, "Well, if you travelled as much as I enjoy doing, you'd get it down to a science, too."

"Hey, I was a soldier. I'm used to stuffing it all into one bag, just never knew a woman who could do it," he said, matching her laughter. Then he hooked one arm around her, looked into her eyes and their lips met. "Thanks for taking a lonely soldier up on his offer, darlin'. We're going to have the best time imaginable."

Huskily, she said, "Yes, I think you're right."

He opened the door and let her go out first, as he carried her bag and watched her walk down the little stone walkway to the car, thinking how he couldn't wait to get her totally alone in a foreign hotel.

She looked back and smiled at him as he put the bag in with his, after she opened the doors. "Do you want to drive, Jerry? With this small car, I'm always a bit nervous on this highway with all those large SUVs and trucks passing me."

"Sure, I love to drive, and they don't intimidate me. They get too close, I'll just pull out my Glock and teach them not to hog the road." He looked over at her and her eyes were wide as could be. "I'm only kidding, darlin', relax, it's going to be a good trip. You'll see."

THIRTY-FIVE

"Well, Maggie," Homer said, "If you want to go shopping on the mainland today, that's what we'll do. Do you think Carolyn might want to tag along?"

"No, I already asked and she said no, she was a little under the weather and just wanted to stay in bed with a good book."

"Oh? Well, I hope it's nothing serious. Never knew her to be sick, before."

"She didn't exactly say she was sick, just that she wasn't herself today and wanted to take a good rest."

"Okay, I'm all set. I suppose you want to go further than Card Sound, right?"

"Of course, I want to go to antique row in West Palm."

"What? Why not antique row in Miami like we usually do?"

"I don't know. Just wanted a change of scene."

"But why West Palm? You haven't wanted to go there since – you know."

"Oh, I forgot about that for a minute. You're right. I don't want to go to West Palm. I know, let's get a hotel on the beach in Vero and drive on up to Augustine. Maybe if we do that, Carolyn'd want to go."

"Sounds good to me. Let's do it. Why don't you go up and talk with her again while I pack us a little picnic lunch we can eat at a rest stop on the interstate."

"Good idea. I'll go see if I can persuade her. We can stay a few days."

After she left the room, Homer dialed the Southernmost Motel. "Yeah, Shirley, we're going to take a road trip to Vero and then the next day go to St. Augustine for a few days. Yeah, she's asking Carolyn now. Can you guys be ready to follow behind us? Good, you check with the lieutenant and I'll call when we're ready to head out."

"Well, "Carolyn said behind him, "it looks like I'm going with the two of you. I guess I could use a trip off the rock the same as you."

"Great! Are you packed already?"

"Sure, only taking a few casual outfits, nothing fancy, since we'll be at the beach most of the time."

"Good. I have our lunch here. Packed extra for the guys. I told Shirley I'd call them when we were ready to head out."

"Is that really necessary, Homer?" They hadn't heard Maggie come back into the kitchen. "I mean, we're not going to be near here or West Palm, so I don't see the point in their following us."

"Boss's orders, Mag." He picked up his cell and alerted Shirley and Joey, who were already in their unmarked car after calling the chief to say they were following the trio. He gave the green light and told them to keep their closest eye on Maggie.

THIRTY-SIX

The drive to Miami was a quiet one for the man who called himself Jerry Stamril and his new companion Sophia MacKowski. They'd passed the time telling each other their personal histories and family tidbits, his totally concocted on the spot, of course, and with all his fictitious family deceased so there'd be no way for her to check to see whether his story was true.

"Well, here we are, the wonderful Miami International Airport, bane of most people's existence," he said, with a big smile for her. "Let me park this in long-term parking. Won't take long", he said, expertly driving the jeep up the curved road to the right area and parking it quickly. He'd decided it might be safer to take it than her little smart car, after all he never knew when he might come back alone from any trip, so might as well have his own vehicle. One never knew when one might have an accident in a foreign country. A lot of women did these days. No big sigh over Lana this time. It was just something he'd had to do and that was the end of it.

He grabbed their bags and they walked across the crosswalk and into the airport. After they were cleared by TSA, they went to the nearest bar and sat there relaxing until their flight was called not a half hour later. "Certainly glad we decided to leave at 8. I didn't think it would take off on time," he said.

"It's nice, though. The sooner we're in the air, the sooner we'll be lying on a white beach in Rio," she said with a big smile that caused a physical reaction in him immediately. This made her laugh.

"Don't laugh yet, woman," he told her. "I might get separate rooms and you'll never know the joy of really knowing me." He grinned.

She smiled back to him. "No, you won't," she said with confidence, causing him to laugh. He didn't say anything but just smiled at her, thinking she's as eager as he was.

Their flight was uneventful and before they realized it was over, they were touching down in Rio de Janeiro. "Oh my gosh," she said, with all the excitement of a child, "It's so gorgeous here."

"Yes, I have to agree," he said, as the cab took them across town to their hotel, which looked more like a private tropical estate. "Well, this is as nice as I remember."

"It's beautiful, Jerry. Thank you for doing this. You have no idea how grateful I am. I'd scrimped and saved and had the money to do it, but I would have used it all, probably, before the month was up."

He put his arm around her as they followed the bellboy to the elevator. "I'm glad to do it for you and this way you'll have a good amount in the bank when you get back and maybe you won't have to moonlight, at all. In fact, after this trip, it might make me a little jealous to see you up there in practically nothing, dancing for everyone else in the place."

She looked up at him in surprise. "Why would it make you jealous? It's not like we're engaged to be married or anything serious like that."

He leaned down and kissed her lightly on the lips, just as the bellboy reached the elevator. "You never know how this trip might change our lives, Sophia."

She was silent on the way up to the twenty-fifth floor and didn't have anything more to say until after they were left alone in their room. "What a gorgeous view!" she said as she looked out at the *Rodrigo de Freitas Lagoon*, that the locals called the *logoa*. She went out on the terrace and looked at the mountains and sea before her. She never really thought she'd make enough to get here but it was great being here, especially after not having to pay out any of the extra money she'd earned.

After they settled in the hotel, with his still not trying to make any moves on her, which surprised her, Jerry took her to see the *Stairway in Lapa,* or the *Escardaria Selaron. Lapa* was one of Rio's small neighborhoods, and the stairway with its beautiful mosaics and colorful tiles were created by an artist from Chili, Jorge Selaron. Afterward, they had a romantic dinner in a quirky little restaurant at Santa Teresa and ended the night seeing a wonderful samba show, before returning to their hotel off the *logoa.*

She stood on the terrace again, alone, as he went down to the lobby "for a little something I forgot," he told her. She was beginning to wonder whether he was interested in her at all, since he hadn't really touched her since they'd arrived in Rio, despite being alone in the hotel for a while before they went to dinner and he seemed to keep disappearing on her.

She was still standing there looking out across the lagoon when he suddenly came up behind her and put his arms around her. "I never even heard you come back in," she said. "In fact, I was beginning to wonder if something about me was turning you off."

"Well, you couldn't be more wrong," he said, as his arms tightened around her. "In fact, I just went to the gift shop and got something for you."

She turned around in his arms and smiled. "Oh you did, did you? Well, this I have to see."

He laughed and said, "Well, some of it you'll have to wait until bedtime to see, but I guarantee you'll love it."

She grinned and said, "When you put it that way, I'm sure I will."

"Close your eyes, Sophia. Let me give you one of your other gifts."

"Okay, I'll play along." She closed her eyes and after kissing her luscious full lips, he took her left hand and put a beautiful emerald ring on the ring finger. She gasped and opened her eyes. "What did you do!"

"I just thought you deserved a sort of promise ring from me. A promise that you'll have the time of your life here in Rio."

She held her hand out and admired the twinkling green stone. "Is this real? Surely not."

"Of course it's real. I don't believe in fake anything. Don't you like it? I can always take it back," he said with a serious look on his face.

"Not on your life," she told him and took his face in her hands. She kissed his lips and he kissed her back, fully and so long she almost lost her breath. "Even if it's just a promise to have a good time while we're here, I still love it."

"I'm glad you do, because it set me back a pretty penny." He held her out and looked serious again. "It was worth every dime to see it on your finger. Who knows? Maybe one day it will mean more than a good time, which will start right now," he said, taking a large sip from his drink.

He steered her back into the room and dimmed the lights. Then he said, "Now, I'm taking what's mine."

Somehow this remark didn't sit well with Sophia, but she tried to let it go and just enjoy herself with him. After all, he paid a fortune to bring her to the place of her dreams and, looking down at her hand, he gave her this gorgeous ring that really did look very expensive. She looked up and smiled at him.

All of a sudden, for no reason, he slapped her face. "Jesus, why did you do that! Are you crazy?' She backed away from him, which he loved. Her eyes were wide and she had that frightened look he craved in his women.

"Shut up, and let me get you out of that dress," he said, to her amazement. How could he change in a flash like that? He knew she was thinking that and loved every moment of her confusion. With one movement he took hold of the dress at the low neck and ripped it in two. It was a lovely little black number and she looked gorgeous in it all night, but it was time to get rid of it.

"My God, Jerry. You didn't have to do that. I would have just stepped out of it. It was a perfectly good dress and I've always loved it."

He slapped her again and said, "Didn't I tell you to shut your mouth? What's it going to take to get you to be quiet, slut?"

"Wh – what did you call me?"

"I called you slut, because you are one. You get up there and prance around before all those men in nothing but a G-string and then you think you're good enough to be treated like a lady."

Still she kept talking, despite her face stinging on both sides. "Look, I don't know what your problem is, but here" she took off the ring and handed it to him, "just take your ring and I'll leave. I have no desire to stay here any longer with someone who beats me up. I've never had anyone treat me like this before, I don't appreciate it and I'm leaving."

She walked away and grabbed a blouse and jeans from her open luggage, and started into the bathroom. Before she got to the door, he grabbed her and threw her onto the bed, causing her to drop the clothing. "Please, Jerry, you're scaring me and I really want to go home."

He whipped out the scarves he always carried with him when he was going to be alone with a beautiful woman like Sophia. "Oh God, please, don't do this. Just let me go and you can find someone else here in the city to spend the month with. There are gorgeous women all around us, everywhere you look. They even are nude on the beach, I'm told."

"And I'll have my fill of them, after I'm through with you, so shut your damned mouth like I told you and hold still."

"No, I won't shut up and I won't hold still. I'm leaving." With that, she reached out with one heel and got him in the leg, but missed his crotch she'd been aiming for.

"Oh, you'll pay for that one, lady. You'll really pay for that one." He finished tying her arms to the bed posts behind her and started on her legs, just as the loose one kicked him in the arm, but he was too fast and it barely grazed him. "You certainly enjoy fighting to the bitter end, don't you." Then, he stood back and laughed like a man who was having a breakdown.

Sophia had to do a lot of things to make her way in life, but she wasn't the loose woman she made men think she was. She was actually quite an innocent. Oh sure, she was no longer a virgin, but she'd always been too afraid of men to get with many of them since she left home. Now it seemed she had good reason to be afraid. More afraid than she'd ever been in her life. How could she have been so happy earlier and believed he must be shy or something because he hadn't made a real pass at her. Now she knew why. And it wasn't anything good. The man was a misogynistic insane criminal who treated women like dirt under his feet. Oh

God, she just hoped she'd live through whatever he was going to do to her. If her pounding heart didn't give out before he did anything at all.

He left her alone again after he went into the bathroom. He didn't say a word, just opened the door after finishing his drink and walked out. As soon as he was gone, she started trying to work on the scarves, but found he'd tied her arms too high and too far apart for her to get to even one scarf. She had to get out of here. She couldn't just lie here like this waiting for God knows what when he came back. Maybe he wouldn't come back. Maybe he'd taken her up on going to get another woman to spend the month with. But then, she looked across the room and saw his bag on the luggage stool and her heart fell.

The room was really cold, as he'd turned down the thermostat as soon as they'd come in from dinner and the show. She wished she could reach a blanket, because she was freezing and that was making her arms and legs hurt even more than they did when he was tying them so tightly. She had nothing at all on after he finished ripping at her clothing, and she thought if he didn't come back and let her loose, maybe she'd freeze to death. He might be gone the whole month and she wouldn't last in this freezing temperature.

While she was contemplating what might happen to her, the door suddenly opened and he walked in, but he wasn't alone. Four other men, very big men, were with him. One of them said, "You weren't joking, were you, senor."

They were all leering at Sophia and she wished she had frozen to death before this nightmare came through the door. "I never joke, my friend. Here, boys, fix yourselves drinks while I tend to our hostess."

As he came near her, Sophia felt herself trying to scoot over to the side of the bed, but her arms and legs were tied so tightly she couldn't move more than an inch away from him. He started touching her and when she turned her head away from him, he slapped her again, causing her to scream and the four men turned to look at each other. One of them said, "Hey, I didn't come up here to beat up on a woman or watch you beat up on her. I'm outta here." Before he could stop him, he was out the door. The other three men looked at each other, contemplating whether to leave, also, since it looked like this guy could be real trouble.

"Okay," he said, as he stood up, "anyone else want to leave?" As he said that, he suddenly whipped out a knife.

"Hey, senor, we don't want any trouble," one of them told him. "Maybe we should all go and leave you and your girlfriend to patch things up."

"Well, look at you three yellow-bellies backing away like you're afraid you're going to get hurt," he said, as he lunged at one of them, clipping him on his arm.

"Hey man, put down the knife," his friend said. "There's no reason to get violent. We thought we were coming up here for a little fun, not to be assaulted and watch you beat up on your woman. We didn't do anything to warrant this," he said, pointing at his friend's bloody right arm.

"Yeah, man," the third man said. "My friends are right. We all just came up to have some fun, you know, like you promised us we'd do. We didn't sign up for no violence. So, please, just put away the knife and we'll all do like you promised – with the woman."

This only made him angrier and he lashed out with the knife again and took a slice of that one's hand.

"Holy – come on guys, let's get out of here before someone gets killed." One of them opened the door and all three ran out and down the stairs before he could come after them.

Hurriedly, he sliced the scarves holding Sophia's arms and legs and said, "Get your clothes on. We're getting out of here. Too frightened to say anything, she hurried and got dressed. He closed their bags and said, "Come on, let's go."

They hurried down the outside steps just as they heard sirens, but he managed to get a cab to stop for them before the cops got to the hotel. "Where to, Pal?" If he was shocked to see Sophia looking so unkempt with the handprints on both cheeks and tears in her eyes, he said nothing. She tried to hold back, but he grabbed both arms and pulled her in with him.

"Just drive," he demanded. "I'll pay you whatever it ends up being. Just drive until I say to stop."

Sophia kept trying to catch the man's eye in the mirror, but he was smart enough to avoid looking at her. The guy with her looked insane and he wasn't taking any chances. He figured if he kept quiet and just drove as he said, he'd get out of this okay. He did feel sorry for her, but hey, he'd seen his share of beaten up women dragged into his cab over the past thirty years, hadn't he? Sure, so how was this different? He wasn't Christ the Redeemer, after all. He couldn't save them all, so he'd never tried. He just kept his mouth to himself and drove his cab. That was his job, his only job. He wouldn't mess with anyone just to save a woman, much as he'd like to save this one. She was gorgeous, despite how messed up she was from the guy's beating, and she looked scared out of her wits when the guy opened the door and shoved her inside the cab. He sighed and kept driving.

Sophia had no idea where they were when he finally told the driver to stop. He handed him $400 and said, "That will pay for your trouble, right?"

The cab driver knew what he meant. "Si, senor, it will pay for it. Gracias," as Jacque grabbed her with one hand and their bags with another, as the driver opened the door for them.

"What? There's nothing here." Just as she said that, she heard the gravel under the cab's tires as he skidded away down the mountain breaking all speed limits as he hurried away from what he knew was coming for that poor lady. But he lived to see another day with his wife and children and that was the most important thing to him.

"Exactly. That's why it's far enough. Look, Sophia, I'm sorry I got rough on you. I don't know what came over me. And you probably didn't deserve any of it." He stared into her frightened eyes. "But this party's over." Before she could utter a word, he grabbed her and slit her throat from side to side, almost decapitating her. Even before he knew whether she was dead, he picked her up and threw her over the wall and down the mountain. He didn't even look down as he had when he pushed Lana over. He had feelings for Lana and like Holly, Sophia was no Lana. Wiping the knife down, he threw it over, also, and started walking to the next town, where he would spend the remainder of his time in Brazil.

151

THIRTY-SEVEN

Maggie was riding her trike along the ocean with Joey and Shirley riding their bikes a block in back of her. Suddenly she stopped, sat there looking out and then waved for them to catch up with her. When they did, she said, "Let's get some lunch at Salute's. I'm hungry all of a sudden."

"Sounds good to me," Joey said with a big grin. "You hungry, Shirl?"

Smiling at the two of them, Maggie said, "Sure she is, aren't you, Shirley?"

"Yeah, I could eat something, thanks." They rode their bikes back the way they'd come until they got to the restaurant. "You want me to call Homer and Carolyn? Won't take a minute for them to walk down here."

"Nah, let it be just the three of us this time," Maggie said, leaving the two cops wondering what she had up her sleeve now. They picked up their orders and went over to sit at two tables facing the water, so it wouldn't look like they were together and they could freely talk, since the ocean's roar would keep anyone from hearing them. "Now, isn't this nice. We've never had lunch together, just us."

Joey looked amused and said, "No, Mag, we haven't and I for one think it's just fine. Thanks for suggesting it. It's on me, by the way," he said, to the amusement of his partner.

"Since when?" she quipped. "We didn't let you pay in Vero or Augustine, and you're not paying now, so just forget it."

"Oh come on, you know I'm a generous guy," he said, chomping down on a large piece of shrimp, and didn't mention it again when he saw the look in her eye. "Man, that ocean looks pretty today, just like a gigantic blue and green lake."

"Yes, it does, doesn't it," Shirley said. Maggie said nothing. Just ate her lunch and stared out to the sea.

"Hey, Maggie, what're you thinking?"

She blinked and looked over at him. "Not thinking a blooming thing."

Shirley laughed and said, "Oh come on, now. We know you didn't just offer to have lunch with us for no reason. 'Fess up, woman."

Maggie laughed, too, but said, "No, no reason. Just got hungry and wanted to stop for a bite. Figured it wouldn't be too polite for me to just stop and eat while the two of you were down the block. Don't you agree?"

The other woman looked at her shrewdly. "Yes, I agree, but I still think you have something going on besides wanting lunch with us."

"Yeah, I agree with my partner, Mag. Come on, you know you can trust us by now. What's in that pretty head of yours."

"Now I know you're putting me on. Remember I'm not a spring chicken, anymore." She opened her mouth in a big ear to ear smile. "And remember my beautiful toothless smile."

"But you look good for your age," his partner said. "And you darn well know it. How many other seventy-one year old women do you see running around with a gorgeous head of hair down their back?"

"Don't forget the lack, of teeth, Shirley," she reminded again. She laughed and they laughed with her. "Not too many running around without them, either."

"Come on, tell us," Joey said, seriously this time. "We'll keep it to ourselves, I promise."

"Oh, all right, I'll talk, but you'd better not mention this to Homer or Carolyn." She hesitated. "And, for heaven's sake, don't tell the chief."

"Scout's honor," they both said and she giggled.

"Okay, I've just been thinking that the longer I stay all guarded and everything, the more futile this whole thing seems. It appears to me that the department is wasting its money having you two valuable detectives sitting over there in the Southernmost Motel all day and night watching me and watching my house."

"How do you figure that?"

She looked at him and then said, "Well, if he was back on the island, don't you think he isn't going to make a move as long as he knows I have bodyguards?"

"Well, you have a point but what else could we do? I mean, you surely aren't thinking you'd be better off if we left and let him get to you, do you?"

"No, but really, think about it. Let's just say, for instance, he is holed up in the Southernmost House. He isn't going to show himself as long as he can see that every time I leave the house there are two cops following behind me."

Shirley said, "That's one way of looking at it, Mag, but we can't be sure of that. He still might try to get to you if he thinks he's closer to you than we are. And of course, we'd nail him, no matter how far back we are. We aren't exactly amateur shots, you know."

She smiled and said, "No, I've seen you in action and you're pretty handy with firearms. I feel safe enough with you near."

Joey threw up his hands, "Then, what's wrong with that?" She grinned at him. "I'm serious, Maggie, what's wrong with that. Don't you want to live through this mess if he is still around? You know the horrible things he's done. Hell, you saw one of them in West Palm."

"Sure, I don't have a death wish. I just think we need to come up with another strategy."

"I have no idea what we could do differently," Shirley told her, as she took a big swallow of her Corona. On undercover assignments they were permitted to do normal things that people do who live on an island and taking a drink in the afternoon was one of those things.

"I don't either, but I figure if we put our heads together without others around us, maybe we could figure it out."

Joey said, "Maggie, that's all well and good, but you're forgetting one important thing here."

"I am? What's that?"

"You're forgetting that we're on assignment and when we're working, whether it's undercover like this or otherwise, we're still supposed to do what the chief tells us to do. We're not independent agents like private detectives."

"I don't see the problem, Joey." She turned around and picked up another shrimp and popped it into her mouth before taking a drink of her own Corona after squeezing and stuffing another fresh key lime down its neck. She loved to visit Cozumel with Homer and Carolyn, and loved that the waiters brought their ice cold Coronas to the table in buckets surrounded by ice and then stuffed the limes in them before handing them to the patrons and leaving the rest of the beer in the bucket beside them on the table. She didn't realize she was smiling and looking like she was far away from Key West.

"Earth to Maggie," Joey said with a laugh.

"Uh, what?"

"Where'd you go just then? It's like you totally blanked out and left us in the dust," he said with a big smile. "Were you thinking of a secret beau?"

"Secret beau?" his partner said, with a laugh. "Which century are you in, partner?"

"Maggie's," he told her. He took a big swig of his beer. "Well, you gonna share with us or not?"

"I was just thinking of Carlos and Charlie's."

"In Aruba?" Shirley was getting a kick out of seeing this side to her.

"No, in Cozumel. Just was thinking how they served the Coronas in those buckets of ice and how cold they'd get. Ever been there?"

"No, I've been to Aruba, but after that trouble they had with that Dutch guy down there, I've never been back."

"You'd love Cozumel." Her eyes brightened. "That's it!"

"What's it?" Joey looked totally confused all of a sudden.

"Why don't we all go to Cozumel? We could take a cruise ship over or fly, either one."

He laughed and said, "As appealing as that sounds, I don't think the chief will pay for us to take a vacation with you to another country."

"He did when you and Homer went to Cuba, remember."

"That was different. He thought the bad guy was there and he was right."

"But see, if we went to Mexico, if he is here this bad guy would follow and it would finally be over. Don't you see?"

Shirley laughed this time and said, "Maggie, I don't think he'd know where we were going, even if we did get on a plane or a ship. It's not like we'd put an ad in the Citizen to announce that we're all heading over to Cozumel."

Joey snorted and blew Corona out his nose, making her look at him in mock disgust. He just laughed and said nothing, as he listened to Maggie and her talk about this proposed trip to Mexico.

"Yes, of course! We could just casually announce in the Citizen that Homer, Carolyn and I are flying to Cozumel for a few weeks. People do that all the time on Facebook. We could do it in the society pages of the Citizen."

He laughed again and said, "What society pages?"

"Oh come on, I read about the comings and goings of people here all the time in the Citizen. If you don't want to talk with the chief about it, I'll do it."

Shirley looked at her aghast. "You're really considering this, aren't you?"

"Sure, why would I bring it up if I weren't?" She reached for another shrimp and washed it down with her fresh Corona.

Shirley looked at Joey and shrugged her shoulders. "She might just have something there, pal."

"Don't tell me you're gonna take this preposterous idea to the chief."

Taking another long drink of her own beer, Shirley said, "Hey, why not? The worst that can happen is he says no, and we continue as we are."

"If I went to Cozumel, you wouldn't have anyone to guard unless you went with me."

"I think it's a terrible idea," he said. "What if he did get wind of it and followed you. If we didn't have permission to go with you, he'd get you for certain and take Homer and Carolyn with you. Do you want that on your conscience?"

She laughed and said, "If I were dead, I wouldn't think about it."

"Maggie, I think Joey's right. Please, don't persuade them to do this with you."

"But I'm tired of just sitting around doing nothing while he just sits and waits – if he is here, and we still don't even know if he is, do we? After all, he did take that trip to Tahiti."

The two officers sat quietly sipping their beers and looking out to sea. Maggie sat looking at it, also, knowing she'd planted a good seed. She just had to let them think about it and talk about it when they were alone and one of them would take the idea to the chief. She just knew they would end up doing it, because even the chief didn't want her to get hurt.

"Well, I guess I might as well head back to the house."

She pulled out some bills and Joey said, "Put your money away, Mag. I told you this was my treat for your wanting us to join you – even if you did have an ulterior motive."

She smiled, thanked him and said goodbye as she climbed back on her trike and pedaled over to the house, a few feet from where they were, as they watched her. She'd get her trip to Mexico. She just had to bide her time and she knew they'd come around. After all, she was not a prisoner. She could go any durned place she wanted to go in this world and they'd either have to let her go without protection or the chief would give in and let them tag along. She couldn't help but smile.

As she neared the house, Homer and Carolyn, who'd been sitting on the front porch wondering what she was up to at Salute's, smiled as she pushed the trike up the ramp to join them. "Well, what have you been up to with our friends," Carolyn asked.

"Yeah, what's been going on over there? We started to join you, but we'd just finished lunch and figured you'd never had them join you for lunch before, so you must have had a good reason."

She looked at both of them and then said, "You might as well start packing your bags."

They looked at her, astonished. "And where are we planning to go?"

"Well, if I'm right, we'll be going to Mexico?"

"Mexico? What on earth did you tell those two to make you think they'd be going to Mexico with us?"

With a sheepish grin, she took the proffered lemonade Carolyn had just put ice into and said, "Thanks, Carolyn. I just let them know I was a free agent and could take a trip if I wanted to, with or without the protection of the KWPD."

"And what did they have to say to that little gem?" Homer didn't like where this was going one bit.

"Nothing, but they'll mull it over and talk with the chief about it. Like I said, you might as well start packing, because we're out of here before the month's up." With that, she finished her drink and rose from the rocker. "I'm going in for a nap. I'll see you later."

"Have a nice nap," Homer told her, and Carolyn said, "Yes, rest well and we'll talk later."

After she closed the door and they heard her walking into her bedroom, she turned to him and asked, "Is she really serious?"

"As a heart attack, my dear. As a heart attack." He gave her a peck on the cheek, grinning after his Clark Gable imitation, and said he was going to drive to Sugarloaf to check on his house and he'd be back in time for dinner. She said she'd see him then and watched him drive off.

Carolyn sat on the swing for a long time, contemplating what their friend said she was going to do. Of course, they'd go with her. That murderer was still out there somewhere. That thought scared her to death. She knew if Maggie has her way, she'd make sure if he were anywhere near their island, he'd find out and follow them. What would they do then? Without having Joey and Shirley looking out for them, he'd probably not hesitate to kill all three of them. Oh Maggie, what are you getting us into?

THIRTY-EIGHT

"**A**re you nuts? And has Maggie gone clear through the turnstile to insanity? My God, man, you know I can't approve such a request."

"Hold on, chief. I gave her my word I'd think about it and after I thought about it, I think she has something there and..."

"Bullshit! Why doesn't she go to Ohio or Montana? Why does she have to go to Mexico where there will be no protection at all from this madman?"

"I have no idea what put it into her head, chief, but if you recall, it was because of her 'sleuthing' that we came to the conclusion Homer was right and the man in black went to Cuba."

"Yeah, what of it? What's he got to do with anything that's happening now?" He reached into his top drawer, pulled out a long Cuban cigar with that power of suggestion out there and lit it.

"When did you start smoking cigars? And I thought this was a smoke-free building," Joey said, trying not to laugh at the way the chief was trying to keep the cigar lit and failing big time. Finally, a giggle came out.

"What are you laughing at, Davidson? I don't see anything funny about this whole situation."

"I was trying not to laugh, but your lighting that cigar is just too funny. For one thing, you need to do this." He grabbed the cigar from his boss' hand and taking a pair of scissors from his desk jar, he cut off the end just a little. "There, that might make it easier to light and stay lit. Not holding it directly under the ac vent might help, too," he said, laughing again.

Finally, Lenny Doan laughed, too. "You know I've had that damned thing in my drawer for probably as long as I've been chief and that's going on twelve years now. Got it from one of the old cigar makers who's still alive. He said, 'Young man, if you're going to smoke 'em, you have to learn to light 'em,' but I forgot how." He laughed again. "That was the last time I had the thing out of the drawer."

Joey snickered as he threw it back into the drawer. "Well, I'd better get back to relieve Shirley, but think about what Maggie wants to do. It just might work, you know. If she's interviewed for the Citizen or even by Jenna on the internet TV, she could play it up about being sick and tired of having bodyguards since she came back from West Palm. Just lay it all out there, since no one in town knew she'd been under our protection. If he reads the paper or listens to Jenna on the internet – and I'm sure if she said something like my guest tomorrow is Maggie Metronia, etc, he'd listen – and if he heard her say she was going to Cozumel without us, well, he just might be tempted to end it all over there away from us meddlesome cops."

"And in this scenario, Shirley and you will still go over there but will sneak in another way than the one she's going on, whether it's by air or by ship."

Joey brightened. "Are you sayin' what I think you're saying? Are you going to let us go? To cover her?"

"I don't know what I'm thinking, but if I do decide to let you go it will have to be on a leave of absence. I can't just order the two of you to leave the country again, especially that far away, to do undercover work there."

Joey dropped his head and stared at his shoes. "Yeah, I guess you're right. Well, they'll just have to take their chances that Homer will see him before he sees them and is as good a shot as he claims he used to be in the Marines. Never knew a Marine who wasn't a crack shot."

"Dammit, I'll think about it, Davidson. Now get back to work."

"Yes, sir," he said, concealing the grin that was threatening to spread before he could turn around and leave. He had a feeling that Shirley and he would be on the next flight out to Cozumel, and would be holed up in a hotel by the time those three stepped from the plane to the tarmac or the ship to the dock, whichever way they ended up going. He couldn't wait to get back to her to tell her the good news – or what he thought would be good news.

What'll she come up with next? I'm sure if I balk at it, she'll just say she's going to South Africa or somewhere further away. Damn, that woman can be so infuriating. Doan's mind was filled with those thoughts of Maggie, when his lieutenant walked through the door.

"Hey Chief, what's got you so stirred up? Haven't seen you pacing the floor like this since before Homer and the guys went to Cuba.

"Try Cozumel, Butler."

"Cozumel? What're you talkin' about? You've decided to take that vacation and go to Mexico?"

"No, Maggie's decided to go and lose Shirl and Joey, and that's what's got me stirred and shaken!" Sweat covered his forehead and his face was beat red.

Lieutenant Butler laughed and threw his arm around his boss's shoulder. "Come on, let's go get a bite of lunch and get you calmed down before you have an MI. The city can't afford to do a chief search right now and you want to see that monster caught, don't you?"

"Sure," he said, throwing up his hand, "let's get outta here."

THIRTY-NINE

As the chief and his lieutenant were having lunch, Maggie was sitting in one of the rockers on her front porch, contemplating her trip to Cozumel. No one was with her. They'd had sandwiches early on the porch while she was with the two cops at Salute. Homer had gone back to check on things on Sugarloaf and Carolyn was napping. This was about the only chance Maggie had of really thinking about anything. She still insisted her little family eat their meals together, well, except for today, but after that she liked to be alone with her own thoughts running around inside her brain.

She smiled as she thought about going back to Mexico. She'd been to a lot of places in that country, but Cozumel had always been her favorite since she was in her early fifties and she and Homer had taken their vacation there. He'd met a pretty senorita and begged off the ship, saying he'd pick her up when she came back into port, so she'd done another voyage so she could sail back with Homer from Cozumel.

Everything was great until she started bleeding during the night. She hadn't gone into menopause yet, but the doctor said she was close, since her periods had started becoming so sporadic and her bleeding amount was so unpredictable. When she did, she told him she just wanted him to do a hysterectomy and get it over with. She knew she'd never marry and have children so she didn't need it. The hysterectomy was scheduled for the following week after her return to Key West.

They'd met the nice ophthalmologist at the clinic hospital the month before when Maggie had her vision checked on their last trip and she liked her a lot. She knew she was married to the only gynecologist on the island, but she never thought she'd meet him, also.

She did meet him and was the first patient to have surgery in the new upstairs surgical suite, after she bled so much on the cruise ship that the ship's doctor ordered her to be taken by the agent to see Dr. Sanchez, the gynecologist, the next morning. Her blood count was so low she almost had to have blood during the surgery, and knew the hospital didn't stock it because, as she'd been told by the clinic director, the only gunshot wounds they saw were self-inflicted and the patients were already deceased so didn't need anyone's blood. If Maggie needed blood, he'd have to recruit the other officers and crew to donate it for her. It turned out she'd barely avoided needing the transfusion and the surgery went well. She did so well that she didn't need it post-op, either.

She felt like a celebrity after being told by Dr. Sanchez that she was the first patient to be operated on in the new surgery suite. She couldn't wait to tell Homer when he came by taxi from the little B&B he'd stayed in all week to pick her up five days later when the ship came back to Cozumel. She was a bit let down when he said the other Dr. Sanchez had already told him, but seeing how her face fell over not being able to be the first to tell him of her celebrity status, he played it up and said they'd have to have champagne at dinner to celebrate how important her role was in that new section of the clinic hospital. They'd even taken her photo and he said they'd probably hang it right inside the hospital door so everyone would know she was the first. They'd always had to ship the surgical patients by ferry or helicopter to Cancun before they built the second floor addition and it was a big deal for Cozumel. Their surgeons now had a state of the art place in which to perform their operations. As it turned out, because of her status, the two of them were invited to dine at the captain's table and her being the hospital's first surgical patient was the talk of the table among the officers and their guests, and they, indeed, had that champagne.

Maggie was smiling as she thought of that night. She seldom was the center of attention and actually had never been comfortable in the role, but she certainly was that night. Of course, that was when she still had her perfect pearly white teeth and she knew her smile was beautiful. Plus, there were no wrinkles at all on her face while she was still in her fifties. There was a large photo of them taken at the captain's table in the foyer of her home right now. It was the most important night of her life, in her mind, so that photographic memory of it held a place of honor at the end of the foyer, right above the arched doorway to the outside, where everyone could see it as they walked into the big white house and she or Homer told the story again if they'd never been to the house before. She felt important every time it was told again.

At this age, there weren't many important events for her to talk about and that was a special one. As her thoughts were on that night in Cozumel, a man walked by on the sidewalk before her, a man who seemed all too familiar to her. He tipped an imaginary hat to her, and said, "Good evening, madam."

Her pulse accelerated as he grinned at her before he continued his walk up the street with his wheeled walker. She couldn't move and was afraid she was going to be taking her last breath within the next few moments, until after he walked on down Duval. Surely he wasn't whom she thought he was, was he? He certainly wasn't a blonde haired man or even a young man, so it must have been her imagination. Still, gingerly, she made herself get up from the rocking chair and quietly open the screen to go into the house. She closed the heavy ornate red door behind her, locking it securely by turning the dead bolt, something none of them did during the day. She suddenly felt as though if she didn't lie down right then she would pass out and they'd find her dead or dying right there in the foyer.

Maggie lay down and whether it was the shock she'd just had or whether she was too exhausted to keep her eyes open, she fell asleep as soon as her head touched the pillow and slept until Carolyn came to her door to tell her dinner was ready.

As soon as she awakened at the soft knocking on her bedroom door, Maggie's mind went back to what had driven her inside earlier. She never mentioned it to either Carolyn or Homer at dinner, as though if she never spoke it aloud, it hadn't happened.

"Have you thought anymore about going to Mexico, Mag," Homer asked as they were relaxing out on the back terrace of Carolyn's apartment, the only terrace from which they could view the ocean and the entire island, depending upon which side of it they were sitting. They could watch the sun set over the water from there, too. Tonight they sat on the south side, watching the few boats still out on the ocean and one cruise ship heading for the western Caribbean and Cancun. They knew from there it would go to Cozumel for a longer port of call, before heading back to Key West and Miami where the passengers' voyage would end.

She blinked and said, "Uh, no, I haven't been thinking of it. As a matter of fact, maybe it was a far-fetched idea."

Her friends looked at each other and Carolyn asked, "Are you all right this evening? You've seemed preoccupied ever since dinner."

She smiled, and patted her hand. "Sure, I'm fine. Just was thinking about how much fun the folks were having on that ship heading for Cancun and Cozumel. It's too far out for us to hear all the music and laughter, but you know they're having a grand time."

Homer said, "Well then, if it's on your mind, why don't I just go ahead and book us a cruise. I think it would do you a lot of good, Mag."

"We'll see. No hurry, so let's just forget about it and enjoy the sunset." Homer glanced at Carolyn again. She raised her eyebrows, but they said nothing more about it. The sky was becoming a brilliant red and he knew this was Maggie's favorite kind of sunset. Soon bright yellow splashed across the sky beneath and through the bright red that was turning into vivid purple. He heard her sigh and knew she was into what was happening before them and thoughts of going to Cozumel were out of her head for tonight.

FORTY

"Well, squad, it looks as though Hamilton Jacques has struck again. The chief just handed me this bulletin. Seems he (or someone who could have been his twin) and a young lady by the name of Sophia Mackowski, a bartender from Cudjoe who moonlighted a time or two at Bare Assets, flew over to Rio. The only photograph of the two of them was taken by a tourist photographer and as you can see, it does look like the original photo we have of him before he adapted into a college professor and killed the other two young women, except for the blonde crew cut."

As the photograph was being passed around the room, the officers were shaking their heads, not believing this guy who'd killed the man in West Palm Beach had struck three times since then and they still could not catch him on a two by four island.

"Here's the photo of young Ms. Mackowski after he killed her. Unlike with the first one, there was no necrophilia on the body and the cause of death is different – before he threw not pushed her off the cliff onto the jagged rocks below on the beach, he slashed her neck so badly she was nearly decapitated. It sounds like his anger is intensifying big time. They also said she was black and blue everywhere and there were bruises in the shape of handprints on both sides of her face and ligament burns on her wrists and ankles where he tortured her on a bed before he took off with her.

"In fact, four island men went to the police and told them he'd asked them to come back to the room for some fun with his girlfriend, and when they came up, she was naked on the bed and tied to the bedposts. They said they were looking forward to having a good time until he started slapping her around for no reason and talking crazy, to quote them. They called him on it, said they didn't sign on for any violence toward her and he slashed two of them on the arm and hand, but they ran out the door. Apparently, knowing they'd probably go straight to the police, he cut the scarves he'd tied her with – they were still on the bed posts – and had her dress and they took off in a cab. A cab driver told police he drove them way out by the cliffs and he made him let them out where there was nothing at all, paid him 400 American dollars and pretty much threatened him with his tone, so he didn't dare say it wasn't enough or say anything at all, except that yes, it was enough and then he took off. He said he was scared for the girl, but he knew the guy would have killed him, too, had he tried to interfere and he has a houseful of little children he had to think of. Can't blame him there. He most certainly would have been killed by this monster had he tried anything at all. They know he was her killer, because they got prints under her knees at the edge of her panties. That's why they concluded she was lifted and thrown rather than pushed off the cliff. Of course, she would have died instantly from his almost cutting her head off, so she wouldn't have known she was being thrown off the cliff as poor Lana did. Either way, he's escalating and we have to find this guy before he gets to Maggie. God only knows what he'd do to her with his anger this intensified. Also, in his rush to get away from there before the police came, he never had a chance to clean the room, so his prints were everywhere.

"Horrible way to die," Shirley Savage uttered under her breath, as she passed the photo to the next cop.

The lieutenant heard her and said, "I couldn't agree with you more, Shirl." After the last officer was finished looking at the crime scene photograph, he cleared his throat. "Okay, let's get out there now and search this island thoroughly for this monster and this time let's get him!"

There was much muttering among the officers as they filed out of the room. "Hey gang," he shouted, causing them to turn around and look at him. "Be careful out there. I don't put anything past this guy and we don't know whether he has a gun. He probably still is carrying around the knife he did poor little Holly and Sophia in with, but so far since he left West Palm, he's never used a firearm on the murders we're aware he's committed. Aware being the operative word with this guy. Who knows how many others there are.

"One more thing," Butler yelled to get them to stop again. "Just keep in mind that sweet cantankerous pain-in-the-rear Maggie Metronia is the reason he's still hanging around here and think how any of us – make that all of us – would feel if we found *her* murdered and mutilated by this monster!"

A shiver went through Savage as he said those words. She felt the weight of the world on her shoulders. She looked up at Davidson, who looked as burdened as she did. "We have to get him, Joey. We just have to. I don't know about you, but I couldn't live with that if it happened."

He half-smiled and said, "I know, and that thought is the worst I've ever had in my life." They told the lieutenant they'd see him later, as he headed for the chief's office, and left the station to hurry back to the motel.

When Butler opened the chief's door, Doan handed him another photo that had just been faxed to his office. "CCTV at MIA caught this a few days ago. This is the two of them walking into the bar. She looks so happy and beautiful. For the life of me, I don't know how he does it."

"Does what? Get them to go with him?" He put the photo back on the desk and helped himself to another cup of the chief's strong Cuban coffee while he was talking.

"Yes, I just don't understand it. This guy's worse than Bundy about that. Bundy could make both men and women think he was this charming highly intelligent guy who wouldn't hurt a living soul, until they were completely alone with him and then they saw the face of the *killer* Bundy."

"I was thinking about him during roll call when everyone was passing the crime scene photos around. You might very well be right about his being worse than Bundy, Chief. I hate to think it, but so far his crimes have been so brutal and yet he seems to somehow get this trust from young beautiful women, so much so that they'll go anywhere with the monster."

"Well, from what that cab driver told the cops in Rio after her body was found, she wasn't very trusting of him by then and she had bruises on her face and very puffy red eyes. They asked him why he didn't report it on his cab radio so the cab company could call the cops before her body was found and he just said, 'he scared me and threatened me in a subtle way and I knew he'd probably kill us both if I tried to do anything to help her.'"

"Yeah, didn't he have the cabbie let them out on a very secluded mountain road where there was nothing around?"

"That's what he told them, yes. Still think he could have called on the way down the mountain after he was safely away from him and told them to get the cops out there to try to help her."

"Well, he didn't and there's nothing anyone can do about it. God, we'd got to stop him, Blake!"

FORTY-ONE

Maggie seemed more relaxed these days since that night on the terrace watching the ship headed for Mexico and into the vivid sunset. Life seemed to be as it was before she left West Palm after having witnessed the murderer tossing body parts down the compactor and then come to the swing to confront her, as he stared out at the lake in front of her after getting rid of the evidence.

Homer and Carolyn were happy she'd begun to be the same relaxed and energetic Maggie who was always up for a fun trip somewhere up the Keys before this encounter with such a madman, and they took full advantage of it, driving or flying off to a destination on the mainland and to other parts of the country, seemingly on a whim, but each trip was planned by them, with the two detectives not far behind them. Not once did she suggest they leave the country again. And although this was a disappointment to Detective Joey Davidson, he knew better than to bring it up since she'd seemed to have forgotten about wanting to go there. On the chief's orders, he and his partner stayed mum about the latest murder by the man who followed her to Key West.

"Ladies," Homer said one afternoon after they'd come back from an excursion to Islamorada to their favorite waterside bar and restaurant, "I told the jury I'd like to play sunset this week. Wanna come down and keep me company?"

"What? Come on, you haven't even looked at those pipes since you became my chauffer. Why now?" Maggie had almost choked on her Sam Adams when he dropped that bombshell on them, because it had been a few years since she heard him play sunset.

He shrugged. "Actually, when I go back home to check on things, I do play them and I sort of miss the celebration. I know I'm getting up there, but as long as I can still walk in circles and blow some noise out of them, I want to play there every once in a while."

"Noise is right," Carolyn teased with a snort.

Maggie didn't laugh as Homer did. She was suspicious of the whole thing. "Are Joey and Shirley going, too?"

"I haven't mentioned it, yet, but of course, if you go, they go. I want to make sure you two are going to be there before I call to let them know."

She shrugged and said, "Well, since you're bound and determined you're going to play tonight, we might as well tag along."

"Sure," her friend echoed, "we wouldn't miss it. I was only kidding about the noise. I kinda like hearing you play and I've missed sitting on the edge of the dock listening to it. "

"Ha! You told me you never heard me play!" he teased.

"Oops," she said, laughing at being busted.

Maggie loved to hear the two of them spar. Although she had no family, as with so many other small groups on the island with no family ties there, the three of them were a family unit, as close as any family could be since they'd become unwittingly involved with the other murders almost two years ago now. She sighed, thinking it seemed like ten years ago since Carolyn and she had been scared out of their wits, afraid a mysterious man in black would sneak up on them and start mutilating them as he had those other three poor souls.

"Mag?"

"Maggie?"

She heard it as from a distance. "Wh – what it is?"

"You just looked so far away there for a few moments," Carolyn told her.

"Yeah, where'd you go, anyway?"

"Nowhere, just thinking about the past two years and happy to have my little family with me," she said with a big toothless smile. "Well, are we gonna get this show on the road or not?"

Homer laughed and picked up his cell to dial the detectives, who said they'd get on their bikes and head out. He relayed that information to the two ladies, picked up his pipes in their case and as soon as the ladies had their hats on, they went out to pedal to Mallory Square, behind Homer on his scooter. One of the detectives was between Homer and them and the other behind all of them. The breeze was blowing against them as they pedaled, slowing down their rides a bit and almost jerking the hat from Maggie's head, but it felt great to the two of them.

"Do you want to take this end of the pier? I don't need to sit there listening to the pipes all night," Joey said, with a laugh. "I can hear them fine at the other end whether I want to or not." Actually, he loved the pipes and had always tried to be near the dock when Homer used to play regularly.

She smiled and told him, sure, she'd cover the end closest to the ladies and she'd love to hear him play the bagpipes for a change. Without looking at the trio, he walked his bike to the far end of the pier, nearest to the Pier House. He missed the days when he could just go into the Chart Room and have a beer, while listening to the chatter about the old days in Key West when Ernest Hemingway and Tennessee Williams, among other celebrities like the great poet Robert Frost, called Key West home. This was before he went undercover and he'd take himself off from the rest of his co-workers on the squad a few evenings a week just because he didn't want to hear any more cop talk and could blend in at the small bar, taking in pleasanter talk among other locals having nothing to do with brawls or homicides, which were few and far between on the small island. Barroom and street brawls among the tourists and occasional muggings and robberies of locals were the top crimes before a person by the name of Hamilton Jacques came onto their radar. He sighed and sat on his bike, his eyes constantly scanning the crowd, as were Savage's, searching for a blond-headed monster who was like a chameleon in the way he could change his looks to the extent that no one could see him. He wondered if the guy was staying further up the Keys and just coming into town to pick up another prey. But that didn't make any sense since Maggie, his ultimate prey, lived on the island. He sighed deeply in frustration.

At the other end of the pier, Maggie and Carolyn sat close to the edge of the dock, but not so close that someone's bumping into them could send them into the water. Maggie had seen that happen to a couple of drunken tourists a few years ago, and the cops and fire rescue had a hard time finding one of them, but it turned out well, though she figured as drunk as they were, the fools would probably do the same thing again sometime.

Their eyes never strayed to the two cops sitting on their bikes watching them and the large crowd. They weren't aware that there were more uniforms walking around the square than usual, after the lieutenant got the call from Davidson that they were going to be there listening to Homer play during the evening, until the sun slipped beyond the horizon and the crowd started to disperse to the bars and hotels. Very few locals attended the Sunset Celebration, preferring to watch the evening's sunset from their front porches with friends and family, at the quiet White Street Pier or Zachary Taylor Park.

Listening to Homer play the pipes amongst all the chatter by the eager and excited tourists who clamored for the best spots to see the sunset, Maggie and Carolyn were able to forget the horror that was Hamilton Jacques for a little while. Carolyn glanced at her friend who looked lovely and relaxed in her floppy denim hat, her eyes out to sea on the large orange ball that could be viewed without her oversized sunglasses now that it was nearly to the horizon. In this relaxed state, even without teeth, she looked younger than her nearly 72 years.

The sky before them was beginning to meld into different shades of red and gold, as the large group became quieter, anticipating what was to come as night approached the small island. When she was pensive like this, Carolyn caught a glimpse of the beautiful woman with the lovely smile Homer had befriended right here at Mallory dock all those years ago. She wished Maggie would let Dr. Troxel put those implants into her mouth so she could have her smile back. She could tell she had plenty of good bone in her upper jaw, still, since her mouth when closed didn't cave in badly like most people without teeth. She sighed, knowing she'd never allow him to do it, believing as she did that they contained microchips through which the CIA could surveil people.

"It never gets old, does it," her friend said now, so quietly she barely heard her.

"No, Mag, it doesn't. Always a different scene every night."

A collective, "Ah!" sounded among the crowd as the last bit of the fiery orb dropped from their vision. "I saw it!" someone yelled, suddenly. "The green flash!" Maggie smiled because although many who'd never seen it said there was no such thing, she saw the instantaneous flash every time she saw the sun set over the water on a clear evening. Everyone clapped and cheered after seeing the last of the sun that evening, as they did every night over the beautiful waters of the Gulf of Mexico, if there was no rain or signs of a storm brewing further out to sea.

Helping Maggie stand as the last traces of red and gold left the palette of color before them, Carolyn smiled. They'd been able to relax for a few hours amongst a crowd without worrying that a man with murderous intent would sneak up on them and kill her friend, and maybe even Carolyn, as well, before anyone could stop him.

"How about grabbing a beer at the Bottlecap?"

"We haven't done that in a long time, Homer," Maggie said. Turning to Carolyn, who never knew them in the days when they did this nearly every evening, she told her, "This was how we spent our evenings before I won Powerball and Homer stopped playing the pipes."

"I know, he told me. It sounds like you had a lot of fun in those days," she said, smiling at her friends. Before you had to think about killers lurking around, trying to get to you, she was thinking. "We'll go home first, so Homer can get out of the kilt and then we'll do that, Mag."

Later, at the large bar on Catherine Street, the trio relaxed under the ever-watchful eyes of Davidson and Savage whom Homer had let in on their plans before they left Mallory pier, as she nonchalantly walked over to drop a dollar bill into his case.

"I'm beginning to think he's nowhere near here, Mag," he said, after taking another swallow and then plopping a peanut into his mouth.

"Why'd you have to go and spoil it? I'd almost forgotten about him."

"Almost being the operative word," Carolyn said. "Let's face it, until he's caught, he'll always be right there in the shadow of our minds."

"Yeah, I guess so." Maggie sighed deeply and finished the last of her Corona, glancing over toward Shirley Savage being flirted with by a pool-shooting patron trying to get her to play against him, not knowing she was actually a cop on duty instead of the tourist from Cincinnati she pretended to be. Her eyes scanned the other side of the room and saw Joey Davidson leaning against the wall, talking motorcycles with another man she didn't know. She sighed again, wishing the two young detectives didn't have to be there making sure she wasn't going to be murdered by a monster, that they were just there doing what they were doing for a fun night away from work.

FORTY-TWO

*L*ittle did they know, a man, who looked to be in his early sixties, with light brown wavy hair sprinkled with gray, mustache, short trimmed beard and wire-framed glasses had watched every move they made at Mallory Square. Once again, Luke Carnett from Boston, as it said on his new driver's license, eluded the vigilant eyes of all the Key West police officers and detectives. He'd sat alone on a bench smack dab in the middle of the square surrounded by them the entire night, his walker by his side.

At the end of the evening, long after the trio and their two shadows left the dock, leaving a sparse group of tourists and cops standing around talking, with a few Cuban locals dancing to the gay Latin music from the little outside bar, the stooped man feigned difficulty standing with the help of his wheeled walker, and one of those nice friendly policemen, who had no clue he was helping the vicious killer they were all searching for, helped him up and took his time getting back to yet another small B&B off South Street not far from all of them, but where he still could see the house from his room on the top floor. He could not keep from smiling at the revelers and cops he passed on his way, feeling smug that once again he'd outwitted the losers and even been helped by one of them. More every day he was thankful for those acting lessons he got before he played community theater back in the day. Man, how he loved this quirky two by four rock at times like this, instead of hating it as he once had! Too bad he'd have to move on permanently after he'd tied up that last loose end. He'd always loved his big spread in Wyoming, though, so he'd soon forget Key West once he was back there.

He'd heard the female cop telling the male that they were headed for The Bottlecap, but he figured he'd had enough entertainment for one night. Maybe this old weary invalid man should just call it a night and get some early shut-eye for a change, maybe even read one of the books he picked up at Island Books the other day until he fell asleep. Yeah, that sounded just right for tonight. No Don's bar, no Bare Assets, just that comfy bed and a good book.

After he brushed his teeth and got into his pajamas, he went through the books and decided on a good mystery by Dashiell Hammill, called Woman in the Dark, about this frightened young foreign woman everyone seemed to be chasing, making him think of that slut Sophia Mackowski, who might be alive today had she just shut up when he asked her to the first time. Women never learned, did they.

FORTY-THREE

Another month went by without a thing happening. No more murders and no sightings of Hamilton Jacques, anywhere. The city police, the sheriff's office and the highway patrol, as well as the coast guard, ATF, and fish and wild life officers – anyone with a badge - looked everywhere for a now blonde-haired man who looked like the photo of him. Everyone came up empty. They had no idea Maggie had seen the man right at the edge of her picket fence and had fought the idea that it was him, so she'd never said a word to anyone. Had she mentioned it, they'd have known he'd changed his appearance again – into an old man with gray hair, leaning on a walker.

One afternoon Maggie and Carolyn decided to go to the Tropic to see a foreign film that had just that one day to go and it would be finished there. They bought popcorn and a glass of wine and walked into the semi-darkness of the largest theater in the building.

The largest theater in the Tropic is not that large, but that was part of the beauty of the small local theater on Eaton Street. The first thing one sees when you walk or bike – few drive – up to the theater is the life-size iconic sculpture of Marilyn Monroe with her white dress blowing above the vent. And the second thing one sees upon entering the theater are the giant black and white photos of the beautiful women and handsome men who were in the '40s movies everyone loved. The real movie stars, Maggie always thought. About the only people in movies today who might qualify for that title were Meryl Streep and Robert Redford, in her opinion. And although she didn't much care for him, she thought Leo DiCaprio was a great actor, who truly became the person he was playing as did the man who played the president in Lincoln, but she could never remember his name.

The Tropic is the go-to place in Key West for most locals to meet for a drink and talk in the expansive lobby with its intimate table settings and comfortable leather seating lining the partition between the lobby and the concession area, where besides their popcorn and candy, movie-goers could order their favorite glass of wine or beer if they wished and could take it into the movie with them.

Maggie was no stranger to the Tropic. One evening while waiting in line for a particularly well-hyped movie most had not seen yet, the entire time she was standing in line, she was being passed from one patron to the other to receive a big hello and an equally big hug. People who didn't know her were laughing and asking if she were in the movie, to others' delight. She really loved the welcoming and old school intimacy of this little theater, where locals were as apt to attend a book signing by a local author as they were to come to watch a movie. She and Carolyn even watched live opera streaming from the Met here. There was no other theater like it anywhere and locals were proud to introduce their out of town friends and family to it.

"This is so nice for a change," Maggie said. Even though their two de-tective bodyguards were sitting in the back and one of the side seats fur-ther to the front, it still seemed as though they were being let out of jail. The manhunt had gone on for so long and they'd almost stopped going anywhere, as they got tired of having someone following them.

"Yes, it is, and we're going to relax and enjoy it, Maggie dear. There aren't many people here this time of day, are there?"

"No, there never are. Most folks like to come later, as you and Homer do, but I always liked the first showing of the day for this reason. Once a nice friend and I were the only ones in the whole theater. I don't think you've met him – John Gish?"

"No, I haven't. What's his story?" Carolyn was enjoying herself already and she hadn't seen Maggie this relaxed in a long time. She took a sip of the chilled wine and listened to her.

"He's a distant relative of Lillian Gish. Your mom would remember her from the silent movies." Carolyn nodded but didn't interrupt. "John came here from New Jersey. Taught English up there in Paramus High School in the sixties and was involved in the gay teachers' movement from the beginning, in the '70s, I think it was. He came here with his long- time partner, John Hanna, and their good friend, Connie Gilbert, who practically started the whole feminist movement so involved was she in it. From what he told me, the three of them lived in Big Coppit, just outside the city limits for years. They got the National Organization for Women started in Key West and they were active in so many different aspects of cutting edge political life on the island. Really interesting man. The two others who meant so much to him and a lot of us here are gone now, sadly. You'd like him. I don't see him very often now. Heck, I don't see anyone very often now, except Homer and you – and our friends, of course," she added with her voice lowered even more than it was. "Sorry, didn't mean to imply that you and Homer weren't important to me."

Carolyn smiled. "I knew that, but I realize how stifled you feel, too. Always having to have someone looking out for that monster so you won't get hurt. Damn." Maggie looked at her, startled for a moment since she'd never heard Carolyn cuss. Not once. She was the one who spewed out the cuss words when things didn't go right or she was frustrated with the situation they were in. With that thought, a string of them went through her mind.

A few more people were coming into the Tropic for the film, among them a man who looked to be in his early to mid-60s. Pushing a walker with difficulty, he went down in front of them to sit in the second row. Maggie sighed. She knew nearly everyone in town, but there were so many new folks moving to Key West now that she didn't know, the disabled man among them. She looked at him carefully this time and knew she'd been wrong about him. He wasn't the monster. Just a harmless elderly disabled gentleman who couldn't hurt a fly. Probably a veteran.

About that time the house lights went down and the screen lit up. Shirley Savage and Joey Davidson kept a sharp eye out, even in the dark, but never saw anyone who looked anything like Jacques. No one with blonde hair, at all, for that matter. Well, that was good. Maybe they could enjoy the movie, too.

Luke Carnett smiled to himself, as he watched the screen. He was sitting directly across the aisle from the red-headed detective who started to get up to help him with his walker, but he motioned her to sit and folded it up expertly, so she relaxed again, giving him a nice smile.

On his way down the aisle, he saw her partner sitting in the back row, also in an aisle seat as was the redhead, behind Ms. Maggie Metronia and Ms. Carolyn Cramer. Everyone was enjoying the movie, so he'd give them that. He was in no hurry to wrap things up. He was still enjoying himself on this two-bit island that was growing on him more every day, so he'd continue to take his time and one day he'd get Ms. Maggie alone without the eyes of the law on her.

At the end of the movie, after he unfolded his walker, he started to walk back up the aisle when the red-head touched his arm. "Why don't you just walk out that side door? It's much easier than having to walk back up the aisle with a walker. It will take you straight to the lobby."

"Well, thank you, little lady," he said, in his older man's voice. "I appreciate that."

"Here, I'll get the door for you."

He smiled, tipped his head in gratitude and went through the lobby and out into the evening light, to choose a little side street restaurant, have a leisurely dinner and go home to watch some TV. He particularly loved "Law and Order: SVU" and "Criminal Minds", and always cheered for the rapists and murderers.

FORTY-FOUR

After he left, she walked back up the aisle to join Joey Davidson in the back. There'd been only around ten people at the early show, so it was easy to see that their target was not at the movies. They couldn't picture him having the patience to sit through a movie, anyway.

"Who was that, Shirl?"

"Who, the older gentleman?"

"Yeah, never saw him around here before."

"I didn't ask his name, tourist, I suppose. Just thought I'd help him a little. He seemed pretty disabled to be on his own with a walker. I'm surprised someone like him doesn't use a wheelchair, instead."

"I think some people use that as a last resort, so they can stay on their feet. I know I would if I had something wrong with one or both my legs. I'd fight like crazy to avoid being pinned to a chair," he said, holding the door for her, after Maggie and Carolyn went through it, smiling at them as they did everyone else they passed, but not paying any more attention to them than that.

They'd been back in the motel for a while, business as usual, with Shirley at the window. "Oh my God!"

"What is it? You see something over there?" Joey ran to the window.

"No, oh God, Joey." She was almost in tears. "I think I messed up. I need to call Butler."

"Wait a minute. Take it easy. Here, have a cold Corona and tell me what has you so upset you're gonna tell Butler you messed up." He handed her the cold beer and sat down beside her at the window.

She took a long drink of the beer. "That old man."

"What old man?"

"In the Tropic, remember, the one with the walker?"

"Oh, yeah, what about him?"

She took a long drink from her bottle and then said, "I think it was Jacques!"

"What? He didn't look anything like him. Why do you think that?"

"Remember what Maggie told the Palm Beach S.O. about his voice?"

"Don't rightly know as I do – oh yeah, she said he made a sound like 'ah' at the end of his sentences."

"That old man did, too. And I let him get away." Tears came to her eyes, suddenly, and she swished a hand over them.

"Guess maybe you're right. We need to get Butler to bring Sam here to sketch him just in case."

She got on the phone and called their lieutenant. "Hi Loo, I don't know how to tell you this, but I think I let our killer get away this afternoon. Yes, I think you'd better, and bring Sam with you."

"Oh my God, I can't believe I did that." He'd never seen her look so upset or so anxious about anything before and they'd worked together for several years now.

"Come on, Shirl, try to settle down. You don't want Butler and the chief to see you this rattled. They might take you off the case if they think you're cracking and can't handle things."

She took a deep breath and another drink from her Corona, but was still pacing around the room, as he kept watch at the window. "Maybe they should."

"Don't be silly. You're human and you might – and I emphasize might – have made a mistake." She said nothing more. He wondered what was taking Butler so long. He thought he'd come right over after she told him what happened.

Soon there was a rap on the door, causing Shirley Savage to start for a moment and then with a look from Joey, she took a deep breath, went to the door and let the lieutenant and sketch artist in after assuring herself it was them.

Their lieutenant crossed the threshold without greeting either of them. "Let's sit down at the table and you can start describing this guy to Sam. You ready?" Sam Tomlinson nodded that he was.

FORTY-FIVE

"Well, how was the movie, ladies?" Homer was in the kitchen, wiping down the counters after their dinner. "Both of you went in for your naps as soon as you got home and I never got a chance to ask you."

"It was a nice one," Carolyn told him. "Thanks for having dinner ready for us. That was sweet of you, Homer."

"Well, I didn't have much of anything else to do after I finished mowing the lawn so figured I'd just get it going so you could both relax tonight."

"Yes, thanks. You would have liked this one," Maggie told him.

"You know I hate foreign movies."

"This one was different. Yes, there were a few scenes with all captions, but most of it was in English and the storyline was great."

"Maybe I would have liked it, then. The last one I went to was all captions and I can't stand that through a whole movie."

"Well, since you're through cleaning up, how about a nice game of cards?"

"Can't ever turn down an offer like that," he said, smiling at Carolyn.

Maggie sighed. She still wished Carolyn would have fallen in love with Homer. They'd make such a nice couple if she'd just give him a chance. They could be married, maybe even have a couple kids she could be a grandma to. But she said two years ago she was through with that

185

part of her life and just wanted friends now, so no need to rehash it with her.

"What's that look for, Mag?"

"Nothing, just waiting for you to stop shuffling and deal the cards," she told him, taking a sip of her tea and biting off the corner of a Baby's cookie.

"Okay, hold your horses, I'm about finished. There, now, we can get this game going." He dealt their cards and Maggie smiled at Carolyn who winked at her. He took a lot of teasing off the two of them, but he loved it, especially now, since it got their minds off that killer for a while. Maggie hadn't had much fun in the past few months and to see her re-laxing was nice.

After she won four hands of gin rummy, they decided to call it a night and each of them went to their respective rooms. Homer didn't sleep on the couch, anymore, but had given in to Maggie's suggestion that he take the guestroom in the middle of the house between her room and the dining room. He slept with his Glock under his pillow and his door open so he'd hear any unusual sound in the house. He never did, al-though sometimes he wished he would and it'd be that monster so they could put an end to this waiting.

Maggie thought she'd go right to sleep, but she was too wound up and after tossing around the bed for twenty minutes or so, she got back up, turned on the light and put on her robe. Not wanting to disturb Homer's sleep, since he slept with the door open, she opted to sit in her chair by the window and read some more of Patterson's book. That didn't work, either, since every time a passage with the killer appeared, her mind would wander and she'd see that man with the wavy gray hair looking at her again as he did when he went by the house and greeted her as she sat on the porch. He certainly did not look a thing like the same man from Windsor Park, but there was just something in his eyes and expression that made her think he'd been taunting her when he spoke. She tried to remember whether he had that strange ah at the end of what he said, but his voice wouldn't come to her. Though she was warm in the air-conditioning with her long chenille robe, just thinking of him caused her to shiver and she had goosebumps on her arms and legs. He was so close, she could almost smell him. She sat in that chair the whole night, dozing occasionally, but mostly her mind would not stop thinking about that day and those taunting eyes.

FORTY-SIX

"Okay, Shirl, start from the beginning and then we'll have Sam sketch him." As much as Lt. Blake Butler didn't want to be upset, because of how long they'd been trying to catch Hamilton Jacques, he couldn't help himself when he realized he might have slipped through their fingers once again.

"Look, I know you're upset with me and I don't blame you, at all. If you want me off the case, I'll go tonight if you have someone to..." She'd never questioned her abilities, but she was now.

"Forget it and just tell us what happened. I have no intention of taking you off the case or replacing you here."

"Okay, thanks. As you know, we went to the Tropic to give them cover, Joey covering the back and I, the front. I saw this guy walking with some difficulty down the ramp to a front seat and at first, not wanting him to fall, I reached out to help him and he brushed it off, folded his chair and sat down."

"Okay, so how does that make you think he was our guy?"

"When the movie was over and the house lights came up, he got up, opened his chair and started back up the ramp. I put my hand on his arm and explained about the door to the lobby he could use without going back up that way, figuring he must be new to the theater or he'd know that."

Butler coughed with impatience and seethed with underlying anger. Dammit, she'd been so close, she'd actually touched the guy! No one else had had direct contact with him. Dammit!

Knowing her boss as she did, she sensed his anger again and wrapped it up for him. "That was the first time I heard him speak and he definitely tacked on an "ah" at the end of his sentences, as though he were short of breath or just had a habit of some kind that made him do this. Again, sir, I'm just so sorry I..."

He lifted his hand to silence her. "Enough. We just need to get this new sketch out there and hope he hasn't figured out you made him and change his appearance yet again."

While Tomlinson sat down with Savage to get the new description drawn, Butler and Davidson sat down at the motel table over a cup of coffee, with Davidson's eyes on the house at the same time. "She really feels awful, Loo. For that matter, so do I, since I saw the guy both times the house lights were up, too. Just never dreamed anyone could fake that much of a disability. He genuinely seemed disabled and we both wondered afterward why someone who has that much of a problem walking would not prefer to be in a wheelchair. Then I tried to rationalize it by saying I'd fight being in a chair, too, since it would mean I'd given up trying to stay on my feet."

"As good as this guy is at these disguises, I'd probably have missed it, too, pal. Look at all the guys who stood right along the street at both entrances to Sloppy Joe's and admitted when they saw the video of his college professor disguise that they'd seen the guy walk out with this beautiful young girl."

"Yeah, I heard them in roll call."

"God, there has to be a way to break through his disguise – if he changes it again – and get this sonofabitch off the streets. I hate how he's playing us. To walk into a public theater, where he knew he'd be seen before the lights went down, you know he's getting more brazen by the day. And it makes me think he knows somehow that Maggie and Carolyn, with or without Homer, are going out and exactly where they're going. It just seems too much of a coincidence that he'd decide to go to the movies the very day and time they'd go when they hadn't been for so long. Dammit, the more I think about it, the more I think he does know."

"I've been thinking that, myself, and I have no idea how he would know that. We've searched every hotel and B&B in the whole city and couldn't be keeping a closer watch on the women unless we moved into the house, which I know you don't want and I doubt they would, either."

"No, I want you to stay where you are. You're close enough to get to them if they call, since they each have you on speed-dial, and you can see if anyone sneaks up to the house from up here and get him before he gets inside."

"You don't suppose he could have planted a bug while we were all away, do you? It's almost always the five of us when they go anywhere. Rarely does Homer stay home. He'd certainly have a chance to get in and plant a bug or several while we were out. We haven't swept the place in a while now."

The lieutenant looked at him and said, "It sure wouldn't hurt to do it, but you'd have to pretend to be a salesman or close relative – something along those lines, which wouldn't make it look like you're there on police business."

"I think that's a good idea. Want me to swing by later to see what we can come up with?"

"Yeah – no, let's just let crime scene come up with a kit of some kind and you could go knocking on the door in your own disguise and stand there showing Maggie all sorts of gadgets and then do a swipe across your forehead and wipe it with the bottom of your shirt or a big white handkerchief, in case the guy's holed up somewhere like a private home or down on the beach with binoculars looking at the house. Then, Maggie can invite you in to cool off and you can do the sweep. Better go alone so Shirl can keep the whole property under surveillance while you're in there."

"Okay, I'll wait till they bring me a kit. Better make the items large enough that if he is watching he can see they're legitimate household products."

"You bet. Hey Sam, you almost through here?"

"Another five or ten, Lieutenant," he said, without looking up from what he was sketching.

"Okay, I'm going back to headquarters. I'll send crime scene or someone by later today. Just relax till then and keep your eyes peeled as you've been doing."

"You got it, Loo. See you later."

FORTY-SEVEN

Because she'd been up close and personal with him, Hamilton Jacques believed there was a chance the red-head was smarter than she seemed and might have "made" him, as cops like to say. He sighed, hating to have to change his appearance again, but knowing it was necessary. He couldn't afford to make a mistake now.

Back in his room at the B&B, he carefully washed out all the tinges of gray rinse from his hair and beard. It took quite a while, and was sorry because he'd enjoyed playing an old helpless man no-one would believe was a killer. He shaved the beard, too, but kept a very small mustache. He'd think about what to do about the hair style on the drive out of town.

He picked up the folded walker, put it back into its original box, which he could easily carry under his arm, and changed into a dark blue sweater and black jeans. He slid his feet into black sandals, combed his hair in a youthful style and left the room with his box under his arm. Not wanting to invite questions about the box, since a photo of a walker was on the side, he slipped out the service door in back, and then walked the few feet to his rental car, where he threw the walker way in the back of the trunk.

Jacques once again drove up the Keys and this time he didn't stop until he got to Sunrise Blvd in Ft. Lauderdale. He hadn't bothered with dinner when he got home from the Tropic, so he drove in back of a grocery store and threw the box into the nearest dumpster he saw. Maybe a guy who needs it will find it. That would be nice. He always enjoyed being benevolent. He grinned to himself. Yeah, when he wasn't doing gorgeous babes and then showing them who's boss. Showing them how contemptuous he found them, out in public bars, drinking and dancing with strangers, maybe even doing other things with them. God, he hated women. Except Lana. She was one in a million. Sadly he thought maybe he shouldn't have done her like that. Maybe he should have cut his losses and kept her around. He was crazy about her and maybe they would have fallen so far in love she'd cure him of what he did to other broads.

He smiled to himself. That's a crock. I live to do other broads and then do them again and again until they have no more to give, not even a breath. That made him itch to find another one soon. He had to find another soon. Maybe tonight was the perfect night. Lauderdale wasn't all that big. He shouldn't have to go far to find someone.

He drove around the strip for a while, watching the babes with short shorts and halters roller blading on the boardwalk. There were a lot of guys, too, but way more gorgeous young women. After a while he tired of just watching and drove west of town to a little mom and pop restaurant.

After he was shown to a booth he'd requested, the waitress came over to ask if he'd like coffee. "No, sugar, I think I'll just have a Bud."

She smiled a toothpaste ad smile and said, "You be looking over the menu while I get your Bud. I'll be right back."

"Don't be long," he said, with a flirtatious wink.

"Oh, I won't. You can count on that." He thought she was giving her behind more of a shake as she walked away from him. He noticed the old man behind the counter was frowning at her. Either he's her dad or he wants a piece of that and she's not buying. When she got to the bar, he walked over and said something to her and she put both hands up in a defensive mode, glanced back toward where he was sitting, and the old man walked away.

"So, tell me, sugar, is he your dad or just someone who wants to be your sugar daddy?"

She laughed loudly and then said, "No, he's my dad and my mom is the cook. You can see her through the long pass through there behind the counter."

"Well, if he's your dad, he's certainly looking like a jealous old coot, if you don't mind my saying so."

"As a matter of fact, I do mind. After all, he *is* my dad. He's just cautious and wants me to be, too." She sighed deeply and said, "Now, what would you like for dinner."

"You," he told her, with a wink. "But since your dad is looking out for you, I guess I'll just have the T-bone special."

She forced a smile, and said, "It won't be long, since you're the only one in here who isn't already eating."

FORTY-EIGHT

Lenny Doan and his second-in-command Blake Butler were combing through video taken at every hotel and B& B again, but kept coming up empty. Then, all of a sudden, Doan said, "Wait a minute. Go back to that last frame. There," he said, pointing to a man walking into one of the B&Bs.

"I think you have something, Lenny." Without saying another word to each other, they got up and hurried from the chief's office. "My car's in front of the door."

They drove up Roosevelt further into Old Town until they reached that block of South Street. The chief walked in ahead of his lieutenant and pressed down on the small bell on the counter. The clerk came out of the back with a smile pasted on his puffy face with the ruddiness of rosacea on his cheeks and a piece of lettuce between his front teeth.

"Is this man still registered – Slim," he added, looking at the name tag. The man had to weigh two-seventy-five, so where on earth did he get a moniker like that? Of course, knowing several men named Tiny who were anything but, he guessed it probably came from his bullying middle-school classmates and it just stuck.

Slim looked through the book, since he'd just been on duty for a couple hours and had spent most of that time in the back room eating his dinner, two hours after he ate a big lunch. Sensing he might have some of his salad between his teeth, he ran his tongue around the inside of his mouth and felt the lettuce sticking out between the two of them. Turning around as though searching for something, as unobtrusively as possible, he took out his handkerchief and grabbed it, putting the handkerchief back in his pocket. Where it would stay until he got home, taking his used and chewed dinner with him.

The chief and lieutenant looked at each other and grinned until he turned around and said, "Ah, there it is." Unlike most Key West establishments, the little bread and breakfast did not use a computer to register their guests in and sign them out. After all, it only had six beds. If they couldn't keep track of things by hand with that small a number, no one could. "Ah, here he is. No, he – oh my, yes he did check out. Or at least, it says here the room keys were found lying on the desk about four hours ago."

"Dammit," Doan said, again, to no one. "This is the most frustrating thing I've ever seen on this island."

"Excuse me?"

"Not you, Slim. It's – it's just a case we're working on, but I'd appreciate if you'd call us if he comes back."

"What's he done, chief?" The clerk looked scared and excited at the same time, thinking a famous gangster or someone had been staying right under their roof. Wait'll he tells that to that jerk-off Roger when he gets here tonight! He never has anything exciting to report, like the day shift guy does and Roger does. Now, he'll get to one-up both of them!

"Nothing of consequence, son. But, I'll tell you what, if we find out exactly what he's done, you'll be the first person we call if you keep quiet about our being here." He handed him a fifty.

"Thanks, Chief Doan! I promise, my lips are sealed." His fingers were crossed in back of him.

"Okay, now I need you to do something else for me."

"Sure, anything you say."

"We don't have a search warrant but do you think, since no one's in that room now so we wouldn't be invading anyone's privacy, that you could give us the key and let us look around the room, before you rent it out?"

He smiled and handed him the key. "Scouts honor, I won't rent it out until after you finish sweeping the room or whatever it is you guys do to a room after the criminal has gone."

Butler looked at him with a stern eye. "No one said he was a criminal, Slim."

"I – I'm sorry, I just assumed he was or you wouldn't want to do this."

"No, we do this for many reasons. Maybe someone is in the hospital and we need to look for the next of kin's phone number and address. Or maybe someone looks like a missing person and we want to get him back to his loved ones, if it is him. See, son, there could be all sorts of reasons for cops to search a hotel room."

The young man puffed out his chest, "B&B, not hotel. There's a huge difference," he said, assuming a proprietary air.

The chief smiled when they got to the elevator. Some people are just way too nosy for their own good. And then there are the others whom you couldn't get a squeak out of if you stood over them all night and wouldn't let them sleep.

"Looks like he swept it clean," Butler said, as he looked under and in back of the last drawer he removed from the dresser.

"Yeah, it was our only chance. I'm sure he's long gone now. Probably figured out Shirl made him in the theater. Well, it would be our good luck if he stays gone, but that hasn't been his pattern, has it. Damn," his boss said as they headed for the door.

"No, I think this guy is so bound and determined to get to Maggie that he'll keep coming up with other disguises and hang around until he gets rid of her. You'd think, though, after all these other murders he's committed, since he landed on the island, he'd figure out we know his name by now, so whether or not he kills her is a moot point."

Doan laughed then. "You'd think, but I don't think this guy's as bright as he thinks he is. He probably thinks no one ever found even a partial or hair to link him to the other murders, otherwise, why continue to come up with a new disguise after each murder and still hang around here instead of head for somewhere far away?"

"On one hand, I hope you're right, but on the other, I wish he'd go so far from the Keys he'd never want to come back here again. I've never been so disgusted with a perp in all the years I've been a cop. And I don't think the body count is anywhere near done, Chief."

Doan said nothing. Just turned from the door and looked around one more time, for what he had no idea since they'd scoured the place and didn't find a hair, even in the drain. He opened the door and the two of them took the stairs down to the lobby.

"It's all yours, Slim," Butler said to him as he handed him the key card.

'Did you find anything incriminating?" He looked like an eager schoolboy hoping the girl who sat across from him would let him carry her books.

"Incriminating for what?" Butler glared at him again and Doan turned toward the door to keep the kid from seeing him smile.

"I – I just thought maybe you found something that would tell you he did whatever you think he did, that's all."

"What'd I tell you about the guy before we went upstairs?" He grabbed him by the collar and said, "Not another word and not a word to your co-workers, either, or I'll come back and you'll be sorry you ever broke your promise when you were given the fifty."

"Okay, okay, I won't say anymore and I won't tell anyone, either, just let me go." Butler turned him loose and he almost fell back into the hot coffee he'd just brewed in the other room. He'd brought the whole carafe in and set it on the counter in back of him, so he wouldn't have to walk the five steps every time to get a refill. It was against the rules, but Slim didn't pay much attention to rules, any more than he'd keep his promise to Butler, and the lieutenant figured as much.

FORTY-NINE

Hamilton Jacques decided against going out again after he found a small motel on a back street, far from the tourist area. He'd wanted that little waitress badly, but with her eagle-eyed father looking out for her, he knew that was not happening.

This time he bought light brown hair color, figuring it was high time he got this thing with Maggie Metronia settled. This would be the last time he changed his looks. First he dyed the small mustache and then the hair. He also bought light contacts, almost a tan instead of light brown with amber flecks in them. The hair was growing out and he had a small wave in it. When he got the contacts in, he took a look.

"Well done, Ham! Ma wouldn't even know you if she were alive! But then since you killed her, she isn't alive, is she." He laughed heinously. "Yeah, I think this is the best, yet. It makes me look a lot younger than I am, so I think it's time to resurrect young Jess Norton. Haven't used him for a dozen years and no one knew about him then. I think he'll be a software exec this time, instead of an insurance salesman. Yeah, that should impress the ladies, since there are so many software millionaires and billionaires running around these days."

He once again laughed heinously at himself in the mirror. No glasses this time, since the eyes are so light. No one would ever think it was Hamilton Jacques talking to them. He wasn't aware that he spoke any differently than the next guy, dropping that ah at the end of each sentence. He poured himself a tall one and turned on "Law and Order: SVU" to relax him. This was a smart move, holing up all the way up here and with this disguise slipping back into good old Key West was going to be a cinch. After he got another rental. He'd have to think about what kind of car a software exec would be driving. Maybe a little red Porsche. Nah, that wouldn't do. A white Corvette? Both way too flashy. And Jess Norton wouldn't drive something that tame to begin with. He had it! A dark blue Mazda convertible. Not too liberal. Not too conservative. Just right for young Jess. A car that would impress without attracting too much attention. He liked that. Zoom zoom! He laughed again. He enjoyed being in this good mood with no one to bother him unless he choose to let them, which was a different story altogether.

Before he went south again, though, he was going to practice his software skills for a while and then maybe he'd take that train trip to Seattle he'd always promised himself. And from there, go on one of those small cruise lines that had ships with a passenger maximum of 80 to 100 people. Intimate enough to get to know a few people, mainly young single ladies, and large enough to have some me time when he wanted it. He had to have that to get his batteries recharged. After all, he'd been going at a mighty rapid pace since he returned from Tahiti and Lana.

Damn, he had to stop thinking about her. He'd never doubted one of his kills before and now wasn't the time to start. She was really a sweet little thing, though. He could see himself with someone like her again, if he could find one that luscious. But first he needed to get rid of that rental and get the Mazda. He'd get some business cards made up and maybe a fake website just in case anyone checked. Wait, maybe he'd better do the business cards and website first and then the car. That'll be a cinch, with his technology skills.

He got out his equipment and began with the cards, first. When he was satisfied with the dark blue card, he started on the website. Make it simple. After all, he was just starting out with his own company and to begin with he only needed a couple pages. The first one described the business. He sure was glad he got that new phone before he got to the motel. He added the new number and email address by the same provider and that was that. The second page was the about us page. Since us consisted of just Jess Norton, that was easy enough. Both parents died in their boat when a faulty wire caused it to blow up in the middle of nowhere twenty years ago when Jess was ten. No one knew where they were heading, since they didn't bother to tell anyone. His father's partner who died of a heart attack the following year was the one who located the overturned and blown-apart boat. There was never a sign of either Mary or Todd Norton. Why would they go off like that without anyone knowing? They did this a lot, young Jess would tell folks if they asked. They were the perpetual honeymooners, always smooching and taking off on mysterious little spur-of-the-moment trips by themselves, leaving Jess in the hands of his old nanny Maybelle, who finally died fifteen years ago at the age of 92, and then he really was alone at the age of sixteen. He'd just had his birthday when she died after baking him a big chocolate birthday cake. He could just taste her cakes, so good they were like eating a light fluffy mousse. There were no other relatives, but he told the neighbors he was meeting his Uncle Jack in St Louis. So, he got in his dad's Chevy Caprice with his bags packed with only the things he wanted to keep, and headed for there. He told the neighbor he could list the house, since he was a broker, and he, Jess, would let him know where to send the check when it finally sold. He said if there was anything in the house that his wife and he wanted, they could have it and just trash the rest or sell it and keep the money they made as payment for cleaning out the place for him. The house sold within the year, after they'd cleaned it out and had done what painting and repairs needed to be done, since it was in a great neighborhood in Columbus, Ohio, and they had to make it comparable to the other empty houses around there. The neighbor sent Jess the check he made in profit on the house, after taking his percentage, which wasn't much because he felt sorry for the lad. This turned out being $65,500 and by then Jess was seventeen and had already started another software company. Now, at thirty-one, he'd started and sold three software companies and now he was a millionaire three times over.

Of course, he didn't put the whole story on his web page; just the basics that parents died in boating accident when he was ten, the worth of the company, etc. The rest of the story he'd tell to the Lana look-alike, if he found her. It would be enough to win her sympathy and then her admiration. Yeah, Jess was going to be fun. None of the other disguises let him have much fun, and certainly not poor disabled Luke Carnett, that's for sure. But Jess Norton; now that guy will party like it's going out of style when he wanted to and he hoped he'd have plenty of time to do it. He'd stay away from Key West for at least three or four months and when he returned he'd frequent just Cowboy Bill's as Jess would do. That should give them plenty of time to figure he isn't coming back, if they did make him. Maybe they didn't and he was going through this for nothing, but he had a strong feeling about it. Wouldn't hurt to have a change of scene, anyway.

FiFTY

"So that's the story, Maggie."

"You really think he believes Shirley's made him and you were closing in on him?"

The chief smiled at her terminology, as he always did. "Yes, we're almost certain of it. Why else clear out of his B&B if he thought he had no reason to run again?"

"Uh, Chief, can you tell us where this B&B was?"

He'd hoped she wouldn't ask that question, but he'd promised when this all started that he'd never lie to her and he hadn't, yet. Maybe now was the time to start. No, she was too smart and she'd know as soon as he got the lie out of his mouth. "It was on South Street."

She gasped, as did Carolyn in the chair nearest hers. "Where he could see my house?"

"Not sure it was close enough for that, Mag. But he isn't there now and you can relax and forget about him."

She knew he wasn't telling all the truth and that both he and Butler probably looked out a window of that room and saw her house. She didn't call him on it, but said, "Hah! You aren't saying you think he's gone for good? You know better than that. He'll never stay away until after he's killed me."

Homer quickly spoke up. "He's saying he really believes he won't come back, that it would be too risky for him – right, Chief?"

"Yes, that's right. We think he's wiped the sand of this island from his shoes and will probably head out west or somewhere else far away, so stop worrying and just live your life."

"But you're not pulling Shirley and Joey off, are you?"

Doan looked down at the police baseball cap he had in his hands. Oh boy, he was up against it, now. He heard her say 'Chief' again and then he looked up. "No, we're not pulling them off, just yet."

"Then don't sit there and tell me you think he's not coming back to Key West, then. You know durn good and well that if you believed for a moment he was gone for good, you'd pull them off and let me live my own life without having to be shadowed every step I took away from this house." She got up and went into the living room, turned on the news and let Carolyn show the chief out. She never said another word to him. What was there to say, anyway? He knew she knew he believed she was still a target for Hamilton Jacques and that was that. Life will never be normal again until she was dead or Jacques was behind bars or dead, himself.

"Carolyn, talk to her and try to get her to see that even though we think he's gone for good, we can't just drop her protection. The guy's been too unpredictable every step of the way and he's always been two steps ahead of us and the FBI every time."

"I know that and you know it, but Maggie's convinced he'll never stay gone from Key West as long as she's alive."

"I know." He put his cap on and patting her on the shoulder, said, "Well, I have a department to run, so guess I'd better get back to doing it. You all take care of each other and we'll be talking if there's any news."

"Thanks for stopping to let us know he's left town. We'll just wait to find out what's going to happen next."

"Hopefully nothing. See you later."

"Bye, Chief." She sighed and went back into the house.

"Well, what did he tell you that he didn't tell me?" Maggie pounced as soon as she went inside.

"He just said he'd let us know if anything else happened. There's nothing more to tell, dear, so just forget about it for tonight, okay?" She put her arm around her and walked back into the kitchen to pour another cup of tea from the pot Maggie made earlier, after she told her she wanted no more.

Homer was sitting there reading the sports page of the Citizen. He looked up but didn't say anything. She heard him sigh before he picked up his Sam Adams and took a drink of it.

"Want to talk about it?"

He smiled and said, "Nothing to talk about, is there? Unless Doan told you something he didn't tell Maggie and me."

"Why do both of you think he told me anything differently? He didn't. He just reassured me that he'd give us a call if anything happened, but he hoped Hamilton Jacques was out west or somewhere else far away from here by now and won't ever come back."

He put down the paper, rinsed out his cup and put it into the dishwasher, and then he kissed her on the cheek. "I'm going out for a while. I'll probably be late getting home, so tell Maggie not to worry when she doesn't hear the Hummer drive up before she's in bed." She looked puzzled.

"What?"

"It's just not like you to say you're going out without saying something like I'm going to run to check on the house or something like that. What're you going to do, Homer?"

"Do? I'm not going to do anything. I just want some fresh air for a while. I might go sit at the BottleCap or something. No need to sit around here wringing my hands with the rest of you, is there?" He stuck the paper in the recycling box in the mud room and went out the back door, got on his scooter and turned onto United from the side driveway.

"What on earth brought that on?"

Her voice startled Carolyn. "I didn't know you were listening to us."

"I wasn't listening, but when I started to walk into the kitchen, I couldn't help hearing the end of the conversation. He's never done that before. I wonder what he's up to."

"Maybe he told the truth. It beats sitting around here wondering whether Jacques is coming back to town, so he's going to get some air and talk to different people than the two of us for a while."

"I don't believe that for a minute. And neither do you. You've lived with us long enough to know his habits as well as mine. He doesn't do things like that when I'm upset about something. He hangs around to see if I'll need him. No, he's not going to the BottleCap. I have a feeling he's heading straight for the police station."

FiFTY-ONE

As he walked into Lenny Doan's office, Homer felt the weight of the world on his shoulders. He had to find out what Doan knows. He didn't think he was telling them the whole story.

"Hey, what can I do for you?" the chief asked when he heard footsteps in front of his desk.

"Were you just fooling with us with that cock and bull story about Jacques staying away for good this time? 'cause I gotta tell you, it smells to me."

"Sit down, and cool off, for heaven's sake. And no, I wasn't just fooling with you. We really do think he isn't coming back this time and we're sure hoping we're right."

"Then why not pull Shirl and Joey off babysitting duty?" His eyes never left the chief's.

"I explained that to Maggie."

"Well, she didn't believe you and I for damn sure don't believe you. You aren't one to waste department funds like that. I've heard you griping for years about funding for the budget never being enough and yet, you're paying two cops to take turns sitting in a window watching the house when there's supposedly no reason for it."

"Wiley, I don't need you to tell me how to run my department. Now, if you don't mind, I'd like to get back to this budget you know so much about. Goodbye and don't forget to close the door on your way out."

He looked back down at the papers spread out before him until he heard the door close, none too gently, but he expected that out of Homer Wiley.

"Damn!" He threw the pen down fifteen minutes later and got up from the desk. Then he leaned down and pressed the buzzer for his secretary. When she walked in, he said, "Ellie, I need to leave. Will you please just put the budget back into the folder and put it away. Sorry to leave you a mess, but I need to get home."

"Is everything okay, Chief Doan?" His secretary had been with him for over a dozen years, but was still as formal with him today as she was when he started in this job.

"Sure, everything's fine. I just have something that needs doing and I'm cutting out a little early to do it. After you get the budget back in order, just go ahead and leave for the day. You won't need to claim time on it." He touched her shoulder and then was gone, with her wondering why he was lying to her.

He really did intend to go home, but then he decided he needed to do something else, first.

"Fancy meeting you here," he said, as he slid onto a stool next to Homer.

"Are you following *me*, now?" His eyebrows shot up and he expected an answer.

"Did you say you were coming here?"

"No."

"Then what makes you think I followed you when you've been gone probably a good twenty minutes and I sure didn't run to the window to see which direction you were taking. Stop being so damned paranoid." He looked at the bartender. "Any hot coffee back there?"

"Coming right up, Chief," he told him, and then walked back into the kitchen for the coffee. When he set the scalding drink before him, he asked if he'd like something to eat. When he was told no, he went back to washing glasses.

The chief took a long drink of the black liquid before he set it down. He sat there looking out at the street, feeling the frustration building again. Where in hell could that guy be? None of this was making any sense. Shirley was nothing but helpful to him in the Tropic until the moment he left, so how could he have thought she made him? But why, if he didn't think that, did he take off within a couple of hours of being in the theater? It just made no sense at all. He set the cup down too hard and picked up a handful of peanuts. The bartender looked at him, but made no comment.

Homer noticed the frustration in the chief's manner and actions. This case was really getting to him. Did he tell them the whole truth as he said he did? What does he know that they don't?

Casually, he opened a peanut hull and said, "Where on South?"

The chief looked up and asked him to repeat it. "What difference does it make where he lived? He's gone."

"Where did he live there? In a hotel, motel or B&B?"

"He was in a B&B. Now, there, are you happy?" He picked up the coffee and took another long drink of it before slamming it back down on the counter. This time the bartender didn't look up. Whatever had the chief upset was none of his affair, so he left him alone. It wasn't his job to meddle into anyone else's affairs unless he was invited, and even then he didn't interfere, just listened.

"Was the B&B within visual distance from us?"

"Oh come on, Wiley, let it go, dammit." He rubbed his eyes that hadn't closed in sleep for way over twenty-four hours. He didn't need this from his friend.

"So, he was spying on us all this time, then."

The chief said nothing, but threw a five on the counter and left Homer sitting there staring at his back as the door closed behind him and he walked back to his car. He knew the chief's leaving like that meant he was right. Jacques had been spying on Maggie this entire time he'd been in Key West. He probably had a room on the top floor where he'd see her every time she went out the door. They hadn't found a bug anywhere in the house, so that had to be the only explanation for his turning up at the theater that day. He watched the house every waking minute, just as Shirl and Joey did from the motel across the street. Now he was angry, too, and just as determined as the chief to find that guy before Maggie gets hurt or worse.

FiFTY-TWO

"Hi Cowboy, haven't seen you in here, before," the cute redhead asked Jess after he sat at the bar and ordered a Bud.

"Maybe that's because I haven't been in here before, darlin." He gave her his biggest smile.

"God, you have the purtiest eyes for a man. Wow, they just look into a person's soul." She returned his smile and went back to her draft, wiping the foam from her mouth after she took the drink.

"They sure like what they see in your soul," he told her, as he peered down her peasant blouse.

She laughed a lusty laugh that at first startled him, because it was like Lana's laugh, but not as soft. Then he recovered his composure and asked, "Wanna dance, beautiful?

"Sure, why not," she said, taking his proffered hand and getting off the bar stool "I'd be a fool not to." He held her tighter than he normally would when he danced, but this was a country two-step and a lot of men leaned into the woman like that when they danced the two-step. He was good at most dances, having taken some time off years ago to be a dancing instructor for Arthur Murray, and teaching a wide array of dances to the ladies.

"You're good at this, you know?"

Why do people end statements like that with a question mark? It always irritated him and it was mostly southern women who did it. "Where you from?"

"Memphis," she said, laughing. "Guess you can tell, huh?"

"Yeah, that southern accent. What brings you down to my neck of the woods?"

"Oh, you're from here? Sure never pegged you for a Florida boy."

"Oh yeah, have been for a long time. Originally from Ohio, but after travelling all over the country after the folks died, I found out South Florida and the Keys suited me just fine." He held her tighter.

"Hey, don't squeeze the merchandise to pieces, cowboy," she said, barely able to breathe.

"I'm sorry. Didn't mean to hurt you. Are you here with friends?"

"No, just decided to take off by myself to get away from everyone. I graduated from college a few months ago and just wanted to get out on my own for a while till I figured everything out," she told him.

"Figured what out, if you don't mind my asking?"

"What I was going to do with my life now?" The music was ending. "I majored in English Lit, but not sure if I want to teach. Might just keep traveling around the country and then go abroad for a while. Maybe I'll go to Paris and try to write a little?"

"Whoa, you do have some big ambitions. That's really fascinating." Just stop with the question marks, lady! You're getting on my nerves and I don't want to be angry right now.

"Oh poo, it isn't, really. Just a young girl's musings. What do y'all do?"

Y'all? Jeez, didn't your English professors teach that out of you? He took a calming breath. "I have a little software company I've just started recently after selling two others," he said, as her eyes widened. He motioned for the bartender to set them up again.

"Wow, you must be very smart and very rich, Mr..."

"Norton, Jess Norton," he said, putting out his hand to shake hers. "How 'bout you?"

"I'm Marylee Tree," she said, after shaking his hand. "My friends call me Mary."

"I love the name Mary," he said, his eyes suddenly watering.

"What? What did I say to upset you?"

"My – my mom's name was Mary." He put his head in his hands and then lifted it, telling her he was sorry. "It's been over twenty years and you think I'd be over their deaths by now, but it's – it's hard." He sounded so convincing he almost laughed.

"Oh, you poor baby, I'm just so sorry? Would y'all like to walk me back to my hotel, where you can tell me more about your business and your folks? It's not far from here."

"I'd like that, Mary," he said, remembering to sound sad. "I'd like that very much."

FiFTY-THREE

Homer was busy mowing the front lawn and Maggie and Carolyn were enjoying lemonade on Maggie's front porch. Their swings moved slowly with the strong breeze. "I love to watch men work," Carolyn said.

"Yeah, I do, too," Maggie echoed with a grin.

"I heard that," Homer told them, as he'd stopped mowing close to the porch to grab a lemonade. "Next time I'll get another mower and I'll watch the two of you, while I sip cold drinks." Carolyn handed him one when he came up and sat in a rocker near them. "Jeez, it's hotter today than it has been. This strong breeze feels really good – as does that ceiling fan!"

They smiled at him and Maggie asked whether he'd heard any news from headquarters. No matter what else they were doing, as much as she hated it, her mind was never far from wondering when the next shoe would fall with Hamilton Jacques.

"I haven't heard a word, Mag, and Lenny promised he'd give us a call if they learned anything new, at all, so I figure not hearing is good news."

"Do you agree with the police that he's out west somewhere and not coming back here?"

He looked at Carolyn for a long pause and then said, "As much as I'd like to believe that's the story, I'm afraid I don't think he'll stay away from here as long as Maggie's still alive."

Maggie started and her breath came out as a loud gasp. "You still think he's going to try to kill me?"

He walked over and sat down by her, pulling her into a hug for a moment. "Yeah, I'm sorry, but I do. He's come back too many times not to think it."

Carolyn shivered but said nothing. She believed as Homer did that since he'd come back to the island several times since this all began, there was no reason to think he was through with trying to tie up that loose end the cops talked about.

Maggie didn't say any more, and Homer went back to mowing. She knew he was right. She'd thought all along that Lenny Doan was just trying to make her feel better, if not safer, by saying he thought Jacques was long gone. And maybe he was. No way of knowing, was there. Well, she wasn't going to let it ruin her day.

"Hey, you two, why don't we get cleaned up and walk up the street to La Te Da and have lunch in the garden. My treat."

Carolyn smiled and Homer said he was about ready to wrap it up for the day, anyway, because it was just getting too hot to walk around that lawn any longer today. "Okay, I'll just run in and get a shower. Give me half an hour."

"I'll go up and freshen up a little, Maggie. Thanks, lunch at La Te Da sounds great. It's always cool in the garden."

It was nice and cool and the three of them were enjoying themselves, as Shirley and Joey were at a table not far from them.

"You three are hard to catch up with," Lenny Doan said, as he pulled out a chair at their table.

"What do you mean, old man, my phone never rang, did yours?" he asked, looking at the two women.

"My ringer is silenced, but I didn't miss any calls, either," Maggie said, looking down at her phone.

"Mine, either," echoed Carolyn.

"Why, chief, any news?" Homer hoped if there was any, it was that Jacques was long gone from the Keys.

"Yes, I'm afraid so," he told him, as he motioned for the waitress.

"Oh God."

"Now, Maggie, try not to get yourself upset."

"How could I not, when you look like the end of the world is coming?"

"Grilled cheese on wheat and a tall iced tea with lemon," he told the waitress. After she walked away, he said, "There have been two more murders."

"Oh my God," Carolyn said. "Where?"

"Well, the first one was in Sunrise three days ago. Another young woman, just out of college, was bludgeoned to death in her hotel room. They found a partial on the door knob."

"Jacques?"

"Afraid so, Homer. But that isn't the only one. Last night the feds identified another young woman, a Tennessee tourist who'd been here a few days ago, stabbed multiple times and dumped in a culvert in Islamorada."

"Oh God, that means he's been back down here and is probably on his way back, doesn't it."

"I'd like to say no, but it certainly seems so, I'm afraid. We're putting more guys on the streets every shift, as is the S.O. and this time we're going to get that SOB and put an end to this once and for all. The feds are just as determined as we are, so if we don't end it, locally, they will." He left them and went over to sit with his two undercover officers to update them.

FiFTY-FOUR

Jess Norton walked into Cowboy Bill's again and every woman's head automatically turned toward him. He smiled at no one in particular and went to the bar. "Bud, please." He turned around in his seat and watched as a pretty scantily dressed tourist rode the mechanical bull. She started to fall when it stopped and he rushed over and caught her.

"Wow, thanks, good lookin'. Where'd you come from?"

He gave her his biggest smile and said, "I was going to ask you the same thing. Would you care to join me for a beer, first?"

"Sure," she said, as she followed him back to the bar. "I guess I shouldn't have tried that bull."

"He did look like a challenge." he said with a laugh behind the remark. "I like the real thing, myself."

"Don't tell me you're a rodeo man?"

"No, not quite, but I've ridden them on the folks' ranch before."

"Where's their ranch? In Texas? I'm from Dallas, myself."

"No," he said, appreciating the view of her naked chest since there was very little covering it and looking down at her, since she was quite short, he could see it all. He adjusted his tight jeans. "They had one outside of Columbus, Ohio, if you can believe that. Had quite a few acres, but after they were killed, I sold it and left town," he told her, putting on the sad face again.

"Oh, I'm sorry. I didn't mean to bring you down." She had a drawl but it wasn't as irritating as that Memphis broad's.

"It's okay. Not your fault. It's been so long since their boat accident you'd think I'd be over it by now, but sometimes the grief just presses in on me. But let's not talk about sad things, pretty lady. What're you doing down here?"

She laughed and said, "Well, I came down for a month with a girl-friend, but she met a fella last week and they took off for the Bahamas, so I'm just trying to enjoy myself by myself."

"Well, that wasn't' very nice of them. The least they could have done was take you with them."

"Oh, they offered, but they were going to Freeport and I don't like it there. I love Nassau and Paradise Island, but you can have Freeport."

"I totally agree. You know, I was thinking of taking a little break, my-self and flying over to the islands this weekend. Would you like to come with me?"

Her eyes widened and she said, with a laugh, "If I knew your name, maybe I'd consider it, but don't fancy taking off with a stranger. I love Nassau, though, so much that, yes, I'll go with you if you meant it!"

"Fantastic! I'll just run back to my hotel and check to see if they have a flight out from here, today. Don't want to drive up to MIA to fly out of there."

"I hate that Miami airport, too," she told him. "I'll go pack a bag, shower and change. Should I meet you back here?"

"Sure, just give me your cell number, so I can let you know for sure we can get a flight out today. If not, I'll just take you to dinner and we'll try for later on Nassau."

"That sounds great. Here's my number," she said, giving it to him. "I'd better go get ready. See you later, cowboy."

Fool woman, you didn't even get my name. Oh well, I'll get going, too, and hope they have a plane out of here, today, as I'd sure like to get you alone off this island. He settled his bill and gave the bartender a nice tip, before he walked out of the bar. He called and there was a flight out within the hour, so he threw some things into a bag and made the call.

"Hello?"

"Hi, I never got your name, either. This is Jess Norton from Cowboy Bill's."

"Oh," she said, laughing. "I'm Roberta Kindle. My friends call me Bobbie."

If there was anything he hated worse than people putting a question mark after a sentence that didn't require it, it was women being called men's names. "I love the name Bobbie. It suits you, darlin'. "

"Thanks, Jess, that suits you, too."

"Well, have you packed your bag? We have a flight out in half an hour, as it so happens."

"Wonderful, yes, I'm all packed. I'll head to the bar now?"

"No need to do that. I'll pick you up at the front of your hotel. Where are you, anyway?"

"Actually, I'm not at a hotel. I'm at Merlinn Guesthouse at the corner of Petronia and Simonton."

"I know exactly where it is. Stayed there a time or two, myself. I'll be at the Petronia side in just a few minutes. Can you be out there waiting? Since I'm not a guest, I don't have a key to the gate."

"Sure, I'll meet you there right away," she said with her excitement building. He was so good looking and seemed like such a nice guy. How did she get so lucky! She went to the desk and told the clerk to hold her room for her, because she was just going to Nassau for the weekend. He assured her she'd have her room to come back to.

FiFTY-FiVE

"Chief, I think you'll want to take this," his secretary told him, looking grim.

He looked up and said, "Who is it?"

"A clerk at the Merlinn." She walked back to her office as he picked up the receiver.

"This is Chief Doan."

"This is Joe, a clerk at the guesthouse, Chief. I think one of our guests might be missing."

"We'll be right there, Joe. Thanks for calling us."

"Butler, we need to go see someone at Merlinn Guesthouse. Yeah, I'll meet you outside."

"I almost hate to hear what he has to say."

"Yeah, so do I. Well, here we are, so might as well get this over with." The chief slammed his door as Butler got out on the other side. They walked up to the office of the guesthouse that always seemed to be on its own secluded island. It was fenced all the way around with gray wooden fencing and had gray wooden walkways leading to the office and the garden area where the pool was. Even when most of the island was covered with bright sunlight, it was always shady in the garden, because of all the lush foliage surrounding it and hanging over the pool. Blake Butler had stayed here many years ago when he first hit town, before he became a cop. He was only fifteen then and his family was visiting Key West for the first time. They liked it so much they never left the island, except to go back to sell their house and pack their things to move to Key West. That was when property could be had for a song. Nothing like today. He couldn't even afford to live here if they hadn't left the big house on Olivia to him.

Walking into the office, they saw the clerk come around his desk. They shook hands with him and he led them back to the office where they could speak in private. "Thanks for coming right over, Chief."

"This is Lieutenant Butler, Joe. You say you think a guest is missing, but you don't know for certain?"

"No, not really – well, you see this young woman, Roberta Kindle, came to me Friday to ask me to hold her room, said that she was just going over to the Bahamas for the weekend."

"And today's Tuesday. That's a pretty long weekend." Hair was standing up on the back of Doan's neck. He just knew where this was going to lead.

"Do you know if she was traveling with anyone?"

"No, she didn't say any more than what I told you, Lieutenant." He looked so nervous, one would believe he'd done away with her, but they knew that wasn't what was going on here.

"Maybe we'd better check out her room, Joe."

"I expected you'd want to, so I told the maids not to go in there, anymore."

"Have they cleaned since she's been gone?"

"Yes, sorry. They cleaned the morning of the day she left and then cleaned again on Sunday morning since she was coming back that day. I'm sorry, had I..."

He interrupted him by raising his hand, "Not your fault. You had no idea she wasn't coming back when she said she was. Oh, I know you said she didn't say she was traveling with anyone, but did you see her with anyone – a man – while she was here?"

"No sir, not while I was on duty and I was only off Saturday and Sunday."

When they reached the room, the clerk said, "I'll leave you alone, but I'll be in the office if you need anything else."

"Thank you, Joe," the chief told him. "Well, let's get this started, shall we."

"I'll take the bathroom."

"I'll check the bedside table first."

"Hope she wrote someone's name somewhere."

"Yes, so do I, but I doubt we'll find anything incriminating here."

They were right, since Jacques purposefully avoided going into the B&B, so he wouldn't leave behind anything. Not even a slip of paper saying whether she took a plane or was going to Miami to take a cruise. Nothing, except a receipt from Walgreen's for sunscreen and a carton of water. And of course, with her going to the Bahamas, she had her ID with her, so they had a lot of searching to do online.

Back at the desk a few minutes later, Doan told the clerk, "We didn't see anything in her room, but I'm sending my crime scene team over, anyway, on the chance there's a print or something we missed."

"Okay, I'll tell staff to stay away from the room until we get clearance from you."

"Thanks. In talking with Ms. Kindle, did she mention any family? "

"No sir, she kept pretty much to herself after her friend left for Freeport. She didn't hang around much after her morning swim. I never saw her with anyone, like I said, even at the pool."

"Did she drive down? And can you give me her address please, if it's in your registration records."

"I already printed her page out, Lieutenant. Here you go. Just call me if you think of anything else I might help with on this. I feel awful that she's missing. Seemed like a nice young woman."

FiFTY-SiX

In the car, they brought her up on the computer. Apparently she lived with her parents, so Lenny Doan called the house. Her father answered.

"Yes, Mr. Kindle, we don't know for certain she's missing. She might have just liked it so much in Nassau that she extended her weekend."

"Well sir," her father said into the phone, "she did love Nassau and had gone there many times by ship, but if she left in the afternoon, I doubt she was taking a ship over, because they would leave before she even got to Miami."

"Yes, that's what we figured, and are checking the flights now. Do you know if she had friends down here, maybe someone she was traveling with?"

"She went down there with a girlfriend, Marie Coward, but she called us a few days ago, bummed out that Marie met a young man who took her to Freeport for a week. They asked Bobbie to go, but she never liked it there so declined."

"Yes, the clerk mentioned that a girlfriend went to Freeport. Did she happen to mention this man's name she was traveling with?"

"Yes, she was laughing because his name was Robert Kincaid, like the photo-journalist in Bridges of Madison County. She told him she didn't believe him, but he produced his wallet and sure enough that was his name on his driver's license and some other thing he had in there. I forget exactly what it was – a membership of some kind."

"Did she happen to describe him, by any chance, or say where he'd been staying here or if he was a local?"

"She said he was around forty, quite a bit older than Marie, totally bald, a little overweight but not fat, Bobbie said. Oh, and she said he was a conch, whatever that means."

"It means he was born here," Doan told him. "Well, I think we've kept you long enough, Mr. Kindle. We'll be back in touch if we find out anything else."

The man thanked him and they disconnected.

"Let's grab a cup of coffee from Denny's and eat a bite. I never even ate breakfast or lunch, so I'm getting low on fuel," Lieutenant Butler said.

"Sounds good to me. I ate breakfast, but no lunch."

They ate a quick dinner, lingered over an extra cup of coffee and then went back to the office to call Nassau P.D., a call Doan hated to make because he just knew what the outcome would be, and he was right. A young woman was found by some tourists tied to a palm tree on Paradise Island on the wide path, canopied by tall royal palms. It was the path tourists took to get to the beach. She was nude and had multiple stab wounds. A scarf was tied around her neck and scarves holding her hands around the slender tree trunk. There was no ID lying around, but they did find a hotel key on the ground near the body. The coroner said a cursory exam showed extensive damage to her genitals. They were able to identify her from the hotel records – Roberta Kindle, from Atlanta. "Dammit!"

Butler said nothing as he looked at the floor. He'd really hoped it wouldn't be her.

"As you heard, I asked them not to do the notification, because we've established contact with the family and we'll do it in person. Why don't you take Parsons and head up to Atlanta. I don't want to tell her dad over the phone. He was upset enough just thinking she was missing. I'll wait here for forensics in Nassau to send me what they have. They said the hotel room was wiped pretty clean but they were able to pull some hair from the drain and a couple prints on the inside of the shower door that weren't hers. He said they looked pretty fresh, so whomever did her got careless and forgot he used the shower."

"We'll head out now, Chief. Don't relish this job at all," his lieutenant told him. "I hate that sonofabitch more every day."

"Might not be him. I'll let you know when I get anything."

"Are you going to talk with Maggie about this?"

"I'll have to if it turns out it is Jacques. And most likely it is. I doubt she'd have flown over to the islands by herself. Women alone usually take cruises if they're going to the Bahamas. Never knew any of them to fly over there alone unless they were meeting someone there."

"Me, neither. Well, I'll get going."

"Have a careful drive up there. Stop on the way to get some sleep if you need it. You don't need to show up at his doorstep too early in the morning, anyway."

"We'll see. Might just go straight to Atlanta and if it's too early, we'll go to a hotel and grab a few winks before going to the house."

"Good idea. See you when you get back."

Doan was in his office just a half hour when his phone rang and it was Nassau law enforcement. "Yes sir, I appreciate that. I'll be waiting for the fax. Thank you. Goodbye." He got up, poured a cup of black Cuban coffee and then called his lieutenant.

"Blake, I just got word from Nassau. The prints are his. The desk clerks described him as a tall slender man with light brown hair and very different eyes – they said they looked tan with a lot of amber flecks in them. Said they'd never seen eyes like that, so he obviously is wearing strange contacts. He signed the register as Jess Norton. This guy has more aliases than anyone we've ever come up against. Yeah, I'm heading over there now. How did Mr. Kindle take it, by the way?"

"I never saw a man so torn up. He started pacing the room, crying real loud and breathing like he was going to have a heart attack. His face was red and he was pale around his mouth. He has no one except his daughter – well, make that had no one. He even said they'd both seen the wanted posters of the guy the FBI was after down there and he'd told her maybe she shouldn't go.

Blake had been alarmed at that. "What did she say to that?" the chief asked him.

"He started crying harder and said, 'She laughed and said, Daddy, we'll be real careful. What can happen to two women together?' Then he threw himself into the nearest chair and just cried like a baby. We asked him if we could take him to the ER just to be sure he was okay, and he threw up his hands and said, hell no, that he wished he'd have a heart attack and die. Said there was no reason to live now that his Bobbie was gone, and said she was his heart. It was really sad listening to him. He showed us her photos and she was stunning, Chief, just like every other young woman that maniac has destroyed. Damn, I want my hands on him!"

"I think that's a common denominator with all of us right now. This time we're gonna get the bastard, if we all have to work 24/7. We'll see you when you get back. I'm on my way to Maggie's now, but you guys take your time getting back here. I doubt Jacques will be back right away, but you can be damned sure he is coming back and this time, we'll make sure he never leaves until he's either dead or in Stark. Even though the feds put that flier up everywhere, I'm calling another press conference and reminding everyone we've a serial killer in the Keys and try to get these young women not to go anywhere with someone they don't know. Okay, see you when you get back." He slammed his cell on the seat and turned onto South Street.

FIFTY-SEVEN

"Hi Carolyn, is Maggie home?"

She could tell by looking at the chief something else had happened. "Sure, chief, come on in and have a seat." She went to the coffee maker and got a fresh cup of coffee and handed it to him, before she left the kitchen.

"Maggie?" She had no response to her knock. "Maggie? The chief's here."

"I'll be right there, as soon as I splash some water on my face."

"Okay, we'll be in the kitchen."

Homer heard her knocking from where he sat on the front porch. "What's going on?"

"You didn't see the chief drive up?"

"No, I was taking a nap and just came out. Did he say what he wanted?"

"No, he came to the back door, and wanted to tell us whatever it is all together, I guess. We're in the kitchen." She walked back and he went with her, nodding to the chief, but saying nothing.

"There she is. Did you have a good nap?" Homer asked to try to get Maggie to relax, since she looked ready to cry. "Here, sit down and I'll get you some coffee."

"I don't want any more coffee. Just bring me a cup of tea, please, if you don't mind."

"I'll get it, Homer. Sit down."

After the tea water was hot and she'd put a tea bag in it and the stevia Maggie used to sweeten it, Carolyn joined the others at the table.

"Well, Maggie, there's no way to sweeten this so I'll just come right out with it. There's been another murder."

"Here on the island?" she asked, biting her lower lip.

"No, not here, in Nassau, but the victim was a young woman who'd been staying over at Merlinn and they found some prints on the shower door in Nassau, so looks like she flew over there with Jacques."

"Oh God, when's it going to end? Was she bludgeoned or stabbed to death?"

"She was tied to a tree, stabbed several times and strangled with a scarf."

She looked as though she were going to faint. "Here, drink some of your tea."

She smiled at Carolyn and drank the tea. "Poor little thing. He's getting worse, isn't he, Lenny."

"Yes, I'd say he was escalating by the day, Maggie. That's why I wanted you to know we're putting more men and women out on the streets and if we all have to work 24/7, we're catching this guy this time. The feds are doing the same thing, Special Agent Metz told me. I was going to hold another press conference, but he asked me to wait until they get there and we'll do it together, like we did after he took poor Lana Carter to Tahiti and then did young Holly." He gulped at the memory of seeing that poor battered and destroyed young woman in the hotel.

"Do you think he's back here now?"

"No, I think he'll lay low for a while like he usually does, but we'll be ready for him when he does come back, if we have to look in every car as soon as it comes to the triangle."

Maggie looked closely at him, with her fist over her mouth, and then she asked. "Has he changed his looks again? I doubt he'd have stayed in his elderly man mode if he was after another woman."

"Yes, he has. He's got light brown hair with a bit of a wave to it."

"It had a bit of a wave to it when he went past the house that..."

Homer almost came across the table at her. "What? You saw him and didn't tell anyone!"

"My God, Maggie, what were you thinking?" Carolyn asked, as she put a hand on Homer's arm.

"Okay, everyone, let's just calm down. I, too, am sorry you didn't' say anything, Maggie, but I doubt it would have changed anything," the chief told her."

"I'm sorry I got upset," Homer said, looking over at her.

"As I was saying," Doan told them," he has a bit of wave to his hair and it's still short. They said he's apparently wearing unusual contact lenses now, because his eyes look almost tan with amber flecks in them. Unless he changes again before he gets back here, he should be easy to spot. And of course, we're checking all the places he could have been staying. We'll get him this time, I'm sure of it."

FIFTY-EIGHT

Once more, back in the states, where he'd flown from Miami to Chattanooga, Jacques was busy dyeing his hair. This time he went dark – auburn – and put in very dark brown contacts. He'd stay in Tennessee until his beard grew out, so he'd have at least a shadow of a beard and mustache, only this time he'd let his mustache grow out more until it was quite thick.

He was bound and determined not to get with anymore young women. He didn't want to even leave his little single wide out in the country, not near anyone who would have any reason to come around. He'd take his trash with the hair dyeing kit and the old contacts out to a dumpster behind a bar tonight and then drive straight back to his home away from home. He'd gone to the store in an old jeep he bought downtown as soon as he got off the plane, not a nice Cherokee like he had, but an old smaller one that was beaten up and fit in around that area. It was old enough he could pay cash for it. He was leaving no paper trail.

"There, Glenn Buckingham, you look just great." He liked the auburn hair and dark eyes. He gathered everything up into a big trash bag and headed out the door in search of that dumpster. He found it on the other side of Chattanooga, heading back down I-75, past the split where 75 coming into Chattanooga became I-24 through the city. The city looked pretty at night right after that split, situated down in the valley with the Tennessee River right there all around it, as he was driving back home. He'd like to go down and explore it, since he'd never been to Chattanooga, but he knew he didn't dare go around people right now.

He took his time driving back across town and to his trailer on the two acres five miles east of Jasper in the mountains. It was back a dirt road and there wasn't a house or another trailer to be found, anywhere. He felt quite safe and had everything he needed. He listened closely to the nightly news and to CNN during the day and nothing was mentioned about the death of Bobbie.

He hadn't thought of her several days. Damn fool woman just had to go sticking her nose in his business and found a couple of his IDs in his suitcase while he was out getting some groceries. Had she not gotten all upset and demanded to know his real name, she might have stayed alive much longer. But no, she got all hysterical when she found them.

When he told her it was not her concern, she tried to run out the door, but he grabbed her, tore off her clothing, raped her several times, once with the end of a broom handle as she screamed and then forced some pills down her mouth and held it closed until she swallowed.

When she was finally unconscious, because he'd forced four sedatives down her, he viciously raped her again two more times even though she was still bleeding from the last time and then when it got very dark, since they used no bright lights around this small hotel, he wrapped her in a blanket and threw her in the trunk of his rental. He didn't check to see if she was still alive. He didn't care one way or the other. He drove as far as he could and carried her way out to where he thought she wouldn't be found for a day or two, at least until the next cruise ships came in and tied her to a tree near the beach. He couldn't believe it when she started coming to, but he started stabbing her and finally because she wouldn't die right away, he put a scarf around her neck and pulled both ends tight. That'll teach her to meddle in his business.

He went back to the hotel to shower and clean the place up, and then he went to the airport and exchanged his ticket for Miami and from there, he flew to Chattanooga, which he picked by closing his eyes and stabbing a place on a United States map. Since he'd never been there, he figured he might as well go. Being it was a city in rural Tennessee, there'd be plenty of little towns around and old dirt roads where he could find an isolated cabin or something. After he bought the old jeep, he didn't drive far until he came to the trailer. He called the number on the homemade sign. When the elderly man answered after several rings, he told him he'd like to buy the place if he'd agree to do it just between the two of them and not involve anything legal, just a gentlemen's agreement between them. He agreed and Jacques paid the man double his asking price in cash. The man looked like he'd won the lottery.

"Now, I can pack my things and move out to Montana to buy a little ranch like I've been wanting to do. Thank you, Mr. Martin. If I can get a plane out tonight, I'm gone from here. Thank you very much. I hope y'all be able to finish your book in record time out here. It's for sure no one will bother you. I think you're the only person to drive out that road nigh onto ten years. I was surprised to hear y'all say you got my number from that old sign in front of it. I figured it had up and flown away with the wind and I didn't rightly care. The old trailer was paid for, so I just never thought about it at all. That road, though, it's always got so many potholes and they're always muddy and slippery, so folks around here don't even bother going huntin' out there like they used to. I'm sorry it's that way but I just haven't had the money to take care of my own place and fix that up, too."

"Don't apologize, Mr. Jenson. Like I told you, I need absolute privacy if I'm ever going to finish this Civil War volume. I've got the other war volumes done, but just can't seem to get this one finished. I know now with this kind of privacy and no phones or anything to bother me out there, I'll be able to concentrate on it."

"I'll be sure to look online for it. Will it be on Amazon? I got me one of them Kindle things to read my books off'fa, so if it is, I'll be able to find it."

"Oh yes, you can be sure it'll be on Amazon, Barnes & Noble and all the other ones. Just look for the title The Real Civil War and you'll find it. It probably won't be out for a couple years, though. My editor and publisher don't work like lightning – you know how those Big Six publishers are or maybe you don't." He laughed like he made a joke, and even though he was ridiculing the old man, he just smiled. "It always takes a couple or more years from the time I finish it, until I see it in print."

The man thanked him again for the windfall, even though he wasn't so ignorant he didn't know the guy was making fun of him. He didn't care. He was getting the hell out of Dodge and soon he'd have his ranch.

Jacques had paid $85,000 for a place that wasn't worth $30 grand. But, he needed the isolation for several months if he were to become as disguised this time as he hoped. Besides, knowing they'd trace Bobbie back to the Merlinn sooner or later, they'd know he'd be coming back, eventually. He laughed. *If* they were able to lay her death on him, which he doubted, since he'd never gone to her room there. He knew for certain the room in Nassau was as sterile as an operating room. But he couldn't take any chances, so he figured he'd stay out here in the boondocks for at least six months. He'd go to one of the dorky little towns to get his groceries far from the trailer. He'd act grouchy and unfriendly, and not give anyone any reason to ask his name. He didn't have any need for a post office box or to have mail delivery back the old dirt road, since he had no intention of turning on the power. He had an outdoor grill to cook on and a large cooler he replenished with ice every time he got groceries. He had plenty of lamps that he had to wind up to turn on and plenty of batteries to keep them going. He even had a little portable TV that ran by large batteries with one of those HD adapters on it, so he wouldn't have to hook up to cable and could still check CNN once in a while. He'd remain totally anonymous until he was ready to drive back to Key West. He wouldn't even bother going back, but of all the murders he'd committed, there was only one witness to any of them and until he got rid of her, he'd never be free. He knew they couldn't pin any of the others on him, since no one saw a thing. He left no fingerprints and all that DNA stuff was just more hocus-pocus, so he wasn't worried about that at all.

FiFTY-NiNE

It was Maggie's 73rd birthday and Carolyn and Homer wanted to give her a big party to celebrate it, since there had been no sign of Hamilton Jacques on the island for over a year now. Everyone was pretty sure he'd given up his quest to tie up that loose end that was Maggie. Cause to celebrate if there ever was one, Homer thought.

"Where do you want to have your party?" Homer hoped she'd say the Bottle-Cap or somewhere equally as large so everyone in town could come to see her.

"I don't want a party," she told him. "All I want to do is to go out to dinner with the two of you and relax and enjoy ourselves. And don't you go and throw me a surprise party, either, Homer. Now just isn't the time."

Carolyn looked up from the novel she was reading as the three of them sat out on the back porch. "Aren't you feeling well?"

"Of course, I'm feeling well, but in case you've forgotten, I'm pretty much living on borrowed time right now and I'm just not in the mood for a party of any kind." How could they think she'd be up for celebrating her birthday with a party? She couldn't imagine doing such a thing.

"Mag, he's nowhere around here. It's been months since we heard about the murder in Islamorada and every cop in the county had an eye out for him, but he never showed himself. Either he got a boat off Islamorada or he simply drove or flew back to the mainland and out of the state before the body was discovered. The highway patrol, nobody, has seen anyone who remotely resembles the guy, so please, just try to relax and forget that low-life. He's ruined a whole year and a half of your life, as it is. Enough is enough." He figured if he was adamant about it, maybe she'd believe the guy was out of Florida.

"Be that as it may," she said, after taking a long sip from her tall glass of lemonade, "I'm still not in the mood for a party and I'll be very upset if you go against my wishes and have one for me. I don't need it and I don't want it."

He glanced over at Carolyn who shrugged and then he said, "Okay, I understand. I won't throw you the party. I'll get on the phone and cancel the 300 invitations I sent out earlier." Then he chuckled, and Maggie smiled her toothless smile at him. Nothing else was said about it.

As the three sat in companionable silence, drinking in the muted colors splashed across the sky, as the cicadas hummed in the fichus out in the side yard, Lieutenant Butler turned off Whitehead and parked his car on United before he reached Duval. "I wonder if he's coming here," she said, her heart starting to pound in her ear.

"Hi, Maggie," he called, "may I come up?"

This must mean trouble, she thought, and almost didn't want to hear what he had to say, but being a good neighbor, she motioned him to ascend the long path and stairway up to the second floor porch. "Have a seat anywhere you wish. Care for some lemonade, Lieutenant?" She had her hand on the pitcher and was reaching for a clean glass.

"Sure, thanks, it looks good for this hot day." He sat in one of the rockers and drank the proffered icy drink. The others watched him, wondering what was happening to bring him to the house today. No one had come near them for months. Maggie hoped he had good news, but wouldn't he have led with that instead of talking about the weather? She sighed deeply and wished he'd just come out with it. She was on the verge of telling him to do just that, when he spoke again.

"I'm sorry to have to tell you this, Maggie," he said. "There's been another murder. This time in Cudjoe. They found the young woman face down in one of the finger canals near the Square Grouper around four this morning. The medical examiner said it looked like, because of the lividity, it probably happened twelve to twenty-four hours before she was discovered lying half in and half out of the canal." Both women gasped.

"And?" Homer was easily irritated by his old nemesis from high school. He always wanted to dramatize everything instead of just come out with it.

"Hold your horses, man. I'm getting there," he shot back at him. He held Homer in no higher regard than Homer did him. "Bartender thought she'd been in there a couple nights before with a guy in his forties with dark brown hair, a beard that wasn't a five o'clock shadow, but that type of one, and the darkest eyes she's ever seen in anyone before. She said she couldn't even see his pupils because his eyes were almost black to her. That's how she remembered them, because she couldn't stop staring at those dark eyes, like she'd picture the devil having. Said they were sitting alone at a table and she thought they were on their honeymoon the way he couldn't seem to keep his hands off her, but since she didn't see rings on either of their fingers to back this assumption, she figured she was wrong.

"So, does forensics confirm it was him or wasn't there any evidence at the scene?"

"No, Maggie, I'm afraid there was nothing at the scene to put him there."

"But if he was touching her all evening like the bartender says, wouldn't there be some partials or DNA somewhere on her?"

"Fraid not. He stripped her naked and must have used gloves, because there wasn't a hair or bite marks or anything – not even sperm – to give us something to work with."

"Damn," Homer said, "what's it going to take for that guy to show himself on this island? I'm so tired of all of us, including you guys, sitting on our hands and just waiting for him to show up here or somewhere else Maggie is and taking her out!" Then he realized what he'd said, looked at Maggie and said, "Oh God, I'm sorry. I didn't mean to say that, Mag."

She waved his apology away. "No need for saying you're sorry, and I don't agree with you that any of the cops are sitting on their hands on this. I think they're all working as hard as they possibly can and we just have to let them do their jobs." Looking up at the one standing ready to leave, she said, "Thank you for coming by and letting us know this, Lieutenant. We were going to go out for dinner tonight, somewhere local on the beach. In your opinion, do you think we'll be safe to do that?"

"If I had my way, you'd never leave this house, but the chief told me to tell you to try not to worry, since no one like that has been spotted. We did take a drawing around to all the bars, though, so someone will recognize him if he does show himself."

"I hate this waiting so much. If you all will excuse me, I need to get on that trike and ride around the island. I'm a bundle of nerves." She stood and started to walk around the porch to the front of the house to unlock her trike.

With his arm out to block her way, Butler said, "Oh no, you don't. That's one thing we don't want you to do. It'd be easier for him to pick you off on a trike than if you were sitting in a restaurant with friends all around and the two detectives at the bar or another table."

"Well, durn it to heck! You're putting Joey and Shirley back on me? I feel like I'm in prison when he's the one who should be locked up!" She stormed into the house, slamming the screen door behind her.

Carolyn started to go after her, but Homer reached out a hand to stop her. She hated seeing their friend so upset. She was so happy for a while after they returned from Cuenca a couple months ago. She'd loved the beautiful colonial city in the highlands of Ecuador with the Andes surrounding it. Every day the two of them had gone to the big outdoor market to buy all fresh ingredients for their dinner, and plenty of beautiful flowers to grace the table.

There'd been only one minor problem. The three of them were walking around the city, looking at the beautiful churches one day and going inside to see the beauty of them up close, when Maggie told them to go ahead, she'd catch up. She said she had a pebble in her sandal and sat on a bench, reaching down for it, as she shooed them away. "I'll just be a minute. You go ahead."

After several minutes went by, Homer got suspicious. When the two of them turned around to see if she was coming, they saw a man walk up to her and the two of them exchange something. They were close enough to hear him say, "Hola, Ms. Maggie," and that's all Homer needed to hear. The man was no stranger and no Ecuadorian. He was from Cuba and obviously the two of them had planned this the moment he'd made their reservations.

"Okay, give it back to him, and you – give her back every penny."

"But, senor..."

"No buts, give it back – now!"

The two of them reluctantly exchanged items again, and he hurried away. "Durn it, Homer, I've had no fun for almost a year and a half and now you go and spoil things for me. He had a beautiful artifact and it wouldn't have hurt a thing for me to take it home with me."

"Yeah, and have Customs and Homeland Security on our backs the minute we stepped off the plane in Miami!"

Carolyn had just stood silently smiling at this little tableau. It was nice seeing the old Maggie again, but she knew Homer was right, even though Maggie was disappointed not to bring her contraband back to the United States. She sighed deeply now, feeling badly for her.

"She just needs a little time to process this whole mess again. After all, we've all been trying to reassure her that he is probably out west somewhere."

"Except for how she was killed, we can't say for sure he's not gone," Butler told them.

"You didn't say how she was killed," Homer bit back, angry that he'd forgotten that detail.

"I know. I just didn't want to upset her more. The victim was stabbed multiple times and had a scarf around her neck, like the victim did in the Bahamas."

Carolyn shivered, despite the heat of the day. "It was him, then."

"I didn't say that, Carolyn. But yes, it does look like it could be. That's why I stopped her from getting on the trike. Even though we can't say for sure, we're all thinking he's back and you just need to keep her off

237

that trike and be with her wherever she goes. After you call Joey and Shirley to back you up, that is."

"Yeah, yeah, we know the drill." Homer sighed deeply and raked his hand through his thick silvery hair that had grown out of its usual crew cut and was wavy and almost covering his neck.

Feeling as frustrated as they were, the lieutenant bid them good evening and walked back down the stairs. Maggie watched him through the window in the den where she'd been sitting since she went into the house trying, but not succeeding, to read a book. She had no idea how she was going to continue being cooped up like that. She was used to riding around the island at least once a day, going to the Tropic to see a movie by herself if she felt like it or going to the playhouse with Carolyn at night to see a play that would leave them laughing all the way home. Now, they never went out after dark and of course, she knew she'd be too good a target on that trike. He'd have her in no time if he was back on the island. Lieutenant Butler was right about that.

"Oh well," she said aloud, as she got up from the chair, her muscles protesting from lack of good exercise on the trike, "might as well go start dinner – or have a swim, maybe."

When she came in from the pool, she found Carolyn chopping vegetables and Homer dusting a large swordfish with flour and the other secret ingredients he never shared. "I was just coming in to get things started," she told them.

"Did you have a nice swim? Oh, I just put the kettle on for our tea, so why don't you have a cup while you're relaxing and let us finish getting dinner going."

She looked at her for a moment, started to say something but thought better of it. "Okay, if you want to, and yes, I had a good swim." She went to the stove and got the kettle. "Do you want me to fix your tea, now, too?"

"Yes, thanks, Maggie. I'll just drink it while I'm working. I'm almost ready to put the veggies on the grill. Looks like Homer's almost got the swordfish ready to put on the table. It won't take more than five minutes to grill these. On second thought, please put mine on the table, too. I won't be that long."

"Okay." She fixed their tea and sat down with her book. She read until Carolyn came to the table, while Homer finished grilling the veggies. He'd already unwrapped the swordfish and set it aside after Carolyn added them. She hated this. They were so stilted, acting like two strangers who were trying not to discuss religion or politics, for fear of upsetting each other and ruining what could have been a nice friendship. This wasn't like her home, anymore. There used to be so much laughter around this table. Now, they seldom smiled, much less laughed.

Carolyn didn't say anything when she came to the table. She didn't know what to say, knowing Maggie was upset. They all were. And she didn't know how much more of this isolation her friend could take. She was 73, after all, not 33. It had to be affecting her worse than any of them. She still was his primary target, although if he came to the house to try to kill her, nothing would stop him from trying to kill the three of them. She shivered again.

"You okay?"

"Sure, I'm fine."

"Well, as far as I can tell it's still 92 out there, so I know you're not cold. I just saw you shiver again like you did on the porch a while ago, so don't tell me you're fine."

"Okay, then, I won't," Carolyn said, with a little smile. "I was just thinking of what Lieutenant Butler told us earlier. I hate to think there's another killer who's targeting young women down here, but on the other hand, I don't want it to be Hamilton Jacques, either, because..."

"Because he's targeting me, of course." She took a large sip of her tea, burning her lips in the process, since it still was steaming hot. "But I'll tell you, I hope he is back. I'm fed up with waiting for him to make a move. If he's back, maybe this time, he'll come after me and they can get him put away, finally."

"You can't mean that! There's no guarantee that Shirley and Joey could get to you soon enough if he came after you. Especially if he came in the middle of the night and they couldn't see him in the dark. He's no dummy. He's alluded every law enforcement agency around the county so far – actually around the state – so he knows what he's doing."

Just then Homer came through the open French doors. "She's right about that. You don't want him coming after you. I might hear him and be able to take him down before he reaches your room if he came at night, and he's too smart, as Carolyn says, not to come at night. Or he might be so quiet that even I, with my good hearing, wouldn't hear him. Then, where would you be? If none of us heard him, we couldn't very well call for help. No, Mag, you definitely do not want that to happen, no matter how much you want this over with. While I was outside, I was thinking about something I want to ask the chief, but I wanted to talk with you first."

She looked puzzled and asked, "What're you thinking of doing?"

"I'm not thinking of doing anything, but I think it's time to get Joey and Shirley to set up camp right here in the house. I've a strong feeling this guy's ready to make his move and I worry we couldn't get them over here fast enough if he does break in."

"The alarm would sound if he tried that, wouldn't it?" Carolyn asked.

"He's smart enough to disarm it in some way, so we can't count on that. He's eluded everyone for almost two years so he wouldn't be like your everyday bungling burglar trying to break in to steal Mag's jewels – if she had any."

"I hadn't thought about that," Maggie said. "Why don't you talk to Joey about it first?"

"I will, but dinner's ready and I was just about to put it on the table. We can talk more about this after we eat."

SIXTY

"Well, what do you think?" Joey was sucking on one of Chief Doan's cigars, but like the chief, he didn't light it, since it was illegal to do so in a public building. Butler had a phone call and had to leave the office for a while, so it was just the two of them. He gave his approval before he left but said it was up to the chief, ultimately.

"I didn't want to chance his being close enough to see the two of you going inside the house, but I think Homer's right. I have a feeling he's ready to strike soon, too. Homer's only one person and he has to sleep sometime. With three of you in the house, one could sleep while the other two sit and wait"

"We're all on the same page then, so?"

"Okay, get with Blake and work out the logistics of it. I'll give Maggie a call and tell her we're ready to make this change early tomorrow morning, preferably before daybreak. Do you know if any of them are up that early?"

"Yes, Homer's always out on the front porch by five or five-thirty, so he can watch the sunrise. After that, he picks up the Citizen from the yard and goes back into the house. "

"That should work well, then. The two of you get packed up and checked out by five tomorrow morning and then walk over. Maybe if he's around, he'll see you. Maybe not, but Homer's right, as usual. It is time we get all of you in one place. And if he is hanging around and does see you going in the back door, he'll know better than to try anything at the house."

"And if he doesn't see you go in, that's good, too, since any surprise attack won't be a surprise for you because two of you will be awake at all times. Between you two and Homer, you can easily subdue the guy before he can hurt Maggie."

"I couldn't agree more, Chief. Do you want me to hang around till the lieutenant gets back or just start packing now?"

"Yes, on second thought, why don't you go ahead and leave, alert Shirley, and get yourselves ready to get out first thing in the morning. I'll go over the logistics with Butler."

"Okay, I'll go talk with her now. And, Chief?"

"Yeah?"

"You're doing the right thing. With all of us thinking he's here and going to make his move soon, it's the right thing to do to protect Maggie from him."

"I sure hope so. Damn, this has to end soon. I'm with Maggie on that. Go on and get things started with Shirley and we'll get this switch going in the morning."

"Will do. You're going to call Maggie now, then?"

"Yeah, might as well get it over with. I hope Homer's convinced her it'll be a good thing."

"It sounded to me like all three of them wanted it, Chief. See you later."

SIXTY-ONE

After they finished dinner and had the kitchen cleaned and shining once again, Homer said he was going to run back to Sugarloaf for a few minutes to pick up his mail and he'd be right back. "Don't get into any trouble in the hour or so it will take me to pick up what I need and get back here, ladies," he teased.

Carolyn smiled and told them she was going up to her place to read a while before turning in and Maggie said, "I'm thinking of doing the same thing, so don't worry. Neither of us will get into trouble in that length of time. I'll leave the lights on in the kitchen if you want a midnight snack. And remember, Joey and Shirley are going to sneak in early tomorrow morning, too, before the sun's up." After the chief called her, she and Carolyn made up two of the guest rooms on the second floor, so they'd not have it to do tomorrow morning. With the room ready, whichever detective had been up all night could go right to bed.

"I know. I'll see you a little later."

They said goodnight to him and he left the house. Being on daylight savings time, it wouldn't even be dark by the time Homer returned, so they weren't worried.

As he was on his way back to Key West from his home fourteen miles away, and Carolyn was upstairs in her sitting room, reading, Maggie was back in the kitchen playing solitaire and thinking. Mostly thinking. She was so weary of this cat and mouse game. No one could convince her that Hamilton Jacques was not back on the island. They wouldn't be going along with Homer on putting the two cops in the house, if they didn't think he was there. She felt his eyes on her so many times. She knew he was just waiting for his chance to grab her.

Little did she know the killer was taking that chance that very night. As she was sitting there playing with the cards, not really paying any attention to the game, he was already standing out in the roots of the large banyan tree in her back yard off the patio and close to Whitehead Street waiting for the lights to go down. For everyone to go to bed. No one could see him, since he was in the shadows, but he could see Maggie. She shivered as she put the cards in their plastic box.

She got up and looked out the back windows. She saw and heard nothing. Then she went to the front of the house. Same thing out there. Chills were moving up her spine, though, as she walked back down the hall. He was out there. She knew he was.

After arguing with herself for ten minutes, her common sense lost the argument. She didn't care if Joey and Shirley weren't in the house, yet. Instead of going to her bedroom as she'd planned, she opened the back door, stood there for a few moments and then closed it quietly behind her. If he was anywhere near her, and she knew he was, then she would make herself available. This whole thing will be over tonight. One way or the other. And if her instincts were right, he'd wait until it got pitch dark out before he'd come near the house. She was so weary of it and she couldn't wait any longer. She was going to force him to make his move. Now.

She sat on the wraparound porch in the glider, her sandal-clad feet barely touching the gleaming hardwoods of its floor. She pretended it was just like any other night. The pastels from tonight's sunset still lingered in the sky and she could smell the frangipani and jasmine as they danced their aromatic waltz with the gentle ocean breezes gliding over the island. In the distance she could hear the laughter of those sitting out on the beach having an after-sunset drink or two and enjoying life on this tropical paradise. As she used to do. Other than that, she heard nothing except an occasional screech from a group of gulls dipping into the sea for their prey and the swishing of the myriad palm trees as their long fronds waved together with each small breeze.

Maggie loved her home and never once regretted buying this wonderful piece of property just steps from the Atlantic that had been all but condemned for years as she rode by on her trike, longing to live there. She smiled as she thought back to that time after she won Powerball and got the contractor to bring his crew over to start tearing down and renovating the beautiful old home, leaving its structure and façade exactly as it had always been since the early days of Key West when so many Bahamian carpenters sailed over from the islands to make this their home and started building all these wonderful old historic houses from wood and their God-given skills, houses that had withstood numerous strong tropical storms and hurricanes that tried in vain to topple them. The Bahamians made sure of that. Now her gleaming white house with its bright red shutters and wraparound porches was one of the most beautiful on the island and that it belonged to her was a miracle and blessing she'd never take for granted.

She sighed now as she, as quietly as possible, rose from her reverie in the glider. It was time. She walked down the wide steps leading to the patio off the lower level of the house. Looking back toward the house, she took a leisurely walk around the patio and pool area, and then walked back up to the back door, started to open it but changed her mind. Instead, she went back down the steps, her soft sandals making no noise, walked further into the back yard beyond the patio and beyond the pool, toward the avocado tree, as if she wanted to pick some fruit from the tree. If he's hiding, he'll be in or near the banyan tree, since no one can see anything at dusk within those roots. This frightened her so she could barely breathe, but she was determined to see this through if she was right and he really was out there. She was still having chills up her spine and the hairs on the back of her neck were standing up.

A few years ago, she'd contemplated having that whole area flooded with motion lights, but then changed her mind. It wouldn't be calming to sit out anywhere with bright lights flooding the whole backyard, including the banyan, every time anyone moved. And with the big sapodilla tree in the middle of everything, it would ruin the affect to have it lit up all the time. So, except for the smallest flood lights she could find on an occasional tree or plant nearest the patio, beyond the pool area was pitch blackness. She still was glad she hadn't done it, but it sure was dark in those massive ancient roots. She couldn't see a thing, but then she wasn't going into them, either. If he was there and wanted her, he'd have to come out into the open where there was a chance Joey and Shirley could take him out if she screamed for them.

Well, I'm out here alone, so if he's going to strike, he'll do it now while no one else is with me. Come on, let's get this show on the road and – what was that? She heard him before she saw him, as he crept up behind her and put his arm around her neck, with his knife in his hand where he could slice her neck in a flash if he wanted to. "Well, hello, Ms. Maggie. It's been a very long time, since you and I were together down by the lake watching that pretty fountain and the sunset at Windsor Park."

His voice startled her. She hadn't heard it for almost two years, since he'd stood beside her at that lake. She would have known it anywhere from the little 'ah' he put at the end of the sentence. Even without his mentioning the murder in West Palm. But he was not going to win this game, she determined. He wasn't quick enough to cover her mouth, so as soon as he stopped talking, she got a good scream out and Carolyn looked down from her terrace and saw what was happening. She speed-dialed Homer, Shirley and Joey. Homer had just pulled into the drive and she told him Jacques had Maggie in the backyard near the banyan.

He grabbed his Glock, and instead of going in through the house and out the back door, he slipped into the next door neighbor's yard and out onto Whitehead. He could head him off by the banyan, if he tried to drag her out to the street. He knew he wouldn't take her out United, so that was the logical route to take. He probably had a car waiting on Whitehead.

As he was positioning himself there, the two undercover detectives ran into the backyard, their guns trained on Hamilton Jacques. "Come on, Jacques, it's over. Drop the knife and let her go."

Jacques didn't move, nor did he release Maggie. She wasn't saying a word, figuring the detectives knew what they were doing. The silence was deafening, except for the gulls and occasional laughter and loud voices from across the street at the bar on the beach, everyone oblivious of the tableau in Maggie's beautiful back yard. Surely he'll not hurt her with two guns trained on him. Surely not. She could feel that knife point on her neck, though.

Davidson thought at first it wasn't even him, because he looked at lot younger, but it had to be. The chief said he had very dark hair, dark eyes and a bit of a beard now. There couldn't be two men after Maggie who looked like that. Even Savage had her doubts, but came to the same conclusion as her partner, though they didn't verbally communicate this. He certainly looked different with all that dark hair and beard. And with their flashlights on him, those eyes looked coal black to them. Charlie Manson eyes.

He'd stepped out of the roots when he grabbed Maggie, so she was facing the banyan tree and his eyes were on the cops. Now, they weren't saying anything and he wasn't saying anything. She thought she'd scream if someone didn't make a move soon, but she stayed quiet, knowing he was so unstable he might just slice off her head if she made a sound. She felt the knife pierce her skin so it wouldn't take much for it to slice through her neck.

All of a sudden, she was so weak she was seeing a mirage. Homer appeared within the roots of the banyan where the flashlights were illuminating it. She blinked very hard a couple of times. Oh my God, it wasn't a mirage. He was really crouching there. He put his finger to his mouth. She kept quiet. She figured if she saw him, with the cops facing that way, they saw him, too, but she hoped that Jacques was too afraid of taking his eyes off them to look toward the tree. He was.

Once again, Joey said, "Come on, Jacques, there's nowhere to go, so just throw down the knife and let Maggie go."

"No point in doing that, now, is there," the man said. "Miss Maggie's staying right here with me. You're not going to take a chance on hitting her by shooting me, are you? So let's just all calm down and stay put.

"Now, if we're all nice and calm, let me tell you what's going to happen next. And if you follow it to a T, no one's going to get hurt," he said, as Carolyn watched with frightened eyes from her terrace in the shadows of early nightfall. "You're going to get on your radio and tell your illustrious chief of police Lenny Doan and his Barney Fife to bring a car around to United right beside us, so Miss Maggie and I can take a nice long ride. You know from seeing my handiwork in those hotel rooms and the Cudjoe canal, I know how to handle this knife. And I promise you, if anyone follows us, her head comes off instantly. Got that? And turn up the volume so I can hear you. Oh, and tell him to have a bag filled with hundreds in the back seat, s'il vous plait. I don't care how much is in the bag, just so there's plenty of it." He laughed, heinously, after saying this. "No tricks now or she pays for it."

Maggie's heart rate was so fast again and pounding so loudly in her ear, she felt he must be able to hear it. Surely Joey wouldn't do what he wants him to do. If they let him take her, she was as good as dead. She knew about those second crime scenes. All the self-defense instructors always stressed that you never let a perpetrator take you to the second crime scene, because if you don't fight your way out of it or if help arriving doesn't stop him, you won't get out of it alive. Surely they won't let that happen to her.

"Okay, you win, I'm calling the chief now. Just stay calm. We don't want anyone getting hurt," Joey told him. He called and they all heard him order the car loaded with hundred dollar bills brought around to United beside the backyard so the man and Maggie could get in and drive off, without an escort. He relayed Jacques' threat to Doan.

He told Davidson he'd send the car around immediately as soon as he could stuff bills from the evidence room into a bag since the banks were closed. He told Jacques not to hurt Maggie, that no one would follow them. Of course, he didn't tell him that besides the car he'd ordered, every cop in town was on the way to the scene, also, including his swat team and someone would take him down from Carolyn's terrace. That is, if the two detectives didn't get the chance to first, because of the way he was holding Maggie.

He'd taken his hand from her mouth since with everyone there, she wouldn't be saying anything, thinking they were going to rescue her. He almost laughed, knowing that was in her head, but there wasn't a chance of that happening. He practically could taste all that money. He still had a lot, but one could never have too much dough, especially if he enjoyed traveling abroad as he did. He almost laughed aloud at that, remembering the things that happened when he did leave the states.

This was not what Maggie wanted to hear from the chief, but under the circumstances, she supposed they had no choice but to do what the madman said, maybe thinking they could talk him down before the car got there. She didn't think she was going to get out of this one, though. She'd gambled on making him try to take her so he could be taken down or caught, but she saw there was little to no chance of that happening now. She glanced up to the third floor terrace and told Carolyn a silent goodbye. She knew she'd never see her again. The poor thing looked terrified standing up there in the shadows.

Then without moving her head for fear he'd slice straight through her neck if she did, she let her eyes travel over toward where Homer was still hiding in the roots of the banyan so she could tell him, her beloved long time best friend, goodbye the same way. Except – except he was motioning to her. Oh my God, what was he trying to get her to do? Yes, now she understood! Pretend to faint and fall backward! Well, what did she have to lose by doing it? He'd never steered her wrong before. Maybe she would get out of this alive, after all – unless it went wrong and her head came flying off her neck!

She said, "Oh, I'm gonna ... "and then she went down, falling against Jacques hoping that would cause him to drop the knife. It didn't drop, but loosened from her neck as she fell, just as Homer took his shot and Jacques screamed and grabbed his chest. He started to grab Maggie again, but Davidson shot him in the head, and he went down, almost falling on top of Maggie, whom Homer ran to pick up at that moment.

"Oh God, Homer, I didn't think I'd get out of that one," she said, hoarsely, and then, the tears that had pooled in her eyes since Hamilton Jacques grabbed her started to fall.

"I've got you, it's okay now, you're safe. It's over, Mag," he said, in a soothing way, as he held her tightly to him. "It's finally over and you're okay now."

As cops ran into the yard from all directions, he pulled her away from the body of Hamilton Jacques and onto the patio, just as Carolyn came running out of the kitchen and down the steps to where they were.

"Maggie, oh, Maggie! Thank heavens Homer got back in time and Joey got his shot in, too! Are you all right?" She grabbed her and hugged her tight.

"Sure, I'm fine. Never really was in danger," she said, to make her friend feel better, as she swiped the tears off her face.

Taking her hand, Carolyn said, "It certainly didn't look that way from my terrace. Had anyone moved a muscle, I think he'd have taken your head off with that knife. When they shined the lights on him, I could even see that little spot of blood where he had the tip of it." She bit her lip to keep from crying now that it was all over and Maggie was safe. She took a tissue from her pocket and dabbed at the tiny speck of blood on her friend's neck.

"Well, I wasn't worried. With those two in front of us and Homer sneaking up on us in the roots, I knew it would end well." She smiled at the two of them.

"Right, that's why you looked like you were going to faint even before I motioned for you to pretend to do it," he said to her, with a relieved laugh.

"Maggie, you were one fine actress there when you fell down on cue and back into him instead of away from him where the knife definitely would have sliced your neck," Shirley Savage told her, with a big smile, as she gave her a hug. "We knew what Homer was trying to get you to do, but were holding our breaths because we weren't sure you'd caught on. We needn't have worried. You're a mighty smart one, lady." She gave her another big smile and Maggie smiled back at her.

Joey Davidson joined the little group by the patio and hugged her, too. "You sure are, Mag! Wow, I couldn't believe it when I got the call from Carolyn that you were in the backyard by yourself and he had you. I was on the window at the time, while Shirl was packing our bags and couldn't see him back there before she called. After that, we just ran for it."

"Yes, and knowing our undercover angel here, you planned it all, didn't you," Chief Doan said, to everyone's surprise, as he walked up to her, Lieutenant Butler on his heels. "Tell the truth, now. You knew he was out there before you came outside, didn't you?"

Everyone's eyes were on her. Surely that wasn't true. "Maggie?" Carolyn asked. "Tell the chief it's not true. Tell him."

Maggie didn't answer her. Instead, she looked at the chief and smiled. "Let's all go inside. I need a Corona." All the other cops were standing in the yard waiting for the medical examiner to come, some doing crowd control as people had run over from all directions when they heard the shots. No one was going anywhere for a while.

The other six looked at each other and shook their heads at the same time. "I'll drink to that," Shirley Savage said.

"I could use one, too," her partner told her, now that their undercover job was finally over.

"After you," Homer told the chief, as they climbed the stairs to the second floor, Maggie in the lead, eager to hold court in her lovely yellow kitchen.

After they were all settled around the big kitchen table and had their drinks in their hands, Maggie asked if anyone wanted anything to eat. "We have plenty of donuts. I know you guys want some."

"No thanks, Mag." Davidson said.

"None for me, either," Savage echoed. Butler shook his head no, without speaking.

"Chief?"

"It isn't donuts I want from you, Maggie Metronia. Now stop stalling and tell us the truth about what happened here tonight." He said it kindly, but she knew he expected an answer.

She took another big drink of her Corona, after stuffing a twist of lime down the neck. "I won't lie to you."

He looked into her eyes, and said, "I know you won't lie, but whether you'll tell me the complete truth is what I'm wondering."

"Yes, you don't have to worry about that, I'll tell you." She looked at Homer who smiled his encouragement. After a deep sigh, she said, "I didn't know he was out there, but I had a chill run up my spine after I was left alone in the kitchen. At first I didn't pay much attention to it. But then, after I got almost to my room, I stopped. I thought if he's here, now's the time to bring it all to a head, so that's when I turned around and walked outside."

"My God, Maggie," everyone said at the same time.

She smiled her big toothless smile at them. "Come on, now. Think about it logically. It had gone on for almost two years and if his thinking I was alone would draw him out in the open, isn't that what you'd have wanted? Be honest now, weren't all of you as tired of waiting to catch him as I was? You know, and I know, durn good and well you were."

No one said anything, except the chief. "Sure, we were all tired of his eluding us, but none of us would have wanted you to put yourself in harm's way with him in order for us to catch him. I told you that when I found you over at the seaport that day."

"I know you wouldn't have, but as I said it was time." All of a sudden, tears popped up in Maggie's eyes, again, and looking up at Homer, she said, "I did fib a little earlier, though." She glanced at Carolyn whose tears fell to her cheeks. "I was so scared, scared as I've ever been in my life. Even more than when I fell overboard in the straits, because that happened too fast to have time to feel anything.

"But," she said, again looking up at Homer, "like then, you saved me tonight. You were so brave, Homer Wiley. You're my hero!"

She threw her arms around him and he held her tightly to him, tears in his own eyes, as they were in the eyes of the small group of friends standing around them, even the tough Blake Butler.

"You're the brave one, Maggie Metronia," Homer said with a husky voice choked by the tears, "and you've always been *my* hero.

ACKNOWLEDGMENTS

I am so grateful for my first readers, Laura Frost Smith, Carol Tavris, Lela Buscemi and Margaret Snow. Writing is a solitary art, but without beta readers reading these manuscripts for us and telling us what you think, rather than what you think we want to hear, few of us would come up with the quality books that finally go to print, so thank you, thank you, thank you!

I'm grateful, too, for Daniel DiStasio, my long-time writer friend who is never too busy to advise if I'm stuck on something or just need him to tell me if I'm on the right track with any of my novels. Danny, thank you more than I can say. You're the best!

Thank you, John Gish, another old friend who shared my love of the Tropic, for allowing me the use of your name in this book.

Thank you, also, to my early morning swimming friends, Carmen, Juana, and Susie who put up with my absence too much while I sit at this computer lost in the creation of these books, never knowing when to stop writing!

Most importantly, thank you to my beloved family who always encourage me in this second career that takes so much of my time: Karen and Stephen, Suzy and Brian, Sam and Rick, Lindsey and Peter, Elizabeth and Bobby, Emily and Caleb, and thank you for sharing those nine precious great-grandchildren whom I adore – you're all pieces of my heart.

And thank you to Sheri Lohr, my first publisher at SeaStory Press, and Shirrel Rhoades, my second, at New Atlantian Library and AbsolutelyAmazingEbooks.com, and Chuck Newman who sadly isn't with us, any longer, who believed enough in me to get me started on this amazing journey of writing, and finally, to all you devoted readers who enjoy my books and ask for more.

I'm so blessed to have all of you in my life,
With love and gratitude,

—Peg/Mom/GP

ABOUT THE AUTHOR

As a resident of Key West for several years after retiring from a lengthy and diverse nursing career in 2002, Peg Gregory began a serious writing career, while covering the Key West City Commission meetings. For a period of time in the mid-1970s she left nursing and worked under the state attorney's office in Palm Beach County as acting coordinator of the newly formed sexual assault assistance program and paralegal counselor to adult and child survivors. She draws from both professions for most of her novels and award-winning short stories. Peg lives in Palm Beach County. She enjoys hearing from her readers by email (put name of book in subject line so it won't be sent to the spam folder) at Pegb.gregory@yahoo.com or on her Peg Gregory Author Facebook Page.

Reviews are the lifeblood of authors and they are how other readers learn of them, so please review this book at www.amazon.com or at the website of the bookseller from which you purchased the paperback or eBook. If you must write a negative review, the author asks just one thing of you, please be kind. Thank you!

NewAtlantianLibrary.com or
AbsolutelyAmazingEbooks.com
or AA-eBooks.com

Thank you for reading. Please review this book. Reviews help others find Absolutely Amazing eBooks and inspire us to keep providing these marvelous tales.

If you would like to be put on our email list to receive updates on new releases, contests, and promotions, please go to AbsolutelyAmazingEbooks.com and sign up.

For sales, editorial information, subsidiary rights information
or a catalog, please write or phone or e-mail

The New Atlantian Library
Manhanset House
Shelter Island Hts., New York 11965, US
Tel: 212-427-7139
www.AbsolutelyAmazingEbooks.com
bricktower@aol.com
www.IngramContent.com

www.ingramcontent.com/pod-product-compliance
Lightning Source LLC
Chambersburg PA
CBHW031055020726
47495CB00007B/1897